— *Wonderful* —
LONESOME

Wonderful LONESOME

OLIVIA NEWPORT

Print ISBN 978-1-62836-631-0

eBook Editions:
Adobe Digital Edition (.epub) 978-1-63058-602-7
Kindle and MobiPocket Edition (.prc) 978-1-63058-603-4

All scripture quotations are taken from the King James Version of the Bible.

This book is a work of fiction. Names, characters, places, and incidents are either products of the author's imagination or used fictitiously. Any similarity to actual people, organizations, and/or events is purely coincidental.

Cover design: Faceout Studio, www.faceoutstudio.com

Published by Shiloh Run Press, an imprint of Barbour Publishing, Inc., P.O. Box 719, Uhrichsville, Ohio 44683, www.shilohrunpress.com.

Our mission is to publish and distribute inspirational products offering exceptional value and biblical encouragement to the masses.

ecpa Member of the Evangelical Christian Publishers Association

Printed in the United States of America.

CHAPTER 1

Elbert County, Colorado
May 1914

The front right wagon wheel, below Abigail Weaver, dipped sharply then lurched out of the hole. At its creak, she winced and eyed Willem Peters on the bench beside her.

Willem pulled the reins in, and the dark stallion responded. "I'd better look."

Willem dropped off the bench, stepped mindfully over the hitch, and squatted to inspect the bent hickory wheel.

Abbie twisted to watch. "Did it break?"

Willem scratched his forehead with his middle finger. "Not that I can see. Maybe the back side of one of the spokes cracked."

Abbie expelled a breath. "When did that hole happen anyway?"

"Who can say? At least it doesn't seem too deep." Willem stood. "We will be all right."

We will be all right. Willem's favorite expression.

Willem hoisted himself up to the bench. "There's an *English* wheel maker in Limon. I can ask him to take a look while you wait for Ruthanna's train."

Abbie nodded, glad to have Willem beside her again. He clicked his tongue and the horse began to move. Limon was only another two miles.

"Do you have your mother's list for Gates Mercantile?" Willem asked.

"She hates having to buy flour." Abbie squinted her brown eyes. "It's like losing last year's wheat all over again."

"Your family is not alone in losing the crop. We all feel it."

"I know. I hope they'll take her eggs in payment."

"They always do. Everybody needs eggs." Willem glanced at Abbie. "Do you think your mother wants to go home?"

Abbie shook her light brown-haired head. "Colorado is home now. She wants to be here as much as I do. I think she's written to every relative we have, though." Abbie reached into the leather bag and ran her fingers along the ridges of the coarse envelopes.

"I promised Albert Miller I would check for his mail. Remind me, please."

Abbie turned her face away and allowed herself a small smile. She liked it when Willem said things like that, the way he depended on her in the mundane.

"Where first?" Willem raised his green eyes in the direction of Limon. "Mercantile? Feed store? Post office? Wheel maker?"

"Someday we'll be able to do more of those things for ourselves." Abbie set her jaw. "Once a few more families join our settlement, we'll have the tradesmen to provide what we need."

"Speaking of tradesmen, remind me to check with our very own cobbler about my new boots. We're blessed to have someone to make our shoes."

"God is *gut*." Abbie peered toward the outline of Limon. "How much time do we have before Ruthanna's train?"

"I'll tell you what. Give me your list and letters, and I'll drop you at the station and start on the errands. That way you can enjoy Ruthanna. She'll be ready to talk your ear off as usual."

"That's one of the things I love about her." Abbie smiled. "Does it count if I remind you now to pick up the Millers' mail?"

One of Willem's cheeks twitched in amusement. "No one can accuse you of not fulfilling your promises."

Abbie stood on the platform and bent at the waist, back straight, to peer down the tracks. Her dark dress seemed somber among the spray of colors and hats of *English* women preparing to board trains, but the sensation was fleeting. Abbie had no wish to be *English*. Perhaps Ruthanna would bring news of other families who wanted to join the settlement. The price of land was certainly attractive. Abbie's father had put his savings into his Colorado farm and tripled the acreage he had owned in Ohio. Willem had rented his acres in Ohio, but here he was a landowner. Every family in the settlement had a similar story.

Twenty-four trains a day shuddered into this station. Limon, Colorado, was on the Union Pacific line as well as the Rock Island. As much as Abbie wanted her Amish church members to be able to take care of their own needs and provide for each other, she knew this town of five hundred was crucial to the settlement's survival. The trains made the distance from their families seem less daunting.

Distant rumbling turned thunderous as the train approached. Abbie sucked in her bottom lip, her stomach fluttering. Four weeks without her best friend was too much time apart. Ruthanna's only letter in that interim had revealed she would travel with cousins into western Kansas and then continue to Limon alone and arrive on this day. Brakes squealed now as the mass of steel slowed to a lumber and halted. Abbie scanned in both directions, not knowing which train car Ruthanna would emerge from. She did know that Ruthanna's favorite apron to wear over her black dress was the blue one. Abbie instinctively looked for fabric dyed in this distinctive Amish shade. Her intuition was rewarded when her friend stepped off the train just two cars forward of where Abbie stood.

In only seconds, they locked in an embrace that wobbled from side to side.

Ruthanna finally pulled back, her blue eyes gleaming under white blond hair. "I'm thrilled to see you, of course, but where is Eber?"

Of course Ruthanna would have been expecting her husband to meet the train. "He's under the weather," Abbie said.

"Eber is ill?"

"Just the last few days, but it keeps him up at night. I saw him this morning and sent him back to bed. He was pale as a corpse, and Willem was coming into town anyway."

Concern flushed through Ruthanna's face.

"He'll be fine, Ruthanna."

"You sound like Willem. I should not have left Eber."

"Of course you should have." Abbie picked up Ruthanna's small suitcase and they began walking. "You must insist that he hire some help, though. A bit more rest would work wonders. Now tell me all about Pennsylvania."

Ruthanna's face brightened. She put her hand on a gently rounding belly. "I am so glad I waited to tell my parents about the baby in person."

Abbie grinned. "Your *daed* loves the *kinner*."

"Now they will have to visit us. Perhaps next spring, after they can see how well we've done with this year's harvest. They cannot resist a grandchild."

Ruthanna adjusted her *kapp*. The train ride had worn her out more than she wanted to admit to Abbie. She had seen other women sick while they were with child, but she had not known how exhausting it could be to fight the nausea for hours on end. At night she slept in exhaustion, but still she dragged through the days.

"Have you heard of anyone who wants to come and join us?"

Abbie's question was just what Ruthanna expected. "Not precisely."

"Is anyone even considering it?"

Ruthanna sighed. "Everyone thought we would have a minister by now."

"So did we. We have twelve households—some of them are even three generations. That's enough for our own minister."

"I'm not sure anyone else will come until we have a minister. They have a hard time imagining how we can go an entire year without a church service and communion." Ruthanna inhaled the loose dirt that always hung in the air on the Colorado plain and coughed. This did nothing to settle her stomach.

"I suppose I cannot blame them," Abbie said, "but surely

God could put the call on a minister to visit us more often until someone from our congregation can be ordained. I shall pray more fervently."

Ruthanna moistened her lips with what little saliva she could muster. "Also, everyone knows what happened to last year's crops. I received many questions about that as well."

"But that is not fair. Even farmers in Pennsylvania or Ohio can lose a crop if the weather is not favorable."

"You have to admit that the advertisements that brought us out here failed to mention some important factors."

Abbie waved a hand. "I do not believe anyone intended to deceive. The first men did not yet know for themselves how little rain there was. Acres and acres of land were available with no need to clear thousands of trees before planting. A new family can get a crop in the first spring they are here. Certainly that's still an attractive truth."

Ruthanna smiled and put a tongue in the corner of her mouth. "You are nothing if not persistent, Abigail Weaver. I cannot think of anyone who wants our settlement to succeed more than you do."

"We are so close! A few more families, a minister, a good crop this year."

Abbie's pace had quickened with her enthusiasm, and Ruthanna could not keep up. "Abbie, I need some cold refreshment and a place to sit that is not in motion."

"Of course! We can find a bench inside the depot. Willem will look for us there anyway. And we can talk about something happier."

Willem watched the two heads bent toward each other as he held the door for a couple leaving the depot with four children stringing behind them. With a tall tin cup in her hand, Ruthanna looked relaxed. Eber had done well to marry her. Ruthanna balanced Eber's subdued demeanor with an exuberance that allowed her to talk to anyone about anything. Between them they had all the traits an Amish household would need to survive on the Colorado plain. Twenty years from now, Willem predicted, they would be watching their firstborn son take a bride in a congregation with three ministers, and they would be hard put to squelch their pride. *Demut,* they would remind each other. *Humility.*

Willem certainly hoped it would be so. Perhaps he and Abbie would follow soon enough. Maybe their daughter would love Eber and Ruthanna's son. A new generation would rise up from the dust of their parents' acreage. *Gottes wille.* God's will. May it be so.

As he walked toward the two friends, Ruthanna's face cheered and incited Willem's curiosity about what the women were discussing. A few seconds later Abbie smiled as well. No doubt Abbie was hanging on every word Ruthanna said, listening to stories, news, information, even gossip from the congregations their two families had left behind when they decided to settle in new territory. Abbie was the intense one. Ruthanna brought her the same balance she brought Eber. Abbie's shoulders now dropped, as if for a few minutes she had released her load. Willem wished she would do that more often. Her head turned toward him in a serendipitous way, and he waved.

"The wanderer has come home." When he reached them, Willem grinned and picked up Ruthanna's suitcase. "I'm sure Eber is anxious to see you."

"Did you mail the letters?" Abbie asked.

"Yes."

"And pick up the Millers' mail?"

"Under the wagon bench."

"And my mother's flour and pickles?"

"Sugar, dry beans, and baking powder, too."

"And the wheel maker?"

"No cracks. A squeaky axle."

Ruthanna laughed. "You two are quite a pair."

Willem gave her a half smile. Most of the community—both Amish and *English*—paired him with Abbie. Many expected him to make a proposal in the fall, after the harvest. After all, he was twenty-six and she was twenty-three, well old enough to begin their own household.

"That's Rudy Stutzman in the ticket line," Abbie said.

Willem glanced toward the counter. Abbie scowled, stood, and marched toward the window. Whatever Rudy's reasons were for being there, his explanation was not likely to satisfy Abbie. Willem admitted his own curiosity and made no move to constrain Abbie.

CHAPTER 2

Rudy, I hadn't heard you planned to travel."

Rudy jumped at the sound of Abbie's voice. "I thought I might make some inquiries about the price of fares."

"Are your parents unwell?" Abbie asked. Rudy had few extended family members, she knew, but he had come west with the blessing of his parents. They would have his two younger brothers to care for them as they aged.

"My family is well. Thank you for asking."

"Visiting someone?" Abbie said. Rudy's pitch sounded distant.

"No, I don't think so."

"Next," the ticket agent called.

Rudy stepped forward. The angle of one shoulder raised a wall between them. When he leaned in to speak to the agent, Abbie could not hear his words.

"Are you sure you just want a one-way ticket?" the agent said at a volume anyone within twelve feet would have heard.

Abbie stepped forward and grabbed Rudy's wrist. "No. Don't do this." Rudy glanced at her grip, and Abbie released it.

"Sir?" the agent said. Two people in line behind Rudy raised their eyebrows.

Rudy sighed and said to the ticket agent, "Perhaps for today you could just tell me what the cost is."

"One way all the way to Indiana?"

Rudy nodded. Abbie's heart sank.

The agent consulted a chart and announced the price.

"Thank you." Rudy stepped aside and Abbie followed.

"One way, Rudy?"

"Abigail, not everyone is as stalwart as you are. After four or five years, some of us are admitting that this is a lot harder than we thought it would be."

"We're all in this together, Rudy. We all need each other. That includes you."

"I am alone," Rudy said. "Willem and I, and Widower Samuels. What good is it for us to have a farm or dairy if we cannot keep up with the work?"

"Then hire somebody to help."

"No Amish families can spare their young men. My cash is in my land. I have nothing to pay an *English* with until the fall harvest. I only have what I make selling them milk."

"All the more reason to stay and make a go of it. You cannot just get on a train and leave your land and milk cows." Abbie's heart pounded. As far as she could influence anyone, she would not let a single settler give up.

"I thought I would make a listing with a land agent. I may not get back everything I put in, but I would have something."

"You know it is not our way to abandon each other in times of need. Speak to some of the other men. They will help you."

"The need is greater than we are," Rudy muttered.

"That is not true. That is never true." Below the hem of her skirt, Abbie lifted a foot and let it drop against the depot's oak decking.

Rudy looked past Abbie's shoulder. "I see Willem. Is he waiting for you?"

"Yes. We came to pick up Ruthanna. Eber is feeling poorly, but you can be sure no one is going to let his farm fail either."

"You cannot fight God's will, Abbie."

"You think it is God's will for us to fail?" Abbie refused to believe the settlers had obediently followed God into a new opportunity only to be forsaken.

"It must be," Rudy said. "It would take a miracle for us to succeed."

"Then a miracle we will have. Believe!"

Rudy leaned back against the wall. He had known plenty of stubborn people in his twenty-eight years, but none was a match for Abigail Weaver. He appreciated how hard she worked helping to bake and clean for the single men of the Amish community, but when she crawled into bed at night, she still slept under her parents' roof. He and Willem had ventured west without parents or wives. Rudy wasn't sure Abbie understood the risk they had taken.

And Willem, apparently, did not understand his ability to make Abbie happy or they would have wed two years ago.

"Abbie," Rudy said, "you are an example of great faith, but there is something to be said for realism as well."

"Not today. This is not the day that you are giving up."

Her dark eyes bore into him, and his resolve went soft. "You're right. One day at a time."

Her face cracked in a smile. "That's right. One day at a time. We *will* get through this summer and have a bountiful harvest. You will see."

Rudy lifted his eyes at the approaching sound of boots. "Hello, Willem. Abbie tells me the two of you have fetched Ruthanna home from Pennsylvania."

"That's right."

As soon as Willem stood beside Abbie, Rudy saw the hopefulness in the turn of her head, the wish for what Willem had not yet given her.

Willem seemed in no hurry about anything except that his farm should succeed. He and Abbie were so different that Rudy often wondered if the predictions that they would one day wed would come true. Abbie's one-day-at-a-time conviction might exasperate her when it came to waiting for Willem, and she might yet turn her head in that way toward another man.

Perhaps even toward Rudy.

When Rudy first arrived in Colorado, he regretted not bringing a wife with him. Then he met Abbie. He hated to think how he might have wounded a wife who saw through him.

"It's good to see you both," Rudy said. "We should all be on our way back to the farms, don't you think?"

Willem squinted at Rudy's retreating back. "Is Rudy all right?"

Abbie pressed her lips together. "I hope so. I suppose no one can blame him for a moment of indecisiveness."

"Is that what it was?"

Abbie was not inclined to answer. Willem was not inclined to press.

"We should get Ruthanna home," he said. "She's worried about Eber."

"Of course. If you are sure we remembered everything."

"Even if we have forgotten something, Limon is not going away. We will be back." Willem followed Abbie's line of sight to where Rudy stepped off the depot platform and stroked the neck of his midnight black horse.

"We should make sure Ruthanna has plenty to drink," Abbie said in a thoughtful murmur. "I can see she is weary, and Eber is ill. They will need something for supper tonight. I'm sure my mother can spare part of tonight's stew."

Willem nodded. Abbie, as always, thought of everything.

When they returned to the bench where they had left Ruthanna, she was standing and engaged in conversation with a man in a black suit. Willem's mind tried to sort out which Amish man this might be.

"Is that Jake Heatwole?" Abbie asked.

Willem nodded slowly as memory came into focus. "I believe so."

"What is he doing talking to Ruthanna?"

"You have to admit, they are two of the friendliest people we could ever hope to meet. They've met each other several times before."

"But—"

Willem cut off Abbie's protest. "But he's a Mennonite minister. Yes, I know. Does it really make a difference when we can't find a minister of our own?"

Abbie drew up her height. Willem ignored the *whoosh* of air she sucked in.

"Jake," Willem said, "what you brings you all the way from La Junta again?"

"Thought I would come and see how folks are," Jake answered with a smile. "Ruthanna tells me Eber is ill. Perhaps I'll pay him a call while I'm here."

"Jake says he plans to stay for at least a week," Ruthanna said. "Of course, I hope Eber will be feeling better long before that."

"He probably just needs his wife back," Jake said.

"If you're planning to stay a few days," Willem said, "why don't you stay with me? My home is small, but there's room for another bedroll."

Abbie barely managed to swallow words she would have regretted and hoped the flush she felt move through her face was not visible. What was Willem thinking? The four of them began moving toward Willem's wagon.

"Where did you leave your horse?" Willem asked.

"At the blacksmith's," Jake answered. "She seemed to be favoring one foot on the ride up, so I thought he should look at her shoes. He should be just about finished."

"We'll give you a ride over if you don't mind sitting in the wagon. I am afraid the bench is full with the three of us."

Abbie admired many things about Willem. He was kind and generous and determined and hardworking. But this was going too far.

"It's only a few blocks," Jake said. "I don't mind the fresh air."

"It is at least a mile," Willem pointed out. "The blacksmith refuses to have a shop closer to town."

Slightly more than a mile, Abbie thought, which raised the question of what Jake was doing at the train station in the first place if he had left his horse. He carried no burlap sacks or packages tied with string from the mercantile. If he had not come to Limon for supplies unavailable in La Junta, then he had only one purpose.

Abbie set her jaw against what she knew to be true.

"In fact," Willem said, "why don't we pick up your horse and then you can ride alongside us? We can chat about how your plans are coming for starting a Mennonite church in Limon."

There it was. Leave it to Willem to speak it aloud. Abbie heard the whistle of an approaching freight train on the Rock Island track.

Jake dipped his head, the black brim of his hat swooping low. "Now that, my friend, is a subject I never tire of talking about."

"Willem, Mr. Heatwole might have other business in town," Abbie said. "We ought not to rush him."

"It is no problem," Jake said. "In fact, I appreciate the hospitality."

The train stirred up the wind around them, and its shuddering volume silenced the moment.

At Willem's wagon, he put Ruthanna's suitcase in the bed and extended a hand toward her. "I promise you'll be home soon."

Ruthanna accepted Willem's assistance onto the bench. "I admit a certain amount of curiosity about the new church myself."

Abbie half rolled her eyes. She and Ruthanna had discussed this topic more than once, and Ruthanna had been steadfast that she would never leave the true church. What was there to be curious about?

Ruthanna swallowed hard. The ride home would be just over eight miles to the point where her farm touched the corners of Abbie's, Willem's, and Rudy's. She had made it dozens of times before with Eber, and the miles always passed pleasantly enough. The child had changed that. Now every jostle, every dip, every sway required utmost concentration to keep her meals where they belonged. It would be good to sleep in her own bed again, beside Eber.

Their small home was hardly more than a lean-to compared to the homes of her parents and their friends in Pennsylvania, but at least it belonged to Eber and her. Ruthanna had a cast-iron stove for cooking, a firm rack for dry goods, a real mattress on an iron frame, and a table and four matching chairs. The baby would not need much at the beginning. Eber would build on next year, after the harvest. The baby would have plenty of room by the time she was ready to walk.

She.

Ruthanna smiled at the thought as Abbie settled in beside her.

"How long did you say Eber has been ill?" Ruthanna asked. "He didn't mention it in any of his letters."

"Just a couple of days, as far as I know," Abbie answered. "I only saw him a few times while you were gone."

"I do not suppose you would have reason to see him often. It's not like him to be sick."

"I admit I've never seen him ill before this, but everyone gets tired, Ruthanna."

"Not Eber."

Willem took up the reins. Ruthanna glanced over her shoulder at Jake stretching his legs in the wagon bed. He was a warm, sincere man with an infectious devotion. It seemed unjust to dislike him simply because he was a Mennonite, so she didn't. Surely Abbie did not truly dislike him, either.

It was the threat that Jake Heatwole carried in his every step that disturbed Abigail Weaver.

Abbie watched Jake Heatwole, relaxed in the wagon, as he conversed with Willem about why he thought Limon needed another church. It mattered nothing to Abbie whether Jake Heatwole started another *English* church. He had left the true faith when he joined the Mennonites. All that remained was to pray that he would not lure any of the Elbert County Amish. Willem had many responsibilities that demanded his best effort. Why would he think it profitable to spend time with Jake Heatwole?

Unless. Abbie sat up straighter. Unless Willem thought Jake would repent and return to the Amish.

CHAPTER 3

Abbie wrapped three still-warm loaves in a soft flour sack and laid the bundle beside two similar offerings on the small table beside the hearth. The day was half gone, its first hours spent making bread dough, waiting for it to rise, heating the small oven, and baking bread two loaves at a time.

Esther Weaver silently counted on her fingers. "Twenty loaves. Nine for the single men leaves eleven for us."

"They came out well this week, don't you think?" Abbie resisted the urge to slice into a loaf that very moment and slather a thick serving with the butter she had churned the day before.

"The way your brothers have been eating lately," Esther said, "they'll go through three loaves a day if I don't stop them."

"I'll make more tomorrow," Abbie suggested.

Esther shook her head. "There's too much to do. We can't get in the habit of giving more than one day a week to baking. It's time the boys learned some self-control."

Abbie had to agree Daniel, Reuben, and Levi seemed to have bottomless stomachs, but she also noticed that all their trousers were too short again.

"Are you taking the open cart?" Esther asked.

Abbie nodded. "I don't mind the sun, and sadly, it is not likely to rain."

"No, I suppose not, though I pray every day for that particular blessing." Esther hung an idle kettle above the hearth. "On baking days at this time of year, the temperature is no different inside or out."

"*Daed* keeps talking about building a summer kitchen. I saw his sketch. It would have shade but no walls."

"He has many plans, but just when we need a summer kitchen the most, he must spend all his time thinking about getting water to the fields."

"He has ideas for an ingenious irrigation system," Abbie said. "It will not always be this hard. Not every summer will be a drought."

Esther smiled and tilted her head. "Abigail, my child, we have been here five years. Have we seen a single summer that was not drought compared to Ohio—and this one worse than all the others?"

"Then we are just about due for a nice wet summer."

"You had better get going. Where are you cleaning today?"

"Rudy's." And she would scrub his home spotless. She did not want to give Rudy any more reason to feel defeated.

Three weeks had passed since Abbie caught Rudy in the ticket line. She saw little of him, but he did not leave her mind. She would give encouragement in any form she could manage, including a sparkling house. Rudy Stutzman had a gift for understanding animals and keeping them healthy. If he left, who would be able to put a hand on the side of a cow and know that the animal's temperature was too high?

The wide brim of Abbie's bonnet, tied over her prayer *kapp*, allowed her to watch the road ahead of her without squinting. When she saw the Millers' buggy swaying toward her in the narrow road, she smiled. In a few more seconds she could see that both Albert and Mary were on the bench. That would mean that little Abraham was with them, probably in the back of the small black buggy.

Abbie lifted a hand off the reins to wave, and the Millers responded almost immediately. She guided her horse as far to the side of the road as she dared to take the cart's wheels. By the time her cart and the Millers' buggy were side by side, eighteen-month-old Abraham was peeking out from his miniature straw hat and had a thumb under a suspender strap in imitation of his father.

"Hello, Little Abe," Abbie said.

The little boy waved, his fingers squeezing in and out of his fist.

Abbie thought Abraham was the most beautiful child she had ever seen, though to speak the sentiment would tempt his parents to pride, so she did not. His chubby, shiny face, with its constant half smile, never failed to charm her.

Abbie raised her eyes to the child's parents. "How are the Millers today?"

Albert gave a somber nod. "We look for God's blessing of rain."

"As do I."

"We have just come from Eber and Ruthanna's."

"I was there yesterday to see how Ruthanna was feeling. How is she today?"

"She was having a good morning. Eber's health is of some concern to her, it seems."

"Yes, I was sorry to hear that he has a difficult day from time to time." Abbie suspected Eber's difficult days were more frequent than he admitted, and that was the reason for Ruthanna's concern.

"They've been hearing coyotes," Albert said. "We should all be watchful."

"By God's grace they will not come close."

Abraham rubbed his eyes, and his mother said, "It's time for us to get this little one home for a nap."

Albert nudged the horse and the Millers moved on. Abbie pulled her cart back onto the road, sighed, and smiled at the thought of Little Abe, and now Ruthanna's baby. These precious children were the future of the settlement. Whatever their parents suffered now would be worthwhile when they had strong, thriving farms to pass on to their sons.

A few minutes later, Abbie could tell from the stillness outside Willem's house that he was not there. Even the chickens had found a settled calm. Willem rarely was in the house when she came. He was running a farm, after all. Yet each time she hoped this would be the visit that he would be there to greet her.

She let herself in, making a point to look for an extra bedroll. Seeing only one, Abbie exhaled in relief. At least Jake Heatwole was not in residence this week. She moved across the undivided space to the area that would be called a kitchen were the structure a proper house. Last week's flour sack was empty, neatly folded, and laid precisely in the middle of the table. Abbie picked it up and put the new sack, holding three loaves of bread, in its place.

Then she scanned the room. Next week would be Willem's turn for a thorough cleaning, but Abbie looked for any task that appeared urgent for this day. Willem had been more generous with space in building his house than many of the settlers, and this pleased Abbie. There was plenty of room for a wife, and even a child or two. Willem also had partitioned off a true bedroom. Abbie peeked in there now, something she had come to be able to do without blushing at the thought that this would one day be her bedroom as well.

She found little to do. Although Willem ate the bread she brought and appreciated her cleaning efforts, he was remarkably neat for someone who lived alone. His habits were thoughtful and purposeful, features she believed she would appreciate even more when she was his wife.

By the time Abbie tidied up at Widower Samuels's house and made the wide circuit back to Rudy Stutzman's farm, bordering in a narrow strip on the Weavers', midafternoon had pressed in on the plain with the fiercest heat of the day. A wisp of humidity made Abbie reconsider her position that there was no reason to think it might rain that day. The whole community would raise hearts of gratitude if it were God's will to answer their prayers for moisture.

Rudy stood in a pasture with two *English* men about half a mile from his house. Abbie slowed the horse and cart long enough to try to recognize the *English*, but she could not see their faces well and could not be sure whether she had ever seen them before. At their ankles nipped a black and white dog. The mixed breed had turned up one day as a pup not more than ten weeks old and attached himself to Rudy. Because of his shaggy coat, Rudy had dubbed him Rug. When Abbie caught Rudy glancing up at her now, she had half a mind to tie up the horse and traipse through the pasture, but she would have no good explanation for doing so. With reluctance, she nudged the horse onward.

Rudy's house was built for a bachelor, one modest room for

sleeping, cooking, and eating, and a functional covered back porch for storing an unsystematic array of household and hardware items. Abbie put the bread in the middle of a table and found the previous week's limp flour sack hooked over the unadorned straight back of one of Rudy's two mismatched chairs. Then she looked in the water barrel and mentally gauged how much she would want for a proper cleaning. She would not use that much, of course. Rudy had a well, and as far as Abbie knew it did not threaten to run dry for household use and watering the animals, but water was too dear to use a drop more than necessary.

Abbie reached for the broom propped in one corner and began carefully dragging it through the dusty footprints on the floor of patchwork linoleum strips. She hung Rudy's extra pair of trousers on a hook, decided that the weak seam in his quilt would have to wait till another day, slid aside the few plates he owned so she could wipe down the shelves, and cleaned the dirty bowls in the bin that served as a sink. Every few minutes Abbie's gaze drifted out the open front door. She wished Rudy would walk through it and she could find out once and for all what was happening in that pasture.

Rudy chided himself. He ought to have known better than to agree to a meeting with the *English* on an afternoon when Abbie was due to come. But the visitors had gone to the trouble to track him down in his farthest field, where he fought a battle against weeds that only grew more futile in the face of strangled crops, and rode with him to the pastures where his eight cows and three horses grazed.

"You have some fine animals," Mr. Maxwell said, "though the coats on several of the cows lack a healthy sheen. That will, of course, affect the price we can offer. We cannot offer top dollar for unhealthy specimens."

Rudy said nothing. The cows were healthy. He would not engage in a discourteous conversation to prove his point. Only two days has passed since he mentioned to the owner of the feed store that he might sell his cows to the right owner, along with one of his horses. With his crop choking, the dairy cows were his livelihood. He would have to be certain of the decision he made.

Nothing required him to accept the offer the Maxwells might make. He was inclined to, though, unless the number they offered was grossly insulting. He could always list the property with an agent on short notice. He would not have to be present for the agent to show the land or close a deal. The animals were another question. If he sold them now, they would be worth more than they would be a few weeks later when they had chewed the pasture's scrabble down to the dust and he had nothing more to feed them and could not keep up with a growing bill at the feed store.

Rudy shook hands with the Maxwells, agreed to wait to hear from them, and watched as they mounted their horses and turned toward the road leading off his land. He had intended to retreat to one of the fields until he was sure Abbie was gone, but he spun around now at the clack of her cart behind him.

"Hello, Rudy," Abbie said. She scrutinized him and then peered down the lane at the dust the two *English* stirred up in their departure.

"Hello, Abbie. Any problems up at the house?"

She shook her head. "I hope you will be pleased with my work."

"You never disappoint."

Abbie searched his eyes. Rudy was not so foolish as to think she had not seen the *English* on his land. "I don't think I've ever seen *English* visitors on your farm before."

"It's the first time."

Indignation welled. Why would Rudy be talking to *English* on his own land if it were not about a sale? "What's going on, Rudy?"

"We had some business to discuss. That is all."

"Business? What are you getting ready to sell to them?"

"I have come to feel that I do not need eight cows."

"Are you giving up on the dairy?"

Rudy waited a second too long to answer.

"Rudy, you cannot live out here by yourself without a cow. Have yours all dried up?"

"No, that's not the problem."

Abbie slipped off the cart's bench and paced toward Rudy. "You are not still thinking of leaving, are you?"

When his response was again delayed, Abbie's stomach tightened.

"I bought a voucher for a train ticket," Rudy said finally. "It does not have a date on it yet, but I wanted to buy one while I could still scrape together the cash to pay for it."

"Oh, Rudy. No. Please, no."

"Why not, Abbie? My wheat looks more pitiful by the day, even though I planted half what I put in last year because I cannot afford to irrigate my acres no matter how much milk I sell. I'm sure your *daed* knows how expensive it is to truck in water."

"But you belong here." Abbie dug her heels into the dirt. "We all do. We are here together."

"And we are stretched thin. Even you cannot dispute that."

"It will not always be this way."

Rudy turned in a full circle, gesturing to the flat dustiness of his land with upturned palms. "It might be."

"You have so much to look forward to here, Rudy. You have a future here." Abbie slapped a hand in Rudy's still outstretched hand.

He looked her straight in the eye. "Do I?"

"Of course you do."

"I mean apart from the land, Abbie." He closed his fingers around hers.

She shrugged, not understanding his meaning.

"Has Willem declared himself to you, Abigail?"

Abbie withdrew her hand and stepped back. "Not in so many words, no."

"But you feel certain that he will?"

"Nothing is certain except God's will."

"What if Willem does not meet your hopes, Abbie?"

Abbie broke her gaze.

As Abbie cut through the back road that tied Rudy's farm with her family's land, the rain started with little warning other than the darkening clouds that blew across the plain on most summer afternoons without dispersing their moisture.

In her cart, halfway back to the Weaver farm, Abbie laughed out loud. She did not care that she had no covering, nor how drenched she might become. Rain! All around the region, farm families would be pausing in their work and looking up in exultation. Abbie turned her face to the sky, closed her eyes, and stuck out her tongue. She had not done that she since was a little girl in Ohio, but it seemed the only appropriate response now. The rain gathered in a thunderous drumbeat, and Abbie hastened the horse. In relief, she realized her dress already was damp enough that it was sticking to her skin.

Rain!

Abruptly the sound changed to a clatter of stones pouring from the heavens. Pea-size at first, then larger. The icy rock that struck her nose made Abbie's breath catch. The horse's feet danced while Abbie's chest heaved in protest. *Not hail. Please, God. Not hail.*

The nearest farm was Ruthanna and Eber's. They kept a hay shed near the road, but it stood empty now. By the time Abbie reached the shed, unhooked the mare from the cart, and dragged the horse under the shed's narrow overhang, tears streamed down her face. Abbie tied the horse tightly so it could not stray, then took refuge in the empty shelter.

She looked out at Ruthanna and Eber's tender crop and knew it could not survive this vicious pelting. No one's crop could.

The force that had destroyed the hope of harvest last summer once again rent in two the yearning of Abbie's heart.

CHAPTER 4

Ruthanna yanked open the door and stood in its frame screaming regret.

"Eber!"

Ruthanna had bitten her tongue two hours ago when Eber said he wanted to walk the fence line. He did not want to take the chance that a neighbor's hungry cow would nudge a loose post out of its earthy pocket in search of a scrabbly patch of grass to nibble on. If he had any grass, Eber would gladly share it with a cow. What he feared was that the animal would start in on his tenuous field of barley just as it showed signs of taking root. Eber had not regained his full strength. That was plain as day. But she could not hold him back from doing the only thing he could think to do as an obstinate summer yawned before them.

"Eber!"

Ruthanna's mind told her it was pointless to shriek into the wind, but she could not help it. The clanging smash of hail dumping from the sky against the tin roof drowned the sound of her voice even from her own ears. Eber had declined to take a horse with him, and he had been gone long enough that he could be anywhere on their acreage. When Ruthanna stepped out far enough to scan the horizon around the house—just to be sure Eber was not near—hail stung her cheeks. White icy mounds swelled around her as ever-larger hail pelted the finer base layer.

With one hand on her rounded abdomen, Ruthanna shielded her eyes with the other and peered through the onslaught of white.

Eber's white shirt would be lost against the hail. His black trousers would be her only hope of glimpsing him. Methodically, she scanned the view from left to right for any movement. Chickens in the yard scurried into the henhouse, but Ruthanna expected at least one or two would not survive the storm. Horses whinnied on the wind in their pasture. Ruthanna offered a quick prayer of thanks that their two cows were safely in the barn at the moment.

But she did not see Eber.

Within minutes, the hail was five inches deep. Ruthanna stepped back into the shelter of the doorframe, watching this mystery of spring. Only a few weeks ago five inches of snow would have been cause for rejoicing. Precious moisture would have melted into the ground and prepared the soil to welcome seed meticulously buried at precise depth and intervals. Even if hail had come before the seeds sprouted, the crop might have survived. But this! This was only terror.

Her father would have reminded her *Gottes wille*. God's will. Could it really be God's will for twelve obedient Amish families to suffer this racking devastation?

And then it was over. The sky had emptied and stilled. Drenched, Eber limped from around the back side of the barn.

Willem shoved open the barn door and hurtled toward the horse stalls. The stallion bared his teeth and raised his front legs in protest against the commotion. Willem slushed hail in on his boots. Frozen white masses in various sizes melted into the straw that lined the barn floor. Willem's tongue clucked the sequence of sounds that he had long ago learned would calm the frightened horse. He would not enter the stallion's stall until he was sure the animal had settled, but Willem spoke soothing words and familiar sounds. In the stall next to the stallion, the more mild-tempered mare hung her head over the half door hopefully, making Willem wish he had a carrot to reward her demeanor.

On the other side of the barn were the empty cow stalls. Intent on farming, not husbandry, Willem only had one cow. The hail's beating had been brief but swift, and Willem could not predict how the cow would have responded. He hoped it had not tried to bolt through Eber's fences.

Bareheaded, Willem stood in the center aisle that cut through the barn and stroked the mare's long face. Only two drops plopped on the top of his head before he raised his eyes and saw daylight through the barn's roof. Dropping his gaze, he saw that his feet stood in a mass of freshly damp hay. Hail had beaten its way through two wooden slats only loosely thatched over. Willem had hoped for proper shingles this year, but that required cash.

He put a hand across his eyes and bowed his head. Any of his fellow Amish worshippers might have thought he was praying, but Willem knew the truth. The thoughts ripping through his mind at that moment were far from submissive devotion to God's will. He forced himself to take several deep breaths before moving his hand from his eyes and again surveying the damage to his barn and the distress of his stallion. He could only imagine what his fields must look like.

Months of praying for favorable weather. Weeks of coaxing seeds to sprout in undernourished soil. Evening upon evening spent bent over the papers on his rustic wooden table writing out calculations and scenarios essential to the survival of his farm.

A hail storm was not part of the equation.

Willem pushed breath out and said aloud, "We will be all right."

The stallion shuffled but no longer protested.

The mare gave up looking for a treat in Willem's hand and nuzzled the straw in her stall.

Willem turned on one heel and left the barn. Outside the sun once again shone brilliant, as if the last twenty minutes had been a bad dream. Willem marched out to the pasture in search of his cow.

Abbie's heart rate slowed—finally.

The clattering of hail stopped as suddenly as it had begun. Cautious, Abbie pushed open the shed door. The extra resistance of several inches of hail required her to put her shoulder into the effort. Outside, fields of white glinted and forced her to squint. Abbie grabbed fistfuls of skirt and raised her hem above the slosh as she moved to where she had tied the horse. The animal was reasonably dry and unperturbed, Abbie was glad to see. As she hooked the cart to the horse again, she inspected her immediate surroundings. The size of the hail and its sheer quantity in the last few minutes twisted a lump in her stomach. In the distance she could see Ruthanna and Eber's house and wanted to see for herself that they were safe before continuing her journey home. The path was difficult to discern at first, covered by hail, but Abbie found signs of the familiar entry and guided the horse. Under the animal's feet and the cart's wheels, each sound of crunching hail reverberated through Abbie's mind with the implications of the storm.

A few minutes later, Abbie pulled up in front of the house. She saw boot prints leading from the barn to her friends' home, where the front door stood open and she could see clear through the structure. On the cooking side of the cabin, Eber sat in a straight-backed wooden chair with his boots off and his shoulders slumped, suspenders down around his waist. Behind him, Ruthanna worked at toweling his head dry. Abbie paused long enough at the door to knock and announce her presence. With a gasp, Ruthanna abandoned the towel and crossed the sparse sitting area to embrace Abbie.

"You're all right?" Squeezing her friend, Abbie felt the growing babe between them.

Ruthanna sniffled. "What does all right mean? Physically we are unharmed, but Eber. . ."

Abbie glanced across the room. "Eber, did you get caught out in the storm?"

Eber responded by putting his elbow on the table and hanging his head in his open palm.

Abbie tried again. "I hope you don't mind. I took shelter in your empty hay shed. You'll be glad to know it seems quite watertight."

Eber stood, pulled his suspenders over his shoulders, and retreated into the bedroom.

Ruthanna turned to Abbie. "What will we do now?"

"You're not alone. We have the church. We are all together, whether rejoicing or suffering."

"I cannot imagine anyone rejoicing today."

"Then we will suffer together and rejoice another day when

God shows us His will for the next step."

"Eber is tired." Ruthanna wiped the back of her hand across her face. "In body and spirit. He is tired."

The bedroom door closed with a thud.

With a promise to return the next day, Abbie said her farewell to Ruthanna. They both knew that a wife should go to her husband in a moment like this.

By now most of the hail had melted and puddled. In some places, miniature rivulets carved a downward path. As thirsty as the ground was, it could not absorb the moisture as quickly as icy chunks transformed into liquid on a warm afternoon. At first, Abbie willed herself to keep her eyes on the road and not to turn her gaze toward the fields on either side.

Ruthanna and Eber's fields.

Willem's fields.

Her father's fields.

What good would come from pausing to look at the damage so soon after the storm? After all, it was possible some shoots would have bent under pressure but might revive during the night, was it not? And Colorado hail sometimes dumped mercilessly in one area, while only three miles away the sun shone uninterrupted. The Amish farms were spread over miles and miles. She would be jumping to conclusions to presume that everyone's farm suffered equal fate. Perhaps the damage was more like a heavy, welcome rain. Surely no one would speculate about the severity or widespread nature of the loss on the same afternoon.

Abbie urged the horse's trot into a canter and kept her eyes straight ahead. She made her ears focus on the rhythmic beat of hooves and the swaying creek of the cart and breathed deeply of the spring scent after a rain.

Only once she turned down the ragged lane that led to the Weaver farm did Abbie allow herself to slow and observe. Her father stood in a field with two of her younger brothers. Abbie pulled on the reins, jumped out of the cart, and stepped delicately into the field.

She could see immediately that she need not have bothered with such care.

"Oh, *Daed*." Her voice cracked as the lump bulged in her throat. Ananias Weaver was beyond hearing range, but Abbie fixed her eyes on him until he at last looked up and met her gaze. Slowly, he shook his head before kneeling. Whether he bent in prayer, inspection, or resignation, Abbie did not know.

CHAPTER 5

Abbie drew a knife through a loaf of bread and laid the resulting slice on the small plate her youngest brother held. Somber faced, Levi carried the plate to the table and sat down.

"Would you like to have two slices?" Abbie poised the knife over the bread again.

Levi shook his head. "We should be sure there's enough for everybody."

"I made four loaves today. You can have more."

The boy declined again.

Abbie laid the knife down. "I suppose we don't want to ruin your appetite for supper."

Levi picked at his bread. At eight, he was a skinny child with a usually infinite appetite.

"What's wrong, Levi?"

"I'm not hungry."

"*Mamm* has a bit of ham for supper, and some vegetables we canned last fall."

"If I tell her I'm not hungry, she won't make me eat."

He was right about that. Esther Weaver did not force children to eat supper, but she did make clear that if they chose not to, they would not have another opportunity until breakfast.

"*Mamm* asked me to give you an afternoon snack." Abbie dropped into a chair next to Levi. "Don't you feel well?"

"I feel fine." Levi put his hands in his lap. "Why don't you wrap this up for someone to have later? I'll go do my barn chores."

Levi nearly knocked his mother over on his way out the rear door of the family's narrow two-story house.

"Did he eat?" Esther set a basket of washed and sun-dried shirts on the floor.

"No. He believes we are running out of food." Abbie caught her mother's hand, forcing the older woman to look at her. "We aren't, are we?"

"The chickens still lay nicely, and the cows give milk morning and night, don't they?" Esther snapped a shirt flat on the table and began to smooth the sleeves. "It's all this talk about losing the summer crop. I've told your *daed* he must be more careful about who is listening."

"It's never been his way to coddle children."

"Surely there is something in between coddling and frightening."

"Yes, I suppose so." Abbie stood and returned to the butcher block to slice more bread. The family of seven would easily consume at least one loaf for supper.

"It's getting hotter every day," Esther said. "We may have to start doing our baking in the middle of the night."

"I haven't seen *Daed* in the fields since the hail."

Esther folded the shirt she had smoothed, wordless.

"*Mamm?*"

"He does not tell me what he is thinking."

"Surely he is going to put in a fall crop."

"Have you put the water on to boil?" Esther abandoned the laundry basket and moved toward the stove.

"I'm going to make a quilt," Abbie announced.

Willem looked up from the patch of ground he was assaulting with a shovel. Sweat oozed out from under his straw hat and down the sides of his face.

"It's a hundred degrees out here," he said. "Just thinking about a quilt is more than I can take."

"But it won't always be a hundred degrees, and we won't always be in a drought."

"Why then, I suppose a quilt is an act of faith." Willem stabbed at unyielding earth once more. It was not too far into summer to put in a few vegetables—something that did not require much water.

"That's exactly right." Abbie folded the empty flour sack she had exchanged for Willem's weekly ration of bread inside his cabin. "An act of faith. It's going to be a tree of life quilt."

Willem chuckled. "The attraction of this land was that we didn't have to clear trees before we could plant. Right now I could do with a bit of shade."

"It's a beautiful pattern. I can make one tree for each of the twelve families in our settlement."

Willem nodded. It seemed unlikely the Elbert County settlement would attract more families anytime soon. He tipped his hat back and looked at Abbie full on. "And what will become of this quilt once it is finished? Will it be big enough for two?"

That blush. That was the reason he said these things.

She unfurled the folded flour sack at him. "You would like to think you're deserving, wouldn't you?"

He grinned. "I'm just choosing my moment."

"And what excuse will you have when the fall harvest is over and it's marrying season?"

"Ministers are as scarce as trees out here." Willem raised the shovel above his shoulders and let its point drop directly into the cracked soil.

"Maybe you'd better start solving that problem now."

"There's always Jake Heatwole."

He heard her gasp but refused to meet her eyes, instead scraping at the thin layer of soil he had managed to loosen. "What if it comes down to a Mennonite minister or no wedding at all?"

"Aren't you getting the cart before the horse? I don't recall hearing a proper proposal of marriage." Abbie folded the sack once again.

"You know I'm irresistible."

"Willem Peters! That is the most prideful thing to say."

"Perhaps. But it is a legitimate question, considering we haven't had a minister even visit us in a year to preach, much less baptize or marry."

"That's not going to last forever. The drought will end. The settlement will grow. We will have a minister."

Willem wiped a sleeve across his forehead. He hoped she was right. He hoped the day would not come that he would have to tell her that the optimism had worn off his own faith.

"Are you tempted to use some prints?" Ruthanna smoothed the folded blue apron one last time before handing it to Abbie.

"Oh my, no." Abbie clutched the apron to her chest. "I don't want to use any fabric that our people would not wear."

"Some do, you know. Nothing too outrageous, but remnants or old skirts from the *English*." Ruthanna sat in one of her four kitchen chairs and wished she had washed the morning dishes before Abbie arrived.

In another chair, Abbie shook her head. "Not me. My tree of life quilt will be a symbol of our growing settlement. I don't want the suggestion of anything *English*."

Ruthanna gave a small shrug. "You wouldn't have to go all the way to the *English*. The Mennonite women are beginning to wear small prints."

"I wish them well in their own settlement, but I do not want their worn dresses."

"I wish I had more to give you. I only have three dresses. I feel I can spare the apron because I spilled ink all over it and couldn't get it out. But there are plenty of unspoiled patches that will do fine in a piece quilt."

"Don't feel badly," Abbie said. "My *mamm* says it is time for her to give her quilt scraps to me anyway. If I have even one item from each of our households, the quilt will truly represent the settlement."

"How much do you have so far?"

Abbie tilted her head to think. "I still need to go by the Millers', but Mary promised me one of Albert's old shirts. And I haven't spoken to Rudy yet." She had contributions from the Yoders, Nissleys, Chupps, Yutzys, Mullets, Troyers, and now the

Gingeriches. Even Willem and Widower Samuels had found something to donate. Her mother's scraps would fill in many gaps.

"Do you really think Rudy will have something you can use?" Ruthanna stroked her stomach. "Most of his clothes look ready for the rag pile as it is."

"I know. I ought to make him a shirt."

"He's sweet on you. You know that, right?"

Abbie bristled. "I most certainly do not. Where do you get such nonsense?"

"I see the way his eyes follow you when everyone is together."

"Without church services, that hardly ever happens. You're imagining things."

"Would it be so bad if he were? Willem is not exactly..."

"Willem is Willem."

"Right." Ruthanna cleared her throat. "Are you sure you don't want a cup of *kaffi*?"

"Positive. I'm perspiring as it is, and I still need to take eggs and cheese to some of the other families of the settlement."

Ruthanna breathed in and out slowly. "Do you think we'll ever stop calling it that?"

"Calling it what?"

"The settlement. Nobody at home in Pennsylvania or Ohio uses that word."

"Because they are all in established districts, with ministers."

"That's what I mean," Ruthanna said. "If no minister ever comes, we'll never be more than a settlement."

Abbie stood. "I am far too busy to let such doubts into my mind, and I suggest you banish them as well. You have a baby to get ready for!"

Ruthanna received the kiss her friend offered her cheek and watched as Abbie skittered across the cabin and out the front door. Last year's failed crop. A horrific winter. Spring hail. Summer drought. Yet Abigail Weaver believed.

Rudy Stutzman leaned on a fence post and wiped his eyes against his shoulder to contain the dripping sweat. Even when he came out to work in his fields at first light, long before the sun slashed the sky with full-fledged rays, he was drenched in his own perspiration before breakfast. Indiana summers were hot, but mature oaks and elms dotted the countryside, and creeks and rivers ran with as much cool water as a man could ask for. Here Rudy reminded himself to swallow his spit because drinking water was scarce and he had the animals to think of—never mind sufficient water to irrigate.

After the hail, Rudy had dutifully begun turning his soil again, inch by backbreaking inch. Not all of it. He did not have seed for a second planting even for half of his acres—not even a third. He only turned as much earth as he needed for sparse rows he could afford. Without any delusions that he would have enough crop to generate cash in the market, he settled for hoping for enough wheat to grind and mill. If the Weaver women were going to continue to bake his bread, he ought at least to contribute grain to the process. He had not intended to be anyone's charity case when he came to this land he could only describe as desolate. Unyielding. Ever-thirsty. Stingy. Yes, desolate.

Rudy wanted to throw off his hat, stick his head in a bucket of cold water, and gulp freely. And when he pulled it out again, he wanted to see the rolling green hills of Indiana, the smile of his mother's face, fresh clean sheets on his bed. He still had the voucher for a train ticket that he bought the morning when Abbie Weaver pleaded with him not to leave. Alone in the evenings, he sometimes took it out of its envelope and fingered the edges.

She still stopped him from going. If he left now, he would never see her sweet face again. In all the weeks since that day, he had heard nothing new about what was between Abbie Weaver and Willem Peters. Perhaps it was not as much as many people presumed.

CHAPTER 6

"Let me help you, Eber." Ruthanna reached for the metal pail.

Eber grunted and turned away from her without releasing his grip on the handle. "Do you think I cannot manage a milk pail on my own?"

"That's just it." Ruthanna moved one hand to the achy spot at the side of her back more out of habit than pain. "It's only a milk pail. I can carry it to the house while you get started with the other cow."

"There's no need. I can bring them both when I come. You have the child to think of."

"The baby is not coming for months," Ruthanna said. "There is no need for me to give up simple tasks, at least not yet."

"You have a tendency to overwork yourself."

Ruthanna bit her bottom lip. How could Eber not see that he had taken his own tendency toward overwork to extremes? Every day that he spent outside in the heat worried her more. Even the brown tones the sun gave his skin did not hide his underlying pallor, and he was breathing too fast for her liking.

"Eber, please let me take the pail. It's not even half-full. I will be careful."

He relented. "We are going to need all the cheese you can make. We may not have much else to see us through the winter."

Ruthanna took the pail before he could change his mind. "Let me bring you some water."

Eber shook his head. "That isn't necessary. We must conserve."

"One glass of water is not going to save the crop, Eber. But it might save you."

He grunted again, running a dry tongue over chapped lips.

Ruthanna pivoted as smoothly as she could with her growing bulk and left the barn.

Inside the cabin, Ruthanna set the milk pail in the corner of the kitchen and took a glass from the cupboard. With the dipper in the water barrel, she filled the glass before looking around for some bit of nourishment to take to Eber as well. He had so little appetite these days. Ruthanna had already taken in his trousers twice. In the evenings, he sat in his chair and stared at her swelling belly. His early exuberance about the child had long ago faded. Ruthanna was sure he would love the baby when it arrived in November, but he wanted to provide a better start for their child's life than a failed crop and a hungry winter.

Ruthanna settled on a boiled egg. They still had hens, and the hens still laid. Ruthanna had boiled a batch that morning, carefully setting aside the leftover water to use again for another purpose. With a glass in one hand and an egg in the other, Ruthanna began the trek back to the barn.

The cow whose udder still hung heavy mooed in protest at Eber's inattention. He sat on a bale of hay with his head hanging between his hands. Just as Ruthanna entered the barn, he looked up for a fraction of a second, then slid off the hay.

Ruthanna hastened her swaying progress, gripping the water glass. She wanted to cast it away and run, but her intuition told her Eber needed the precious water more than ever. When she reached him, she cradled his head in her lap and slapped gently at his cheek.

"Eber! Open your eyes!"

He obliged, to her great relief. He was breathing far too heavily, and his skin was clammy under her touch.

"You must drink some water. Don't argue with me." She gripped the back of his head and raised it, while at the same time tipping the water glass against his lips. But he seemed to part his lips only to let his faltering breath escape. Water dribbled down his chin rather than down his throat.

"Eber! You must drink!"

He seemed to want to speak, but he did not have the strength.

Ruthanna's heart pounded. Her husband needed help. The closest neighbors, the Weavers, were miles away even by crisscrossing the back road. She picked up the hem of her dress and dipped it in the water glass, then moved the damp fabric around Eber's face and against his lips. When his mouth opened again, she squeezed the hem so loose drops would fall into his throat.

He closed his eyes again.

"Eber! No!"

He moaned but did not open his eyes. His head fell to one side.

Ruthanna laid his head back in the straw and opened the front of his shirt before drenching her hem again and dabbing his chest. He breathed evenly now and not so heavily, but Ruthanna was not fooled. He was not simply asleep.

She pushed herself upright and left the empty water glass beside the egg in the hay. The buggy was outside the barn, and the horse in the pasture. Ruthanna mustered a whistle, and the horse turned his head. She whistled again, and he began to trot toward her. She opened the gates. The hundreds of times she had fastened horse to cart guided her muscles now with efficiency beyond her thought. Ruthanna could not get herself astride a horse in her condition. The buggy was her only option.

She drove recklessly, abandoning all sensibility to the thought of losing Eber. Even when she turned into the rugged lane leading to the Weaver home, she did not slow down. Chickens in the yard scattered. The young Weaver sons looked up from their chores. Ruthanna screamed her friend's name.

The front door opened and Abbie appeared.

Abbie drove the rig with firm determination and little sympathy for the performance she demanded from Ruthanna's horse. Beside her, Ruthanna gripped the bench with both hands, and behind them, Abbie's mother clutched a large jug of water and a sack of herbs and cloths. Esther had refused to stay behind, and Abbie was grateful. Her mother had far more experience coping with a crisis than she did. Ruthanna's face was a sopping mess of tears by the time they turned toward Eber and the barn. Abbie pulled the buggy up as close to the barn as she could. Even in her clumsy state, Ruthanna was out of the rig before it fully stopped, and Esther clamored out behind her. Abbie opted to leave the buggy harnessed to the horse in case they should need the animal's service again soon, but she allowed a rapid gesture to tie him to a post while Esther and Ruthanna ran into the barn.

When Abbie entered, she could not see Eber. Ruthanna and Esther were on their knees, bent over him.

"Is he—?" Abbie asked.

Ruthanna gave a cry. "He's still breathing. We're not too late."

"Hold his head, Ruthanna." Esther fished in her bag. "He's burning up. We have to get him cooled down before we do anything else."

As Ruthanna arranged her lap under her husband's head, Abbie fell to her knees on the other side of Eber. "*Mamm*, tell me what to do."

"Get this cloth good and wet." Esther flung the scrap of an old flour sack at Abbie and thrust the water jug toward her.

Perspiration drenched Abbie's dress as the afternoon's heat pressed in. She handed the sopping rag back to her mother, who exchanged it for a dry one. Abbie drenched the second rag as her mother opened Eber's shirt as far as it would go. With cool damp rags on Eber's chest and face, Esther proceeded to force water down his throat a spoonful at a time.

"Shall we try to take him into the house?" Ruthanna asked.

Esther nodded. "Soon. I hope it's cooler in there."

"It is," Ruthanna said. "Eber insisted on building a generous overhang for the extra shade."

"His own wisdom may help save his life."

"I should pray." Ruthanna looked stricken. "I can't think what to say. Why can't I pray when I have never needed to pray so hard in my life?"

"God hears your prayers." Esther handed a rag to Abbie to dampen again. "Words are not necessary. Now, Abbie, you help me get Eber upright. Ruthanna, you make sure a damp rag stays on his head at all times. Do you understand?"

While her mother tended Eber, Abbie finished milking the cow Eber had left in distress. With three younger brothers she did not often milk a cow anymore, but she managed. Then she took a slop bucket out to the chickens and made sure the horse had food and water.

Evening's waning light gave way to blackness, and still Eber's skin threw off heat. Each time he moaned, the three women jumped to their feet. Ruthanna pulled a chair up to the side of the bed and draped herself across her husband, finally finding words for her prayers. Abbie watched her friend's lips move silently but steadily.

Well after midnight, Abbie lit a lantern and rummaged around Ruthanna's pantry. She found the boiled eggs and a wedge of cheese and prepared a plate, which she set on the bed next to Ruthanna.

Ruthanna shook her head, struggling to swallow. "I cannot eat."

"You must. For the baby."

Ruthanna slowly drew herself up. "I am not sure I can."

"You must try. You must."

"Abigail is right." Esther Weaver's voice came from a dark corner at the foot of the bed.

Abbie peeled a boiled egg and handed it to Ruthanna. "I'll get you something to drink."

"Take care of my Ruthie." The sound from the bed startled them all.

"Eber!" Ruthanna put a hand against his face then turned toward Abbie. "He's cooling off!"

Esther laid a hand across his forehead. "She's right. The fever has broken."

"Will you drink something now, Eber?" Ruthanna asked.

He nodded. "If you will."

Abbie let out a joyful breath. "I will be right back with two glasses."

Esther followed Abbie out of the cramped bedroom and into the cooking area.

"Do you know where to find the doctor in Limon?" Esther whispered.

Abbie swallowed. "I think so. But Eber is better. Haven't we sat through the worst of it?"

Esther glanced toward the bedroom. "I am concerned that he is truly ill."

"He was too much in the heat," Abbie said. "He'll listen to Ruthanna now. He'll be more sensible."

Esther shook her head. "The Lord whispers to my spirit that it is more than that. You should go at first light."

CHAPTER 7

Three days later, Abbie hung up her apron and brushed the loose flour from her skirt. While the bread rose, she had time to go visit Ruthanna and Eber, particularly if she took a horse and buggy rather than walking the miles between the farms. Outside she stood for a moment surveying the Weaver land. The barn and chicken coop were close to the house. Beyond them her father had marked off the corners of a proper stables and training area for new horses. Abbie knew he had hoped to build the structure by now, rather than cramming horses into the barn at night and leaving the weather-beaten buggy outside.

Abbie blew out her breath, swallowed, and crossed the yard to the barn for a horse. Inside, the barn was dim, and it took a few seconds for Abbie to realize that her father knelt next to an open sack of seed. He scooped up a handful then spread his fingers and let it run back down to the sack. She watched him do this three or four times before she spoke.

"*Daed?*"

He looked up.

"Is it all right if I take the buggy? I want to check on Eber and see if Ruthanna needs anything."

"That is fine, daughter. I am sure God is pleased at how you are caring for your friend. You make sure they are following the doctor's instructions."

"I will." Slowly, she reached to remove a harness from the wall. "Are you getting ready to plant again?"

He resumed the rhythm of lifting and sifting seed.

"*Daed?*"

"This seed is the most valuable thing I have. Our family's future depends on the decision I make."

"It's not too late. Others are planting again now."

Ananias Weaver lifted his head and looked at his daughter full on. "It is difficult to discern whether that is foolishness or faith."

"If we don't plant, we won't have a crop."

"And if I cannot irrigate sufficiently, and we don't get rain, we will have wasted a valuable resource."

Abbie moistened her lips. For all of her childhood, her father had held closely any hint of difficulty in the family's finances from year to year or the reasons for his decisions. But she was no longer a child. She was of an age where she could have married and remained in Ohio. Abbie had chosen to move to the new settlement as an adult. At the time, she thought she knew the risks. They all did. No one could have foreseen the difficulty they would face in the quest to root an Amish congregation in the unyielding Colorado plain.

"Take the dark mare, please," Ananias said. "She hasn't been out of the pasture for several days. I don't need a horse that becomes accustomed to idleness."

Willem Peters stabbed a pitchfork into the soiled hay in the end stall of the Gingerich barn. The stench assaulted his breath. Willem was well accustomed to the smells that came with housing and caring for animals, but this seemed extreme. He could not help but wonder how long it had been since Eber felt well enough to adequately muck stalls. The doctor Abbie had fetched from Limon three days ago was clear that Eber needed complete rest for the next few weeks. Word of Eber's decline had spread quickly through the Amish families, and the men soon enough volunteered for the outdoor work to keep the farm operating. Eber would have no crop again this year and had no seed to plant again, but his animals would be milked and fed and cleaned up.

Rudy positioned a wheelbarrow as close to Willem as possible.

"We should have come sooner," Rudy said.

"*Ya.*" Willem emptied the fork into the wheelbarrow and attacked the stall with the implement again. "Eber doesn't like to ask for help."

"He should know that pride is a sin."

"He only wants to know he can take care of his family. You and I are not married men. We don't know what that responsibility must feel like."

"I guess not." Rudy picked up a shovel and began to work alongside Willem. "Why have you not married?"

Willem shrugged. "Perhaps I feel as Eber does—I want to feel sure I can provide."

"So you are waiting for the right time?"

"I suppose so."

"Not the right girl?"

"Of course I want the right girl."

"But haven't you found her?"

Willem eyed Rudy in his peripheral vision. "Do you mean Abigail Weaver?"

"No man could ask for a finer wife. Lovely in appearance, loyal in spirit, unafraid of hardship, devoted to the church."

Willem diverted his gaze now. "You seem to have given a lot of thought to Abigail."

"I am merely an observant man. I have not yet drawn a conclusion about the extent of her patience." Rudy dropped his shovel and gripped the handles of the wheelbarrow again. It was full enough to take out and dump in a place where the manure could do some good.

Willem watched as Rudy navigated down the short length of the barn and turned out of sight at the open door. He stood the pitchfork straight up and leaned on it, wishing Rudy would just say what was on his mind. What did he mean about Abbie's patience?

Willem heard a buggy clatter to a stop outside the barn and abandoned his task to see who had arrived. Abbie Weaver descended from the driving bench and leaned her head attentively toward Rudy.

A week later, Ruthanna worked as quietly as she could along the one wall of the cabin that she called her kitchen. It was a far cry from the sprawling kitchen of the home she grew up in and that she had always imagined her own kitchen would be like.

She *would* have a kitchen someday. Ruthanna refused to believe that she and Eber would have anything less than what they dreamed of when they left Pennsylvania. After all, they had a baby on the way finally—and owned more land than they could have hoped for in Pennsylvania. If they had to live in a small cabin for a year or two longer than they expected, that was not too great a sacrifice.

Ruthanna glanced toward the bedroom. If Eber were well, he would scowl at the thought of two men cleaning out his barn. He might even be displeased at the dishes of food that had been turning up in the hands of Amish visitors eager to be of some practical help during his illness. As it was, he did not question the origin of the food his wife offered to him at frequent intervals and ate very little before saying again that he wished to sleep.

The doctor had been vague. Ruthanna was not persuaded he knew what was wrong with Eber. Prescribing complete rest and generous food was safe advice. Anyone could see Eber was exhausted and thin. Rest and food could not possibly hurt him, but was it enough to help? Ruthanna murmured prayers every time fear welled within her. Eber *would* get well. She would not let her mind dawdle over any other possibility.

The knock at the door was soft, and Ruthanna knew it was Abbie before she turned to look. Abbie had heard the doctor's instructions with her own ears. Each time she visited she kept her voice low and movements soft. The door opened and Abbie entered.

"How are you?" Abbie touched Ruthanna's cheek. "Are you taking care of yourself?"

"I'm fine." Ruthanna gestured to a chair for Abbie to sit in. "The men have been coming to do all the chores. I barely have to leave the house."

"Good. If Eber needs you, you want to be here."

Ruthanna nodded.

From the bedroom came an insistent, deep-chested cough.

"When did that start?" Abbie looked alarmed.

"During the night."

"It sounds terrible."

"It is not constant. He has a fit every few hours. I think it is only the dust. I can't seem to keep it out of the house."

"I will ask my *mamm* if there is something else you should be doing."

"Thank you." Ruthanna swallowed. "I wish I could ask my own *mamm*."

"Have you written? I could mail a letter for you."

Ruthanna shook her head. "I don't want to alarm anyone at home. By the time a letter reached Pennsylvania and my *mamm* could write back, Eber will be well."

"Levi asked me to tell you he is praying in his heart all day long."

A strained smile stretched Ruthanna's lips, and she put her hand on her abdomen. "I hope my *kinner* is as sweet as Levi."

Abbie did not stay long at Ruthanna's. She knew her friend well enough to know she needed to use nervous energy by keeping her hands busy and feeling that she was accomplishing something. While Eber slept, Ruthanna would sweep and scrub and mend and cook, and Abbie would not suggest she should do otherwise. Abbie chatted with Rudy and Willem while she served them cold water and cornbread, provisions sent by her mother. Something was odd between the two of them. Whatever it was, they would have to work it out. Abbie had more on her mind.

Leaving Eber and Ruthanna's farm on the main road, Abbie saw Albert and Mary Miller approaching. She reined in the mare as she came alongside them and could see that Mary held in her lap a dish wrapped in towels. The generosity that poured out of all the Amish neighbors nearly made Abbie's chest burst. They might not have a minister of their own or the twice-monthly worship services they all yearned for, but they could still be a church and care for each other.

Little Abe peeked out from behind his mother and gave Abbie a grin. She grinned back. He lifted one bare foot for her inspection.

Mary laughed. "We were talking about having the cobbler make him some shoes. We have a piece of leather he can use, but we have not had time to take Abe to be measured."

"Why don't I take him?" Abbie said. "I could come by tomorrow and pick up Little Abe and the leather. I would be delighted to do it."

Mary glanced at her son. "He always loves spending time with you."

"Then please let me do this for you. I'll come in the morning so I can have him home in plenty of time for his nap."

CHAPTER 8

It all seemed so secretive, and Abbie did not understand why.

She put her father's breakfast plate in front of him and waited for his silent prayer before she asked, "What will the men be talking about this morning?"

"Church matters, of course." Ananias looked over his round-rimmed glasses at his daughter.

Abbie poured coffee and pushed the mug toward him. "Are we going to get a minister?"

"That is a question for God." He bit into his toast.

"We've been praying for a minister for years." Perhaps it was time for God to answer the pleas of the believers.

"In God's time."

Abbie thought back to more than a year ago. Her father and a few other men gathered on a morning not so different from this one. Hot. Dry. Cloudless.

But a bishop had been with them for that meeting. The men were behind closed doors for hours with Bishop Lehman. He had come from Kansas, which was not so far compared to Ohio or Pennsylvania. Even still, the bishop had not visited for months before that. Another minister, also from Kansas, had come to preach during a break in the February weather. By June of 1913, the twelve Amish families scattered around the outskirts of Limon ached for worship, for the discipline of hearing sermons, for the slow, careful harmonies of their hymns.

For communion, the body and blood of the Lord.

But the bishop cut his visit short without explanation. None but the handful of men on the church council knew the nature of the conversation that would cause him to leave abruptly without preaching and leading the communion service.

And none of them would speak of it, not even to their wives. Abbie had heard enough whispers among the women to know that her ignorance of the circumstances had nothing to do with her age or marital status. The men simply would not speak. Not a word for over a year.

"Maybe a minister would visit us again," Abbie said now, "if we asked."

Why had the ministers stopped visiting the new settlement? The question rang in Abbie's mind, though she dared not ask it aloud.

Ananias cleared his throat. "Abigail, I can see that you are disturbed by your own curiosity. I will not satisfy it, so you may as well release it and put your energy into something needful."

Abbie turned around and set the coffeepot on the stove. Did her father think the women did not miss having church services? Did he believe them incapable of understanding whatever had sent the bishop away?

This time all the men, even the unmarried ones, would attend the meeting. As her father finished his breakfast and put on his hat, Abbie cleaned the dishes with a minimum of water and pondered whether to ask Willem or Rudy later to tell her what happened.

Sitting on the wooden stoop outside his cabin, Willem raised his eyes to the sun. He judged he had a good thirty minutes before he must leave for the meeting and raised his coffee to his lips. It was strong and black and bitter, and he relished the sensation of its thickness oozing down his throat. Before too many more hours, the day would be blistering and he would not want coffee. In this moment he could enjoy it as he gazed across his land and watched as shadows dissipated and the day came into crisp focus.

Open on the step beside Willem was his mother's latest letter.

His brother was considering taking a job in an *English* factory to pay the bank what he owed on his farm. To finance new farm equipment, one of his cousins had sold a parcel of land that had been in the family for 150 years. Willem's gut clenched at the thought of those enchanting rolling acres lost to the Peters family forever. His cousin had been threatening to sell for years and even offered the acres to Willem. But they would have made for a small farm with no good place to situate a house, and Willem wanted a large farm. He wanted plenty of earth to receive as his own, a gift from God. He wanted more than to eke out a living. His parents had taught him generosity from before he ever held a coin in his hand. Over the years since he became a man, Willem had come to see that generosity was a measure of the spirit and not of land or money. Nevertheless his heart swelled with yearning to give. If God blessed him with abundance, Willem would gladly give to all in need.

Eber, for instance. Willem wished he could do something for Eber and Ruthanna. They deserved to know their child would have everything he needed.

Willem took another gulp of coffee. He was not a man for meetings. Last year, when the church council met, Willem had no curiosity about their discussions. He was as surprised as everyone else that the bishop left without serving communion, but Willem never thought to ask about the meeting. Like all Amish men, when he was baptized, he agreed to serve as minister if he should ever be called on, but the possibility could not be further from his mind. Especially now. A minister would have to be ordained, and if they could not even get ministers to visit and preach every few months, it was unlikely a bishop would suddenly agree to ordain one of the men. Besides, Willem was not married. No one would think to nominate him to be minister.

The coffee mug was empty now. The four men who made up the council had been firm that all men should attend this meeting, so Willem stood up, tucked in his shirt, raised his suspenders, and trudged to the barn for his horse.

"I am sure the council will understand if you are not present for the meeting." Ruthanna followed Eber around the cabin, hesitant about every unstable step he took. "They shouldn't even have come out here to ask it of you."

"They asked all the men." Eber leaned over to pick up a boot and sat in a chair to put it on. He turned his head to cough.

"You are not well, Eber." Ruthanna presented herself in front of him with hands on hips.

"I have been in bed for weeks while other men do my work. I believe I can manage to sit upright for one meeting."

"Eber, you barely stay out of bed long enough to eat a meal at the table with me. You cannot even walk to the outhouse."

Ruthanna regretted pointing out this last reality.

Eber's eyes flashed at her. "Perhaps you can find it in yourself to leave me a small portion of my dignity."

"I'm sorry, Eber. You know I love you. I want you to be well. I want you to be strong. Then you can do all the things you want to do."

"Today I want to be strong enough to go to this meeting." Eber laced his boot and tied it snugly.

Ruthanna briefly considered blocking his view as he looked around for his second boot. He had not even had them on since the day she found him collapsed in the barn, yet he thought he was recovered enough to travel twenty miles and sit upright and awake. He did not know what the meeting was about. How could he be so sure he must be present? When Willem Peters delicately asked if Eber planned to go and Ruthanna immediately brushed away the impossible idea, Eber had announced his startling intention.

She stepped across the room and fetched Eber's other shoe. When she handed it to him, she said, "Why don't you let me drive you? I'm sewing for the baby. I can take my things and find a bit of shade to wait for you. That way, if you tire, I can bring you home."

He eyed her briefly before returning his attention to his feet. "I will drive. But you may come."

"Do you promise to let me drive home? You'll be exhausted by then."

Eber put his hand on his stomach and groaned. Ruthanna

winced at the sound.

"All right," he said. "Bring some food. For the sake of the baby."

When Ruthanna carried food and a jug of water out to the buggy, she also took a quilt and a pillow. Even if Eber did not want to admit it, she knew he was going to need them.

Rudy did not see the point.

What could the men possibly have to talk about that would make a difference?

Crops? As far as he knew, no one seriously believed there would be a harvest.

A prayer meeting? Perhaps they intended to pray for the miracle of favorable weather. Rain to drench the fields and fill the water troughs. The stilling of the incessant wind. Clouds to protect their burnished faces from further assault. Such an effort would require more faith than Rudy could muster.

News of a visiting minister? That hardly required a meeting of all the men. The council would have arranged that.

A particular financial need? Rudy could not think what he had to share. Perhaps he would slaughter a cow to mercifully save it from starving to death and revive the long-forgotten taste of meat in everyone's mouths.

Whatever decision was to be made could be made without Rudy. He would go collect the morning's eggs—oh, how he was tired of subsisting on eggs—and go back to bed for another hour. There was no point in going into the fields.

The day's yield was seventeen eggs. Rudy placed them in a tin bowl and shuffled back toward the house, turning only when he heard the sound of a horse and buggy.

Willem Peters.

"You're a mess," Willem said. "Have you even washed your face this morning?"

"I'm not going." Rudy reached for the door.

"Of course you are." Willem dropped down from the buggy bench. "I'll wait for you."

"Willem—"

"Rudy, you're an able-bodied Amish man. The council has asked us to attend, and we will respect them. We knew when we joined the settlers that we might face some difficult decisions."

Rudy did not appreciate Willem's authoritative tone, but he took his point. "I think I have a clean shirt."

Or at least one that was less thick with dust.

CHAPTER 9

The Weaver house filled with women and small children. Abbie knew her mother had invited Mrs. Chupp, the cobbler's wife, and Mrs. Nissley to stop by while their husbands were meeting. The others must have come out of anticipation for what the men's conference might yield. Abbie put a fresh pot of coffee on the stove and fanned herself with an envelope from her cousin Leah in Indiana. Abbie would have to cut the coffee cake and canned apples into small portions to extend hospitality to a dozen extra women and children. The house was crowded and tepid, but Abbie did not mind. Having so many of the Amish women together in one place was almost as satisfying as a shared meal after a church service, an event beginning to fade in memory.

When Abbie heard one more buggy clatter into the yard, she threaded her way through the visiting women to look out the front window.

Mary Miller. And Little Abe.

Abbie grinned wide as she held the door open for them and scooped up Little Abe as soon as his bare feet and wiggly toes crossed the threshold. He showed her all his teeth and put a playful hand over her face.

"He is so adorable that I don't know how you can stand it," Abbie said. She slobbered a kiss on the boy's cheek.

Mary laughed. "He is not always so well tempered. When he has a tantrum I'm grateful we live miles from anyone else or we would have to supply the neighbors with something to plug their ears."

"We'll have to see if we have a treat for you." Abbie gently poked the child's tummy. She looked at Mary. "I'll bring you some *kaffi*. Mrs. Chupp is here. Perhaps she knows when her husband will have Little Abe's new shoes ready."

"He's excited to have shoes, but he is so used to bare feet that I don't know if he'll wear them."

"It will be good for him to have them. The ground here is not like the soft grass at home. Anything that grows is scratchy, and there are so many pebbles. Once he has shoes you can let him play more freely."

"He's not a baby anymore." Mary looked around. "Speaking of babies, is Ruthanna here?"

Abbie shook her head. "I'm sure she wouldn't want to leave Eber at home just to visit. She hasn't left their farm since the day he fell ill."

"I want to ask her what she needs for the baby. I would be happy to share the things Little Abe has outgrown."

"I'm sure she would be grateful."

Little Abe wriggled out of Abbie's arms and squatted to touch the nearest pair of shoes.

"How is your quilt coming along?" Mary asked.

"I have almost all the pieces cut out." Abbie tickled Little Abe under the chin. "I can't wait to start piecing."

"I'm eager to see your progress." Mary looked around. "I suppose everyone is here for the same reason. It's too nerve-racking to wait alone at home for news of what the men are discussing. I hope it is news of a minister. Without church for over a year, this is a wonderful lonesome place to be."

The men gathered on a motley arrangement of chairs, milking stools, barrels, and bales in the Mullet barn. It was the only space that would allow them to sit in a lopsided circle where most of them could see each other's faces. Willem sat beside Rudy at the curve in the circle nearest the open barn doors. He had also carried two jugs of water in from his wagon and now offered this token of refreshment as he studied the mostly bearded faces of the assembly.

Only two gave the slightest sign that they knew the purpose of the meeting. Everyone else appeared as uninformed as Willem and Rudy were.

Eli Yoder cleared his throat. As one of the first Amish men to arrive in Elbert County five years ago, Eli held a certain if unofficial role when the families gathered. Around the circle, conversation ceased as he commanded attention by the gutteral signal that he was ready to begin.

"I thank you all for coming." Eli nodded at Eber Gingerich. "We are blessed to have some among us who have been ill and brought back to us by the grace of God."

Murmurs confirmed the shared gratitude for Eber's presence.

Eli continued. "We will begin with a time of silent prayer so that we may know that we are acting in accordance with the Lord's will in our decisions today."

Willem glanced at Rudy, while around them others bowed their heads. Willem was accustomed to prayer, and he supposed Rudy was, too. Living and working alone on a wide expanse of plowed land allowed ample time to hum the hymns of the *Ausbund* and speak the words of Holy Scripture as prayer. Generally, though, when Willem was instructed to pray he preferred to know what he was praying for. What decisions did Eli Yoder expect they would be making? Willem inhaled softly and bowed his head. He could pray for the Holy Ghost to make His presence known. Such a prayer seemed relevant to any situation Willem had ever encountered.

Eli waited a good long time before speaking an audible "Amen." Willem heard the relief on the breath of other men that they would now find out why they had gathered.

"We need a minister," Eli said. "I have come to feel certain that if we were to nominate a faithful man from among our midst, we could invite a bishop to come and ordain him."

Rudy's hand went up.

Eli raised his eyebrows. "Do you have a nomination already, Rudy?"

"No sir. I have a question."

Eli shifted his considerable weight on the small wooden chair.

"A year ago a bishop was here and left without preaching or

giving us communion. I would be dishonest if I said I have not been wondering for many months why this was so."

Heads turned from Rudy to Eli.

"We are not here to discuss the past," Eli said. "Our need is for a future, and if we have no minister, we have no future. Now, I myself have come prepared to make a nomination."

The only shade Ruthanna saw was in the shadow of her own buggy. She kept her word to Eber and did not situate herself anywhere near the Mullet barn. This was the first time he was out of her sight since that day in their own barn, and every moment stretched interminable. At intervals that did not exceed fifteen seconds, she lifted her eyes to make sure Eber was not emerging from the barn overheated and freshly ill.

Ruthanna spread the blanket on the ground beside the buggy, lowered herself onto it, and unfolded the bundle of sewing she had brought. She was nearly finished with a small quilt and just had to put the hem into two long white infant dresses. Feeling the tension rising in her chest with each glance toward the barn, she began to recite Psalm 23. When she came to, "Yea, though I walk through the valley of the shadow of death," Ruthanna stopped. A lump rising in her throat threatened to cut off her air and she skipped ahead to, "Surely goodness and mercy shall follow me all the days of my life."

Then she made herself take a deep breath and begin stitching without looking up at the barn. She determined to finish a six-inch row of binding along the edge of the quilt before she raised her eyes again.

The wind was oddly still for the Colorado plain. Ruthanna was not sure whether to be grateful not to have hot, dusty air blasting into her face or to think that any movement at all would bring some relief to the perspiration trickling down her neck. She moistened her lips and focused on her row of stitching.

Ruthanna never knew what it was that made her sit up straight and look over her shoulder, through the undercarriage of the buggy, and into the eyes of a coyote. She froze, staring into the unmoving animal's eyes. Every farmer in the region knew what it was like to have a coyote get into the henhouse before dawn—and in one attack destroy the steady flow of eggs that fed the family. Ruthanna had not heard any tales of settlers coming face-to-face with one in the day's light, though.

If she moved, she might startle him into attack. But if he attacked first, her swelling belly and aching back would slow her down. And what was to keep him from leaping into the buggy if she tried to drive away? If he would come this close to begin with, what else might he do?

She started again at the beginning of Psalm 23, speaking the words in her mind over her pounding heart. This time she did not skip the unpleasant part as she held perfectly still and locked eyes with the coyote.

Finally the animal lost interest, turned around, and sauntered away. All Ruthanna wanted was to feel Eber's arms around her.

Rudy meant no disrespect, and he did not pursue his question. Eli did not intend to respond, and the only other two men present who knew the answer would never defy Eli. Unsatisfied about why the rest of the men should remain uninformed and confused, Rudy crossed his arms and tilted his stool back on two legs while Eli made his nomination.

Noah Chupp. The cobbler.

Eli methodically listed Noah's virtues. His mild temperament. His patience. His spiritual depth. His friendly relationships with everyone in the community. His family heritage of ministers, and the certainty that had he remained in Pennsylvania he would have been a minister before now. His grandfather had even been a bishop.

Noah Chupp humbly responded that he would need time to seek out the will of God in this matter. The assembly agreed that of course he should take as much time as he required to be sure. No one wanted to misinterpret the leading of the Lord.

As the meeting broke up, Rudy leaned toward Willem.

"Do you think we will ever know what happened last year?" Rudy asked.

Willem shrugged. "Do we need to?"

"If there is a reason why we have not been able to establish a true church before this, it affects us all. There may be division among us."

"Everyone seemed of one accord about Noah Chupp," Willem said softly. "Unless you are not."

Rudy scratched his chin. "Noah is a fine man."

"Then what is your hesitation?"

"I sense something must come into the light."

Willem stood. "Let's see what comes of praying over this matter. In the meantime, let's see if Eber needs help."

CHAPTER 10

But I thought Noah Chupp was to be our minister." Abbie scrunched her face in confusion.

In Mary Miller's arms, Little Abe twisted to lean over and touch his new brown leather miniature boots.

"Mrs. Nissley says her husband believes it would be better if we began our church with a more experienced minister," Mary said. "He thinks one might come from Kansas."

"Does this minister know. . .the challenges of the settlement? He might need to find a way to make a living other than farming." Abbie tried to picture where a new family might live. Plenty of land was for sale closer to Limon, or perhaps in the other direction toward Colorado Springs. Considering the nearly nonexistent crop yield last year, the price per acre might even have fallen since her father purchased land.

"I don't think Mr. Nissley has anyone particular in mind just yet."

Mary relented and set Abe on his feet, which Abbie thought sensible. That was the point of having shoes made. They stood beside the treeless cow pasture on Weaver land, so the boy would not wander out of sight.

Abbie's confusion compounded. "If Mr. Nissley does not yet know of anyone willing to come, isn't it premature to talk about the possibility? Besides, we all heard what the men decided. Noah Chupp was to pray over the matter and give an answer in two weeks. What if he says yes? Wouldn't it be easier to find a bishop to ordain him than to persuade a minister who is already serving another district to move out here?"

"What if Noah says no?" Mary countered.

Then they would be back where they started. But if Adam Nissley thought enticing a minister from Kansas truly was an option, surely it would have happened by now.

"Let's walk a little bit," Abbie said, "and let Little Abe try out his shoes."

"He has learned to say 'off,' but I want him to be used to them before the weather turns." Mary began to amble in the direction her son led.

Abbie scanned the horizon. At winter's worst, it was hard to imagine the days would ever blister this hot again. Now it was difficult to think of the weather turning. Snow could fall as early as mid-September—too late for the crop and too soon to hope a minister might come before spring.

"I think Noah Chupp would do a fine job," Abbie said. "He makes wise decisions, and he was one of the first settlers to come. He loves the church, and he listens to the Holy Ghost."

"I wonder why they didn't think to ask him before this." Ahead of them, Mary's son lost his balance and fell on his bottom.

Abbie watched the tenacious child. While other toddlers might have wailed at falling in the dirt, Little Abe did the obvious thing. He put his hands on the ground and pushed himself upright again. Abbie's imagination drifted forward forty years when Little Abe would just be Abe, or Abraham, and he might be called upon to lead the congregation that nurtured him from infancy under the leadership of many ministers.

"We all must pray," Abbie said. "We followed God's leading to come and settle here. We must not think that He would abandon us. Finding the right minister is a matter of God's timing. Perhaps God has only begun to prepare the heart of our minister."

"I long for communion." Mary put a hand to the side of her head and pushed an errant braid into place. "I long for the unity that comes when we gather around the Lord's table."

"As do I," Abbie murmured. Without a spiritual leader for much longer, she hated to think what would happen to morale among the settlers.

The knock on the door startled Ruthanna. It was a man's knock, heavy fisted and insistent. She put down the baby's quilt and pulled herself out of the chair before Eber stirred. Though he would deny it, in Ruthanna's opinion Eber's outing to the men's meeting had sent him back to his bed in worse condition. He simply did not have the strength to spend half a day riding in a wagon and sitting upright. By God's grace Ruthanna had refrained from chastising her husband about his choice, instead caring for him with the same tenderness she offered before their disagreement. She did not tell him about the lurking coyote that day, though she had folded the blanket and moved back up into the buggy, and instead of watching for Eber every fifteen seconds she moved her eyes back and forth across the horizon, turning also to look behind her.

She opened the door now expecting Willem or Rudy or one of the other men inquiring whether she needed help with anything beyond the usual chores.

Instead she stared into brown eyes above ruddy cheeks on the face of Jake Heatwole.

Jake offered a warm, broad smile. "Good morning, Mrs. Gingerich. The Lord's blessing be on you."

"Thank you." Ruthanna moved aside, wondering what refreshment she might offer. Perhaps bread and strawberry preserves. "Please come in."

"I suppose you're surprised to see me."

Jake stepped into the room and removed his black hat nearly identical to Eber's. He wore the same collarless black suit and white shirt the Amish men wore. The townspeople of Limon never understood the difference between Amish and Mennonite, but Ruthanna did. The Amish had parted ways from the Mennonites more than two hundred years ago. Ruthanna did not claim certainty about the original dispute or the sometimes hostile chasm it opened between the two groups, but she did feel certainty that she belonged to the heritage her family had claimed for generations. She had no need to test the liberties the Mennonites might allow upon which the Amish would likely frown—especially if they had a minister. Ruthanna would much rather rest secure in belonging to the true church.

Still, it was hard not to like Jake Heatwole. She wondered why he had never married.

"I've just come from Willem Peters's," Jake said. "He tells me that your Eber is still ill and that he has not truly been well since that day we all encountered one another at the train station."

Ruthanna nodded and gestured to the only chair with a hint of padding on its seat. "Let me get you something. *Kaffi?* I have fresh cream."

Jake sat in the chair but waved away her offer. "I have not come to cause you inconvenience. Quite the opposite. I want to help."

"The men are doing the essential chores until Eber gets back on his feet."

"So Willem tells me. He also says that he looks around and sees work that they cannot keep up with because of their own farms. The henhouse, for instance, has a hole in the roof that is only going to get bigger. And he says you never leave the farm because you do not want to leave Eber alone."

Ruthanna nodded. This was all true. She depended heavily on Abbie and Esther to stop in and see if she needed anything from town before they went. Rain was unlikely, so she had not worried about the hole in the henhouse roof, though since her encounter with the coyote she wondered just how much of an opening the animal would require to wreak havoc.

"We're getting by." Ruthanna wiped her hands on her apron, turned a chair toward Jake, and sat down. "The others are doing everything they can to help."

"Of course they are," Jake said. "That is what the church does. I am here to help for the same reason."

Ruthanna furrowed her brow. "But you are Mennonite. We are Amish."

"We serve the same God."

"But your own farm—"

"It's in the capable hands of my two brothers. They know that I will move to Limon eventually to open a church there. They hardly let me lift a hand around the farm anymore."

"Surely you must have a thousand things to do."

"No doubt." Jake leaned forward, his elbows on his knees. "But this comes to the top of my list."

"Mr. Heatwole, your offer is most generous, but—"

"We can talk it over with Eber. I propose to camp out behind your barn for two weeks. I won't ask anything of you in the house except a bit of water if you can spare it. I'll give the other men a break by looking after all the chores, and if you need to go into town or want to visit with your friend Abbie, you can do so knowing that someone is here with Eber."

Ruthanna swallowed as she considered. What he suggested had merit. "Only for two weeks. Not a day more."

Jake turned a palm up. "We all hope Eber will be better soon."

"And only if Eber agrees."

"Of course."

The committee assembled at the crossroads that joined three farms. Two miles away was Noah Chupp's land, with a promising vegetable garden despite the drought and a separate structure he used for a small tannery and cobbler's shop. He made shoes for the *English* as well, along with other leather goods, and it seemed to Willem that Noah's livelihood was thriving better than most. Willem was glad for the whole Chupp family, which included seven children under the age of twelve.

Willem never intended to be on this committee. Certainly he did not volunteer for it. Unlike Rudy, Willem hesitated to decline anything Eli Yoder asked him to do, so here he was with Eli. They stood beside their horses as they waited for the widower Samuels to join them. The trio would proceed together to hear Noah's discernment of the Lord's leading about becoming the first minister of the fledgling congregation, provided a bishop would agree to ordain him.

Martin Samuels trotted toward them, slowing his gelding but not dismounting.

Eli crossed his wrists in front of him. "Shall we have a word of prayer before we proceed?"

Willem hoped God had already made His will plain to Noah Chupp. Most congregations chose their ministers by lot, and the man chosen rarely had grounds to refuse. Noah already enjoyed the privilege of private discernment. But once again Willem found it impossible to refuse Eli.

"I agree," Martin said. "If Noah feels the calling of God to take up this mantle, he will bear the burden of healing the divide among us. It will not be an easy task. Will we wait until he agrees before we explain why the bishop left last year?"

Eli's eyes flashed at Willem before lowering in a posture of prayer. "We will not speak of that. We will pray only for our future."

Willem would have been hard-pressed to say he was praying in the moments of silence that followed. Too many questions flashed through his mind. He did not even close his eyes, instead gazing first at Eli and then at Martin. Eli stood motionless, head bowed, eyes closed, feet shoulder width apart. On his horse Martin leaned over the horn of the saddle, one hand crossed above the other, with his eyes squeezed in peculiar fervency.

Rudy's barn door was wide open in the middle of the morning. Abbie glanced at the cows dotting the nearest field and then turned toward the smaller horse pasture. The animals were all where they were supposed to be. She knocked on the house door as usual, heard no response, and went inside to leave the bread. Coming out again, it disturbed her to see the barn door open, and rather than climbing back into her cart, she strode over to the barn.

"Rudy?"

"In here." A grunt accompanied his reply.

Visions of Eber sprawled in the straw spurred Abbie into the depths of the barn. "Where are you?"

"The end stall."

Abbie kicked straw out of the walkway. When she saw him, Abbie gasped. A cow was secured in the stall, and Rudy had one arm well inside it.

"Time for the calf?" Abbie said. She had seen calves born on her own family's farm in Ohio, but the wonder of it mesmerized her every time. "Is she all right?"

Rudy nodded, his eyes closed.

He was visualizing the position of the calf, Abbie knew.

"I have one foot and the nose," he said. "Ah. There's the other foot."

Abbie moved into the stall. "How can I help?"

"Hand me the rope," Rudy said. "It's there on the wall."

Abbie handed it to him and then leaned over his shoulder to peer into the mystery of life. Rudy secured the feet and prepared to pull if necessary. The cow began to strain, and as she did, Rudy checked the position of the calf once again.

"Will it be a normal birth?" Abbie asked.

"I think so. The mother is doing well. This is her third calf."

Abbie held her breath, awaiting the cow's next round of exertion.

"Here we go," Rudy said, readjusting his position to brace for delivery.

Abbie stepped back to watch without further chatter until first the face, then one shoulder, then the other emerged. Rudy kept his hands positioned to respond to distress but otherwise let the natural process take its course. Within a few minutes, the calf lay in the straw beside its mother. Rudy examined the newborn quickly.

"Is it all right?" Abbie asked.

Rudy looked up and grinned. "A female, and she's perfect."

Abbie squatted to look more closely, taking in the angles of the legs and the curves of the head. "God is good."

Rudy calmly tended to the mother. "I'm glad you were here to see the birth."

"I am, too. I would have come ready to be more help if I had known."

"She was fast. I only started watching her closely last night, and not much happened until this morning."

"God has blessed you." Abbie stepped out of the stall. "I'll heat some water so you can clean up."

"*Danki.*"

Abbie turned for one last look at mother, calf, and Rudy, a triangle of tenderness in a bed of straw. She had not seen such contentment on Rudy's face in months—but perhaps she had not been looking.

CHAPTER 11

Thank you for taking me to town with you." Ruthanna offered Abbie a grateful smile.

"It was no trouble. I was going anyway, and it's so much more fun to have you with me." The reins were nearly slack in Abbie's hands. Their business in Limon complete, they were in no rush to return to the chores that awaited them.

"We both did well with our eggs today," Ruthanna said. "It seems to be the only thing that gives us a bit of cash these days. Imagine what would happen if the townspeople figured out they could keep chickens in back of their houses."

"They don't like the smell and the mess. So far there are enough merchants to take eggs from both us and the *English* farmers. God provides."

"It doesn't hurt that the railroads will buy as many eggs as they can get to feed their employees."

Abbie chuckled. "Blessing comes in many forms."

Ruthanna spread her arms out in front of her. "Fresh air! I've barely been out of the house in weeks. Jake insisted it would be good for me to have an outing. He promised he would stay inside the house with Eber the whole time I was gone."

Abbie bit back the response that sprang to her mind. If Ruthanna had wanted to go somewhere, Abbie or one of her parents gladly would have stayed with Eber. Abbie visited every day, sometimes collecting eggs to sell in town, and Ruthanna never said she wished she could go, too. But she took advice from Jake

Heatwole, that Mennonite minister who obviously was looking for people to help him start a congregation of his own.

"Have you heard anything new about Noah Chupp?" Ruthanna asked. "It's already been four days since he told the committee he needed more time."

Abbie nodded. Talking about the possibility of their own minister was a far more pleasant topic. "I think he wants to be very sure, and I cannot blame him. It's an honor to be asked, and he will want to be sure of his motives before the Lord."

Ruthanna peered down the road at her approaching farm. "I do hope Eber is all right."

"I'm sure he's fine." Abbie clicked her tongue to speed the horse for Ruthanna's sake. "He seemed much better this morning when we left."

"He enjoys Jake's company, even if he has reservations about the Mennonites."

"If Eber is feeling well enough for company, I am sure our own men would be happy to see more of him."

"Willem and Rudy have been by, of course. We're out of the way for everyone else."

"Nonsense. I will mention to my *daed* that Eber might benefit from some male company." She turned into the lane that would take them to the Gingerich home. To her surprise, Eber was sitting in a chair in the yard.

When Abbie stopped the buggy, Ruthanna got down as gracefully as possible in her condition.

"Eber! You're outside!" Ruthanna closed the yards between them and put a hand on her husband's head.

"Jake carried the chair outside," Eber said, "on condition that I agree not to lift a hand with the work."

Abbie followed Ruthanna's eyes as she smiled at the Mennonite minister.

Jake picked up a rag and wiped it across his forehead. "I thought I would make some repairs to the henhouse. Hail damage, I think."

"I'm sure the hens will be grateful," Ruthanna said.

"Maybe they've gotten used to seeing the stars at night."

Ruthanna laughed. Still in the buggy, Abbie clamped her jaw

closed. This was not the time to impress on Ruthanna that Jake Heatwole's motives might include recruiting the Gingeriches.

"I should go." Abbie rearranged her grip on the reins. "As soon as I hear that Noah Chupp has officially accepted, I'll let you know."

Willem looked up when the shadow across the barn door interfered with the light he was depending on. "Noah! Good afternoon."

Noah stood in the doorway without stepping into the barn. "Do you have a few minutes, Willem?"

"Certainly." Willem laid down the short stool leg he was carving to replace one that had cracked on his milking stool. "Shall we go in the house? It's humble, but it's out of the sun."

Noah nodded, and Willem led the way. Inside, Willem turned two narrow wooden chairs toward each other. He saw the perspiration seeping through Noah's beard.

"Let me get you a glass of water."

Noah put up one hand as he sat down. "There is no need. I'm on my way into town to deliver some boots and will not take up much of your time."

Willem scratched the back of his head and occupied the other chair. The space between them would have accommodated one pair of stretched out limbs, but Willem took his cue from Noah and sat straight and upright.

Noah cleared his throat. "I told the committee I would let you know when I made a decision."

Willem held his face in solemn stillness, already suspecting that Eli Yoder was going to be unhappy with what Noah was preparing to say.

"Yes," Willem said, "we are anxious to hear what sign the Lord has given you."

"I came here because I believe you are the most sensible man on the committee who visited me four days ago."

Willem waited.

"I must decline the gracious invitation to serve as the settlement's first minister."

Willem sighed. He could not think of one settler who would

not be disappointed to hear this decision.

"People will have many questions," Noah said.

"Yes, I suppose so." Willem waited as Noah shuffled his feet and rubbed his hands down his legs.

"We each must serve out of our conscience," Noah said. "My conscience will not allow me to accept such a grave responsibility while my spirit is home to the least bit of doubt."

"Doubt?" Willem had never known Noah Chupp to be filled with anything but devout faith. "Are you doubting our Lord?"

Noah shook his head. "Our Lord is faithful, and my faith in Him is firm."

"Then what troubles your spirit, Noah?"

"Our settlement is as fragile as an old stalk of wheat."

Willem leaned forward, elbows on knees. "Yes, we are precarious. I would have to agree. But we all feel that a formal church with a minister will only be to our good. When we hear the Word preached and sing our hymns together, our bonds will surely strengthen."

Noah tilted his head. "I realize that is the prevailing sentiment."

"Is it not more than sentiment? Is it not faith?"

"Therein lies my doubt," Noah said. "We are few in number as it is. No one else is coming. We need members. We need crops to feed our families and take to market. Frankly, I believe we will lose families rather than gain them."

Willem also suspected this to be true, so he offered no dispute.

Noah licked his lips and glanced around the house before meeting Willem's eyes again. "My family will be the first to leave, Willem."

Willem sat up and scraped his chair back a few inches. "Have you already decided? I thought your livelihood was going well because you took in work from the *English*."

"It is. But I need a church as much as anyone. My seven children need a church. In a few years my eldest daughter will be looking for a husband. Am I supposed to marry her off to Widower Samuels? Or that bundle of nerves Rudy Stutzman?"

Willem had no response.

"I am on my way to Limon to mail the documents to finalize

the purchase of land in Nebraska. I am already talking to an *English* interested in my land here. He won't pay what I paid per acre, but I will go away with something to start again."

"I see. You've given this a great deal of thought."

Noah rubbed a knuckle against the side of his nose. "I may as well tell you the whole truth."

"There's more?"

"I am leaving the Amish."

"Leaving? Altogether?"

Noah nodded. "I believe the Mennonites are fine people, and not so different from us. Even the Baptists are true people of God, and many of them live as plainly as we do. I am sure we will find a spiritual home."

Willem felt his jaw drop open. He never suspected Noah Chupp would consider anyone beyond the Amish to be true people of God. He cleared his throat.

Noah stood. "I thank you for not trying to talk me out of a decision I have wrestled with in prayer for long hours."

Willem stood as well. "I know you can't have come to this easily. What would you like me to do for you, Noah?"

"Speak to Eli Yoder, please."

Willem's heart thudded. "Perhaps we can go together to speak to him."

Noah waved off the idea. "I realize he will come directly to my shop as soon as he hears, and I will have to talk to him. But I trust your sensibilities to break this news to him first."

Abbie clenched her fists and glared at Willem.

"Don't look at me like that," he said. "Noah Chupp's decision is not my doing."

She kicked a rock down the rutted lane of her family's land. Willem had waited until they were beyond earshot of the rest of the Weavers to tell her the news. She huffed out the air pent up in her chest.

"I'm sorry. It just would have meant so much to the community for him to become our minister." In an established district, church members would have chosen their minister by lot from among the men. Declining would have been far more difficult. Sadness crept through Abbie that time-tested traditions of their own faith had failed to answer this need.

"I know how much you wanted Noah to accept," Willem said.

"To discern that it was not God's will is one thing. But to move away and join the Mennonites? Or the Baptists?"

"He remains a man of deep faith, Abigail." Willem reached for her hand and pulled her to his side. "*Gottes wille.* If Noah is not to be our minister, God still has a plan. We will be all right."

"Why won't any bishops come to us, Willem? That's what I want to know." She searched his face for any sign that he knew the answer to her question. "We don't live in the wilderness. Colorado Springs is not so far, or Denver. Limon has twenty-four trains a day! Traveling to us is not a great difficulty."

She could see he had no response, but the rampage in her heart was too full blown to stop. "We *need* to worship in our traditional ways. We need to go to church. We need to hear the Word preached. Our settlement could bear everything else that is happening to us if we just had our spiritual life together."

Willem nodded and lifted both her hands, turning her to face him. "Jake Heatwole is a minister. He knows all our hymns. He speaks our language. We could have church."

A *Mennonite* church service. The thought of it almost caused physical pain in Abbie's chest. She wondered if Willem knew her as well as she thought he did.

Abbie stitched feverishly that night on the tree of life quilt, full of defiance of what Willem implied. His words would not be enough to diminish her faith.

CHAPTER 12

Abbie swiped a rag cut from a flour sack across the wide-planked table one last time. Rudy Stutzman lived simply. Cleaning his house never took long. He was not particularly organized, but he was more inclined than most men to push a broom across the floor occasionally or brush bread crumbs into his hand and shake them outside for the birds. Abbie had not seen Rudy that morning. She supposed he was in the fields, though it was possible he had decided to go into Limon. His horses were not in the pasture where Rudy usually left them during the day.

She gathered her pail of cleaning supplies and stood on his narrow front step for a moment, her mind flashing to the day she had found him inquiring about train tickets. That was weeks ago. Surely he was not still thinking of leaving, not after the joy she saw on his face when the calf was born. Abbie heard chickens clacking in the yard and saw Rudy's cows nuzzling the ground for something to chew. When Rudy acquired more than one cow, many had thought it was an odd choice for a bachelor. How much milk and cheese would he need? Abbie had smiled to herself at the time. Eight cows were Rudy's investment in a future. Before long he was selling milk, butter, and cheese to *English* neighbors, claiming that the distance he had to drive to do so was well worth the income. Sometimes they paid him in meat or beans, which was almost as good as cash.

With her pail beside her on the floor of the Weaver buggy—in the heat of midsummer, she preferred the shade of the buggy to the open-air cart—Abbie picked up the reins. She was on her way next to Mary Miller's farm, having promised to sit with Little Abe for a few hours while Mary went to work on a quilt with Mrs. Nissley. Abe was past the age of sitting quietly to play on the floor while his mother concentrated on something besides him, and Abbie loved to be with him. With a glance at the sky to judge the time, Abbie opted for a detour that would take her well out of her way. Once she had made up her mind, she shut off any thoughts of reasons not to.

Forty minutes later, Abbie pulled up to the Chupp property, swinging wide away from the cobbler's workshop and instead aiming for the house. Sarah Chupp was in the yard hanging the sparse laundry she had indulged in washing. In a household with seven children, a certain amount of water had to be allotted to washing. At Sarah's feet, her youngest child pushed a fist-sized rock around in the dirt. What would Little Abe Miller do without his favorite playmate?

With a dark brown dress slung over her shoulder, Sarah turned toward Abbie. Taking in a deep breath, Abbie stepped down from the buggy's bench in no particular hurry.

"Hello, Abbie." Sarah took a clothespin from a basket and used it to hang a towel. "I suppose you've heard the news."

Abbie nodded. "I'm sorry that I didn't notice you were unhappy before it came to this."

"It hasn't come to anything. We made a decision, that's all." Sarah pinned up a tiny white shirt.

"I hate to see you go. You are a precious family. The church loves you all."

Sarah lifted her basket and moved it down the line. Abbie picked up a damp towel and two pins.

"There really isn't a church, now is there?" Sarah's tone was soft, but her words stung Abbie.

" 'Where two or three are gathered,' " Abbie said. "We could be the kind of church we all want if your husband were the minister."

Sarah sighed and scratched the top of her head just in front of her prayer *kapp*. "Noah made up his mind."

"You're his wife. He would listen to you."

"You presume I would want him to change his mind."

Abbie forced down the lump forming in her throat. "Your families have been Amish for two hundred years."

"I know."

"Then you know what it means to belong, to help each other through hard times, to care for each other."

"We have seven children to think of." Sarah bent for a moment to run a hand through her son's hair, smoothing it out away from his face.

"I am sorry we failed you," Abbie said. "I hope you will accept my apology on behalf of the whole church."

"Don't be silly, Abigail. No one failed us."

"But you want to leave us."

"It's not anybody's fault, Abbie. We made a choice to move out here three years ago, and now we have made a choice to try another place."

"But to leave the Amish church—is that not extreme?" Abbie fought the lines forming in her face.

Sarah reached out and took Abbie's hand. "You're very kind. No one is more committed to this settlement than you are, and if it succeeds I suspect it will be because of you."

Abbie's shoulders fell. "But you do not believe we can succeed."

"*Gottes wille.* But no, Noah and I both feel it is only a matter of time before the families of the settlement will face the same decision we faced. We simply have chosen to decide sooner."

Abbie failed to stifle her gasp. "Do you really think others will leave?"

"Abigail, you're an intelligent young woman." Sarah raised her palms toward the blistering sun. "You know about the drought. You know the damage the hail did. You know that everybody owes money to the bank. You know that not everyone will have any crop to sell this year."

"But your husband has a trade," Abbie protested.

"And no money to buy hides to make leather, and nine mouths to feed. Our own people cannot even ask him to make shoes because they have nothing to pay him with. We did not come all the way out here to make shoes for the *English*. Noah can do that in a place where we can join a church and teach our children the life of faith. We've made our decision, Abbie."

Sarah put her empty laundry basket on her hip, reached for her son's small hand, and began to walk toward the house.

By the time Abbie reached the Millers' house, she made sure her to banish her tears. Mary met her at the door with her quilt project bundled in her arms.

"Little Abe is down for a nap," Mary said, "but he should wake up in about half an hour. Thank you for coming!"

Mary left, and Abbie moved to the doorway of the room where Little Abe slept. She leaned against the doorframe with her hands behind her waist and watched the little boy's chest rise and fall. He was too little to know he was losing a playmate whom Abbie had hoped he would know for his entire life, too innocent to realize how precarious his own family's existence was. Abbie's mind drifted to her own quilt, the one she worked on in the evenings. Twelve trees of life were to represent the twelve founding households of the settlement. Eleven would be all wrong.

The evening cooled, though the air remained arid. Willem rode over after supper, as he often did, to see if Abbie would like a walk. One look at her face told him that Noah Chupp's decision still crushed her.

"*Gottes wille,*" he said. "We will be all right."

"It's wrong, Willem." She paced so briskly that Willem expended more energy than he wished to keep up with her. "Can't you talk to Noah again? It's been a few days. Maybe he would be ready to listen to reason."

"Each man should follow his own conscience." Willem reached for her hand, trying to slow her down. "You know Noah is a man of prayer. He did not make the decision on a whim."

"But what about our community? It is the way of our people to have a commitment to one another. We all knew that a new settlement would face challenges. We must face them together, not surrender to our individual interests."

He took her by both shoulders now, stilling her and turning her to face him. "Abbie, can you honestly say that your family's life has been as you pictured it when your parents began talking about moving to Colorado?"

"That is not the point I'm trying to make." She tried to worm free, but he would not release her. He held his gaze steady until hers settled and she looked him in the eyes, unblinking.

"We all came out here not just to begin a new church," Willem said, "but because we believed we could have a more prosperous life. More land, lower prices. We have to be honest about our motives before we judge Noah Chupp."

"Of course the men must make a living and provide for their families," Abbie said. "Life here on the plains is a great deal of work for the women, too. But how can we so easily lose sight of the church? If everyone gives up and moves away, what will these years have been for?"

"God has His purposes. Even suffering forms us into His image." Willem moved one hand up to the side of Abbie's neck, and he felt the tension ease beneath his fingers as he knew it would. "Abbie, no matter what happens, we will be all right."

"You always say that." Her lips pouted, but the fight had gone out of her tone.

"Because it's true. If it is God's will for our settlement to succeed, then it will. And if everyone moves away, God will not care for us any less."

Her lips moved in and out, but Willem could see Abbie had no argument against the simple truths of his statement. He raised a thumb to her face and gently drew it across her lips before covering her mouth with his and feeling her remaining resistance dissipate.

They jumped apart at the sound of a throat clearing.

Willem peered over Abbie's shoulder. "Jake."

Abbie exhaled and took a farther step back.

"It's a lovely evening for a long walk, don't you think?" Jake smiled at both of them.

"How is Eber?" Abbie asked.

Jake tilted his head. "Today has not been as bad as many."

"Has the doctor been back out to their place?" Willem asked.

"Several times. He does not seem to have anything new to say. It may be a disorder of the stomach."

"Eber is under too much stress," Willem said.

"How much longer will you stay?" Abbie asked.

"A few days." Jake ran one finger around the rim of his hat. "I will let you know, Willem, so you and the others can sort out what to do about the chores. I don't want Ruthanna left with the heavy work."

"Of course not."

Abbie raised a hand to adjust her prayer *kapp*. "I think I'll turn in early tonight. I'll see Ruthanna in the morning." She turned to go.

"I'll walk you back," Willem said.

"That's not necessary. There's plenty of light left. You two must have things to talk about." Abbie had already recovered her brisk pace of earlier in the evening.

Willem watched her go but made no move to follow.

Jake's mouth twisted in a smile. "Where's your horse, Willem?"

Willem dipped his straw hat. "Outside Abbie's front door."

"She's a woman with a mind of her own."

"That she is. She's worried about the church more than anything."

Jake nodded. "I heard about Noah Chupp. I would offer to try to help folks, but I suspect I would only feed the discord in the council right now."

Willem swiveled his head to look at Jake. "Discord in the council?"

"My presence suggests that some believe true faith is possible outside the Amish church," Jake said. "Is that not what causes the bishops to refuse to come to your congregation?"

Willem scratched his forehead. "It would certainly be an explanation, though not one that I have heard."

"Then I hope I have not spoken out of turn." Jake lifted his own hat off his head in a farewell gesture. "Keep your distance. Don't let her catch you fetching your horse."

CHAPTER 13

Standing in the Chupps' barren yard two weeks later, Abbie refused to let tears well. Noah double-checked the harness that strapped two horses to an overloaded buggy while Sarah kept the youngest two children where she could reach them easily. Abbie stood with Rudy Stutzman apart from the mass of families who had come to bid the Chupps farewell.

"They aren't taking very much with them," she observed.

"An *English* family came in and bought it all for half what it was worth." Rudy kicked a pebble back and forth with one toe. "Noah wanted every penny he could scrape up for traveling costs."

"Will they drive the buggy all the way to Nebraska?"

"I believe that is his plan. Nine train tickets would be costly, and he wants the horses."

"What will he do for work? Do the *English* in cities even use cobblers anymore? Don't they have factories for things like that?"

Rudy shrugged. "Noah is not afraid of hard work. He will find something."

"But they cannot even go to their families if they are still intent on leaving the Amish church."

Rudy turned to look at Abbie. He gestured toward the buggy. "They are truly leaving, Abbie. You have to put them in God's hands."

"If they were in need, the rest of us would do anything we could to help, just as they would have for us. A family with seven children—they have to know what a loss this is for our community.

Why should they leave when the rest of us are here? I had hoped they cared more than that."

"Your own love for the church cannot force anyone to stay."

"You stayed," Abbie said. "That day at the depot, you were thinking of leaving, but you are still here."

Rudy said nothing.

"Rudy, you're staying, aren't you?"

"I don't want to quarrel, Abigail."

Her heart raced. "We are not quarreling. We are talking about the good of the community, about not thinking only of ourselves but how our choices will affect many other people."

Rudy gave the pebble a swift kick with the side of his shoe. "You should talk to your own Willem about that. He will do anything it takes to save his farm. Surely you know that."

"We all share that goal. If we save our farms, we save our settlement, and if we save the settlement, we save the church."

"In your mind everything is tied together like so much string in a ball. Willem doesn't see it that way."

"Who are you to say how Willem sees our life here?" Abbie ground her teeth together. Who was Rudy to think he knew Willem better than she did?

"I thought we weren't going to quarrel." Rudy spoke softly.

Abbie swallowed. "We're not."

"Ask Willem yourself, unless you are afraid to hear what he would say."

"Of course I am not afraid to ask Willem." Abbie flipped a palm up. "I'll do it tomorrow."

"Ask him what choice he would make between his farm and the church."

"Why should he have to make that choice?"

Rudy was not looking at her any longer. "The Chupps are ready. We should go wish them Godspeed."

"Does *Mamm* know you are taking salt pork?" Levi Weaver raised his blue eyes with the question.

Abbie put the lid back on the wooden barrel outside the Weaver back door and made sure it was closed tightly. "Yes, she does."

"Is she sure we have enough food for you to take some?" Levi thumped the barrel lid himself.

Abbie carried a hunk of pork into the kitchen, where she had left a knife on the butcher block. Levi followed. "As you can see, I am only taking a little bit."

"But *Mamm* always says every bit of food counts." Levi's tone carried no accusation.

"And she is right." Abbie drew the knife through the pork and carved off five modest slices. She held one out to Levi.

The boy shook his head. "I wouldn't feel right."

"I am sure *Mamm* would want you to have it. She said only yesterday that she doesn't believe you are eating enough."

"I'm fine."

Levi was such a serious child, Abbie thought. He was not anything like the two brothers in between the family bookends that Abbie and Levi formed. Daniel and Reuben were hardworking and respectful, but they did not carry the weight of the world on their shoulders.

"Levi, we have enough food. It probably feels like we eat the same things all the time. I suppose that's true, but we have enough."

"It can't last forever."

"We have to eat, Levi. That's what food is for."

"But you're taking a picnic for Willem. Is he running out of food?"

Abbie wrapped the pork slices in a flour sack towel. "I don't think so. But he's a bachelor. We often share food with him and the others. You know that."

He shrugged one shoulder and looked at his feet.

She sat in a chair and pulled him onto her lap. "God will provide, Levi. You must believe that. God gives us food to nourish us, and when we eat it we show that we are grateful for God's gift. Do you understand?"

Levi dragged his bare toe in a circle on the floor. When had he gotten tall enough to still reach the floor when he sat in Abbie's lap? He was going to be lanky like his brothers.

"I hope Willem is grateful for the food you're taking him."

"I'm sure he will be. Now help me pack the picnic. Get me a jar of apples from the back porch, will you?"

"We didn't grow those apples," Levi said. "*Mamm* had to buy them from the *English*."

"They were too small for the *English* to sell in their market, and she got a very good price on the whole bushel. Now go get me a jar."

Abbie ran down the mental list of foods she would use to entice Willem on a midday picnic. She had fresh bread, egg salad, spiced apples, half a sponge cake, and salt pork. And she would be sure to take plenty of water. It would be an act of faith that surely God would soon send rain.

Abbie smiled down at Willem from the buggy bench, and he leaned on the fence post with both arms.

"You must have driven halfway around my farm to find me out here," he said.

"I very nearly gave up and thought perhaps you had gone into Limon and didn't mention it to me."

"Now why would I do that when you make such fine company?"

"What are you in the middle of?"

Willem liked the way her nose scrunched when she asked questions instead of coming right out with what was on her mind.

"I can't seem to grow anything," he said. "But I'm thinking of marking off a road from the back side of my property."

Abbie smiled. "We go that way all the time anyway. Might as well make it a faster way."

"I was pretty sure you would figure that out." Willem raised his hat and ran a hand through his hair. "Why have you tracked me down out here in the far corners?"

She brightened further. "I packed a picnic. Let's drive somewhere and find a nice spot."

"A picnic? For no reason?"

"Your favorite cake. Admit it. You can't resist."

Willem looked over his shoulder in the direction of his future road. He had wanted to pace off his planned route and begin calculating how many stones he would need to line the edges for the entire length. If conditions persisted, dry soil would blow off toward Kansas and leave stones uncovered. He would rather have had a good crop and have to dig rocks out. Willem looked again at Abbie's face shining under the brim of the bonnet she wore over her prayer *kapp* and admitted what he was doing did not qualify as urgent. And a man did need to eat lunch, after all.

"All right, then." He brushed his hands together to clear them of dirt. "But I want you to let me drive."

"Of course." Abbie slid over on the bench.

Willem hoisted himself into driving position and signaled the horse to make a wide turn. Abbie was a good driver but too slow. She would wander all over searching for the perfect spot—which of course did not exist. A picnic called for temperate weather, not oppressive heat. A picnic called for shade, not one exposed field after another. A picnic called for a cool breeze off a lake or river, not dust blowing in their eyes. Had Abbie even thought about these realities, or did she see in her mind's eye the river and oak trees of Ohio rather than the dried creeks and half-dead scrub oak of Colorado? Willem wondered how long it would take to grow a decent shade tree in this part of the country. Maybe their grandchildren would be able to sit under one.

Abbie spread a quilt out on the ground. The spot of shade Willem had spied was barely big enough for the two of them to sit beside a large bush, but she did not complain. They had not passed any more promising options, and at least it was a patch of green instead of unending brown dirt. Abbie still did not know the names of all the odd vegetation of the Colorado plain.

She had used an empty fruit bushel to hold the picnic food. It had seemed like plenty in the kitchen, but out here it appeared sparse. *Gratitude,* she reminded herself. At the bottom of the bushel basket were two plates, and she handed one to Willem. They paused for a silent prayer. Abbie asked for the assurance her heart craved. Of Willem's love for her. Of his faithfulness to the church. Of the only choice she could bear to hear him voice. She waited until she heard Willem moving before she opened her eyes.

"Eat!" she urged.

"This is quite a feast for a simple bachelor's lunch." Willem laid two slices of pork on his plate.

Abbie let her breath out. Willem did not require fancy food. Why had she let herself fuss? She spooned egg salad onto his plate, and he selected a thick slice of bread.

"I suppose I must eat my lunch before I can have cake," he said.

Abbie chuckled. Her own plate was still empty.

"Aren't you going to eat?" Willem set his plate on the quilt and reached for the jar of apples and twisted off the cap.

"Yes, I will." She made no move to serve herself any food.

Willem set down the apples. "Abigail Weaver, something is on your mind."

She took in a deep breath and let it out slowly. "There's plenty of time to talk. I want you to enjoy your lunch."

"I thought the purpose was to enjoy lunch together."

"It is." Abbie reached for the egg salad and a slice of bread. "How long have you been thinking of making a road?"

"It has always been in the plan, when I found the time. I might get started on it this year, but soon we will all have to start laying in coal for the winter, and that's a lot of work."

"Will we have a harsh winter, do you think?" Abbie used a fork to spread egg salad around on her plate without moving any to her mouth.

"*Gottes wille.*" Willem put a piece of bread in his mouth, chewed slowly, and swallowed. "Perhaps we should talk about whatever is on your mind."

"All right." Abbie set her plate down and looked Willem in the eye. "If you had to choose between making your farm successful and staying with the church, which would you choose?"

Willem did not shift position, but Abbie could see that he was moving his tongue over his teeth, first the bottom then the top.

"Come with me," he whispered.

CHAPTER 14

"Come with you where?" Abbie felt her heart skipping beats.

"Think of the life we can have together." Willem put one elbow down on the quilt and leaned toward Abbie.

"I don't understand. Do you want to follow the Chupps to Nebraska?"

He shook his head. "I want to make my farm work. We may be peaceable people, but I am going to fight for my land. Everything I have is invested there."

Abbie moistened her lips and set her untouched plate aside. "Then what are you saying?"

Willem held her gaze with his green eyes as her breaths grew shallow. Finally he turned his head and looked to the horizon.

"Would it be so awful to be Mennonite?" he said.

"So you've made up your mind?" Abbie's heart pounded. She had waited all this time for Willem because she never doubted they would one day be together—not until now.

"I haven't decided anything," Willem said, his voice thick with earnest conviction, "except that I want this farm to work more than anything I've ever wanted."

More than you want me. The truth clanged in her mind like *English* church bells. "What has that got to do with turning Mennonite?" Abbie asked.

Willem picked up a twig, snapped it, and flicked half of it away. "Noah Chupp's decision to move away was disheartening to some of the other men."

"To the women as well."

"Noah did not think the settlement will succeed. What if he's right?"

"He will be right if we allow ourselves to think that way." Abbie stood up, unable to keep her feet still. "We'll fight this drought together. We will be all right. That's what you always say."

Willem pulled his knees up under his chin and wrapped his arms around them. "What if the threat is more than the drought? Bad weather is not the only thing that can break the back of the most determined of men."

"Willem Peters, you must not allow your mind to dwell on such things. We must encourage one another, now more than ever." Abbie paced three steps away from the blanket and pivoted sharply to return, forcing herself to sit down and discuss Willem's concern like a calm adult.

"Not everything we first heard about Colorado has proven to be wrong," Willem said. "It is a different kind of beautiful than Ohio or Pennsylvania, but it is the handiwork of God. We could have a good life here. You and me, together."

This was not the sort of proposal Abbie had always supposed she would eventually hear from Willem. His words were far too conditional. She eased pent-up breath out of her chest.

"Why should we not have a lovely life here if we choose to spend it together?" she said.

"Because the church may not be here, Abbie. You have to see how precarious the situation is."

"One family left. That changes nothing."

"It changes everything. The solidarity is broken."

"Perhaps Noah was not a true believer after all. Perhaps that is why it was so easy for him to leave."

"Easy?" Willem shook his head. "It was not easy. And I do not believe you could doubt the faith of a man like Mr. Chupp."

She flushed, knowing he was right about Noah.

"The bishop of the nearest district has not visited in over a year," he said. "We have had no visiting ministers in all that time. Noah was our best hope for a minister of our own. Adam Nissley's notion that a minister will come from Kansas denies reality. People are discouraged. Even if their farms were flourishing, they would be longing for a real church."

"As do I." Abbie laid a towel over the egg salad and started to wrap up the bread.

"As do I, as well."

Abbie stilled her hands and looked at Willem. "Then what is our point of disagreement? Why were we talking about the Mennonites?"

"Because the others may decide to sell their farms and move back to a thriving district, but I don't want to go back. I only want to go forward. I want to stay here, no matter what. If I have to go to the Mennonites to do that, I would like nothing more than to have you with me, but I will not propose marriage under false pretenses."

Abbie began to stack dishes in the empty bushel basket.

"You didn't eat anything," Willem said.

"I have no appetite. You should take the food home for your dinner."

He reached for her hand. "The last thing I want to do is upset you, but I have to be honest."

Ruthanna sat on the lone chair in the yard, her hand on her abdomen. Beneath her touch the baby kicked, and her lips spread in a smile though no one was near to see it. For the third day in a row, Eber had risen at dawn. He had done the early morning chores, and when he returned, Ruthanna cracked one egg after another into the sizzling skillet and pulled fresh biscuits out of the oven. Eber guzzled coffee with a glow on his face she had not seen in many weeks.

After breakfast Eber returned to bed for a long nap, but Ruthanna had been confident he would rise again bubbling over with tasks he wanted to accomplish around the farm. A poor crop was no reason to let the fences go untended, he said, and he was going to see about getting a couple of roosters and more hens. They could do more than eat eggs the chickens produced. They could raise chickens to see them through the winter and to share with others who might have already begun to consume hens that stopped laying despite their tough meat. Eber and Jake had gone off together to cut a window in the back side of the barn. More natural light would allow Eber to create a workshop in an empty stall so he could begin building some decent furniture out of lumber he had stacked months ago, before he first fell ill.

Ruthanna hardly let herself admit that she had worried Eber would not rally. He was so weak for so long. But during these last few days he was showing signs of his old self, and Ruthanna murmured one continuous prayer of thanks all day long.

Jake approached, and she smiled.

"You have been an angel of the Lord," she said. "You brought hope when I needed it, and look at Eber now!"

Jake nodded. "He is much better, but he is not as strong as he thinks he is. You must watch him carefully and make sure he rests. I look forward to hearing good news when I return."

Ruthanna stood, one hand on her aching back. "You are leaving, then?"

"I believe it's time. Eber wants to work his own farm again."

"But you'll be back?"

"I expect I will be coming more often. I am thinking of moving to Limon soon. If I am going to open a Mennonite church, I must begin making real plans not just talking about it."

Ruthanna's throat thickened. "I am sure you will do well."

"You will always be welcome, you know."

She shook her head. "We have our people and our ways. I have faith that God will send us a minister."

Jake pointed over his shoulder toward the barn. "Eber is cleaning up. There's a place in Limon where he can get glass for that window when he's ready. I'll help him finish out the day and then be on my way in the morning."

Somber muteness swathed the ride back to Willem's farm. Abbie had run out of words, and Willem seemed to know that he should hold his. When he got out and handed her the reins to the Weaver buggy, she pointed to the basket behind her.

"Please take it," she said. "We hardly touched the food. There will be plenty for your evening meal."

"I'm sure your brothers would be happy to have it."

"But I want *you* to have it." She heard an edge in her tone she had not intended and took a deep breath to restrain it. "Things are not so dismal that we cannot afford a token of generosity. Please enjoy the food. It would make me happy to know you have it, especially the cake."

He nodded and lifted the basket from the buggy. She did not look at him again as she nudged the horse forward, back toward the road that would take her to the Weaver farm.

Rudy Stutzman was right.

If Willem had to choose between his church and his farm, he would choose his farm.

Even if that meant leaving her.

Abbie felt foolish for all she had presumed in the last several years. Putting clean sheets on his bed and imagining the day it would be her bed as well. Cleaning the corners of his sitting room and seeing herself seated in a chair beside him, perhaps with a toddler at her feet. Imagining the joy of spending three days cooking when it was their turn to host their fellow Amish worshippers.

In the beginning, they were fellow settlers facing a challenge that left little respite. On neighboring farms, of course the Weavers got to know the determined bachelor. Life on the Colorado plain toughened Abbie, made her feel grown up. And of course she was grown up—old enough to have married years ago in an established Amish district. When her eyes turned to Willem in something other than a neighborly manner, he was looking back at her. Abbie knew she would marry him someday.

In all the episodes where she had let her mind drift toward a future with Willem, never had she supposed he was capable of turning his back on the center of her heart. Never.

Willem loved the Lord. Abbie was sure of that. And he loved her as much as she loved him.

But he would choose his farm. He would choose the Mennonites.

As she turned into the lane leading to her family's house, Abbie wiped the backs of her hands across her eyes and cheeks, trying to banish the heartbreak her family would see in her face.

Daed met her in front of the barn. "How was your picnic?"

"Hot. I should have known it would be difficult to find shade."

"I will cool the horse for you."

"Thank you." Abbie handed her father the reins. "*Daed,* can I ask you a question?"

"Of course."

"I know we have not been getting any new settlers because people back home have heard how difficult the drought makes everything. Is there another reason why no one wants to come?"

"What do you mean, daughter?"

"Did something happen? Something to cause division?"

"We are a people of forgiveness."

"I know. But all this time without a minister—can it not cause doubt?"

"Are *you* doubting, Abigail?"

She was quick to shake her head. "I am confused, that's all."

"Whether we have a minister, are we not still in God's hands?"

"Yes."

"And whether we have drought or rain, are we not still in God's hands?"

"Yes."

"Then, my daughter, what is there to be confused about?"

Abbie brushed dust off her skirt. This was her father's way of saying what Willem always said. We will be all right. She trusted both her father and Willem, but standing in the blazing sun at that moment, she found scarce comfort. Would her father also say, "Whether you have a husband or not, are you not still in God's hands?" She wasn't sure.

"Thank you for letting me take the buggy," she said. "I'd better go see if *Mamm* needs some help." Abbie gave her father a halfhearted smile and let him kiss her cheek.

Despite all the chores awaiting her attention, and the heat that made her feel as if she were walking around in an incinerator, Abbie chose to walk through the fields to Rudy's farm the next morning. She found him in the barn with the new calf.

"How is she?" Abbie said when he looked up.

"Healthy and happy." He stroked the calf's nose.

"Good."

She watched his gentleness, never more evident than when he was caring for his animals. Abbie had thought to tell him that he had been right about Willem. Now the words caught in her throat.

"I remember the first time I helped a calf feed," he said. "I was about nine. My *mamm* thought I should stay out of the way, but my *daed* insisted I needed to learn. After that he let me help with all the new calves, helping them suckle at first and then weaning them and feeding them with a bottle."

It was a sweet picture. Abbie welcomed it into her mind. Rudy as a little boy, learning to feed a calf on a farm in Indiana, with his father watching over his shoulder and murmuring patient instructions.

"I found a scrap I thought you might use in your quilt," he said. "It's just a bit of red. I'm not even sure why I have it, but if you still want it, I'm happy to give it to you."

She smiled. "*Danki.* Yes, I would love to have it." His was the only square she had not finished cutting pieces for, waiting because she hoped he would find something to give her—and because it might mean he had surrendered his notion of leaving.

He might have been right about Willem, but the moment when she wanted to give voice to his insight eased away.

CHAPTER 15

The number of winters Willem had spent in Colorado equaled the fingers on one hand. Even in mid-August heat, his mind was on the coming cold season. The hope of a crop was gone weeks ago. He needed to keep his animals alive and healthy and try not to get frostbite himself. In many ways the Colorado climate was more temperate than eastern Ohio had been, but it seemed that seasons could shift during a casual gaze at the horizon. Winds would gust, clouds would swirl in, and a winter storm would release its fury when only hours earlier the day had promised fall pleasantries. Willem would be ready whether that day came in mid-September or late October.

The last three weeks had not been wasted. Willem had picked through his paltry wheat fields, gleaning dry wisps that might contain seed to use next spring when he would try again. And he *would* try again. His pile of stones to mark off his back road had grown considerably. Though he might not get them all laid before winter, he was now able to estimate how many more times he needed to fill his cart, and he had taken his horses back and forth over the route he planned to tramp down the straggly weeds and make the rough places plain. But soon he would interrupt this task to begin gathering coal for the minimal cooking he did, warming his cabin for the winter, and selling to the *English*.

Soft brown coal was in plentiful supply. All the Amish farmers lived within a few miles of a ravine where lignite coal was free for the digging. In places it was only a few feet below the surface, rather than thousands of feet down. Still, digging it out and transporting it to a useful location was tedious, backbreaking work, and because lignite burned quickly the homes required considerable supplies. A year ago Willem had discovered that many of the *English* around Limon were willing to pay someone else for this labor even if they had a vein on their own land. This year Willem had already made inquiries and committed to dig lignite for three families in addition to what he would need for himself. They would pay him either in cash or supplies. He preferred cash, a scarce resource among the Amish, but Willem had already parlayed his friendliness into a network of information about who possessed particular kinds of goods and who sought them. He was confident he could trade to get what he needed not only to survive the winter but also to make improvements on his farm that would last long into the future.

Willem hated to see anyone so discouraged that they would give up on their farms, but even if all the rest packed their belongings and traveled eastward, Willem would remain.

Was that not a commitment strong enough even for Abigail Weaver?

Ruthanna could hardly believe the difference the last three weeks had made in her girth. After months of feeling sick to her stomach most of the time, the sensation settled at last. She made one batch of biscuits after another and fed her ravenous appetite with them while the baby kicked to make his presence known almost incessantly. When the motions stilled, alarm flashed through her, but she reminded herself that even a babe yet in the womb would sleep at some point. Her gait reminded her of a waddling duck, but she reveled in the movement, perhaps even exaggerating it. Well past the halfway point of her pregnancy, she had begun to realize she would miss the wonder of a child growing within her. So many weeks were consumed with worry for Eber rather than rejoicing together in this mysterious fruit of their love. She wished she had savored more.

Eber was better. He was. But he was not well. He learned to pace himself so that he did not fall into exhaustion and have to return to bed for days at a time, but his energy was not what it had been. When he sat across the table from her, his shoulders stooped. His hand went to his stomach in moments of pain. In his workshop in the barn he sat on a stool rather than stand. After supper, when he read aloud from the German Bible, sometimes she could barely hear him. Then he went to bed earlier than Ruthanna had ever known him to do.

The baby would help. Ruthanna rubbed her firm, expanding middle. Eber would hold their child in his arms and dream beyond the future he could see now. This would spur him to new strength. They would warm themselves at the stove and pass the baby back and forth while one or the other of them tended to chores and they waited for the winter to pass. At Christmas they would remember the birth of God's Son by cradling their own child in love. Spring would come and they would find the money to buy new seed, even if they had to borrow it. They would plant. They would harvest. They would build. Day after day Ruthanna focused her energy on believing this.

Still, in the night as she listened to Eber's erratic breathing, Ruthanna's heart clenched. *Gottes wille.* Why would it be God's will for Eber to be ill? She knew she ought to rest in God's will, and she did not confess even to Abbie that this troubled her. A minister might be able to answer her question, but whom could she ask? Jake Heatwole was a warm, generous man, but he was a Mennonite. Ruthanna lacked confidence that she should open her soul to anyone outside the Amish church.

And who would dig their coal for them? Eber would want to do it, and Ruthanna would worry what the effort would cost them both.

Willem did not rush the team of horses. They would be working hard enough in a few hours when the wagon was full of coal. He calculated where along the ravine he should begin. All the men had their favorite spots. It was not a question of whether they would find coal. Geology reports assured them their farms were on the eastern edge of the great Denver Basin and lignite was abundant.

They had all found this to be true in previous years. The worst of the work was clearing away earth and rocks to expose the vein. Even though the depth to reach coal was only a few feet, the labor of making a hole large enough to work in meant that most of the men brought their sons or relatives to guard an exposed hole while they carried a load home and then returned to dig more.

Willem slowed along the side of the ravine, wondering if he should have partnered with Rudy as he did last year. They could have looked out for each other. But he was here now and might as well do what he could. He took the team down the slope of the ravine and looked for a spot to claim for his day's labor. There was nothing to tie the horses to, but unless they were frightened Willem doubted they would drift too far.

When he got out of the wagon, he took his axe with him. Spreading his feet and bracing himself, he swung the sharpened edge in rhythmic, circular strokes until he began to feel the surface give way. He pounded and loosened and shifted dirt until he spied the promise of lignite. In his mind, he pictured his wagon full and overflowing and then the pile he would have behind his house. Once he exposed the lignite it would be soft enough to break in his hands. At that point he could shovel for as long as his back would tolerate.

Willem heard the approaching horse before he saw it. Determined not to give way to distraction, he tossed another shovel of coal into his wagon without lifting his head and listened for the sound of the rider passing by.

The sound stopped. Willem shoveled.

"Willem!"

At the sound of Abbie's voice, he looked up. They had not spoken since the day of the picnic. His last view of her had been a face wrenched in disappointment, shoulders slumped in dismay. Now she sat erect and controlled on her horse.

"You look well," he said. The sun magnified the light in her wide brown eyes.

"As do you." She looked around. "Are you working alone?"

"For today." He took advantage of the interruption to wipe his dripping face.

"Reuben could help you."

"Your brother must have a list of chores taller than he is." Willem jabbed the point of his shovel, and lignite tumbled out of the wound he made in the earth.

"My father has three sons," Abbie said. "I'm sure he can spare one of them for a few hours."

"I'll keep that in mind the next time I come out to dig."

"I'm on my way home now. I'll tell Reuben you're here. I'm sure he will come."

Willem nodded. Reuben was good company, even if he was easily distracted.

CHAPTER 16

Willem waved up at Reuben. Abbie must have gone straight home and urged her brother to hurry to the ravine.

Reuben slid off his horse and peered down.

"Did you bring any tools?" Willem asked.

"A shovel. Abbie didn't say to bring anything else."

Willem tossed another shovelful of coal into the wagon. "That will be fine. I have an axe."

"Should I bring my horse down?"

"Maybe later. Right now it would make things crowded."

"Be right down."

Willem jabbed at the vein of coal with the point of his shovel, testing the resistance of the next section. Behind him he heard Reuben controlling his slide down the slope of the ravine, his shovel sometimes thudding against the wall of dirt.

"Did you help your *daed* last year?" Willem looked at the boy out of the side of his eye as he raised his shovel once again.

"Once."

"So you know what to do?"

Reuben nodded. "You already have the hole exposed. That's the hard part, right?"

"It's all hard." Willem reached for his axe. "You dig out the coal you can see. I'm going to try to widen the hole so we both have room to work."

"Your wagon is more than half full already." Reuben probed the vein with his fingers.

"I've been here quite a while." Willem paused to run the rag over his face again. He could not go more than five minutes without sweat dripping into his eyes and blurring his sight.

"Maybe you should have some water."

"Later." Willem laid his shovel down and picked up the axe, bracing again to swing it at the side of the ravine.

They fell into a pattern, swinging in opposite rhythms and keeping their hands out of the way of descending implements. Widening the hole seemed to be less intense than starting it had been, and Willem allowed himself to feel the relief that Reuben's help would bring to the task.

His axe head stuck in stubborn earth, as if it knew Willem was feeling encouraged. He yanked on it and pushed the handle back and forth trying to loosen the tool. When it did not yield, he leaned into it—and immediately regretted the movement.

Reuben froze with his full shovel in midair. "Did it crack?"

Willem sighed. "Yes." With one more twist, the split axe handle came free in two pieces.

"We can still dig what's exposed." Reuben emptied his shovel into the wagon.

"I should have brought two."

"How could you know the axe handle would break? No one expects that."

"This is going to slow us down."

"I'll come back and help you another day."

Willem shook his head and glanced up at the sun. "We still have several hours of good light before your mother will expect you home for supper. Can you stay while I ride home for another axe?"

Reuben nodded. "I'll keep digging what I can get to."

"Thank you. I don't want to leave the wagon unattended or have someone else find the hole waiting after I've done all this work."

Willem removed the harness that strapped his team to the wagon and pulled out an old saddle he stored under the bench. Unencumbered and on his stallion, he could avoid the roundabout roads and gallop across open country.

Rudy knew Jake Heatwole had left the Gingerich farm. He also knew, from Abbie, that Ruthanna still was nervous about Eber's vitality. What harm could it do for a neighbor to drop by and see if he could help with something? Rudy threw down a fresh layer of straw from the barn's loft and spread it around the empty stalls his animals would occupy in a few hours. Then he went outside and whistled for his horse.

When he reached Ruthanna and Eber's place a half an hour later, he saw no sign of activity. The barn was closed up. Even the chickens were sluggish in the afternoon heat. Rudy dropped from his horse and rapped on the door, where he could hear Ruthanna's cumbersome movements within. When she opened the door, he kept his voice low.

"Have I disturbed Eber's rest?"

Ruthanna puffed out her cheeks and blew out her breath. "He's not here."

"Oh?"

"He wanted something from Limon."

"I wish I had known. I would have gone to get whatever he needs."

"That's what I said. He wouldn't wait. I didn't even want to ask what it was that could be so urgent." Ruthanna stepped outside the house to share the small space of the stoop with Rudy.

"I'm here," he said. "I may as well see if there is something I can do to help."

She shook her head. "Thank you, Rudy. That's very kind. But Eber is feeling sensitive these days. I don't want to have to explain to him how the chores got done."

"I see."

"But since you have ridden all the way over, I hope you will let me get you a cold drink." She laughed. "Or a lukewarm drink, at least. I have some tea that used to be cold."

"I would be obliged."

As Ruthanna retreated into the house, Rudy spied the chair that sat out in the yard and moved it close to the stoop where it would be in the shadow of the house. Then he sat on the step and set his feet on the ground below. Ruthanna reappeared with a glass in each hand. Rudy wondered how much time she had left before her baby would come, but it was unseemly to ask.

"Is Abbie still stopping by to check on you?" he asked.

Ruthanna sat in the chair. "Nearly every day. And we've been into town together a couple of times. She is such a sweet friend."

Rudy took a long gulp of liquid. "I am glad you think so."

"I cannot imagine how I would get by without her."

Rudy had pondered the same question lately.

Willem wasted no time at his farm, going directly to the barn to pull another axe from the rack and throwing himself astride his horse before the animal had time to even nuzzle the barren ground. As it was, more than an hour would have passed by the time Willem got back to Reuben. Even if the boy had worked steadily in Willem's absence, they could continue at least two more hours before abandoning the exposed hole. Willem was already calculating when he could dig again. If he went soon, perhaps no one else would discover that he had begun and he could exhaust that section of the vein. He dug his heels into the horse's flanks and spurred speed.

At the ravine, Willem pulled up on the reins, confused. He was sure he returned to the same place where Reuben had left the Weaver mare. His wagon should be down below.

Except Reuben's horse was missing.

"Reuben!"

Willem listened for a response that did not come.

"Reuben!"

Willem left his horse and scrambled down the side of the ravine. Reuben was nowhere in sight. And Willem's wagon was empty, with his second horse content to stand still and swish her tail. Fury rose from his gut. Everyone knew it was unsafe to leave a wagon of coal without someone to watch it. Too many came to this vein for coal who would find it much easier to take what someone else had dug out, not to mention the risk of losing his horse. Even when Amish men were the only ones digging with no *English* around them, none of them left a load of coal that represented as much as a day's labor. With two wagons backed up against each other, two men—or even one—could shovel the soft coal from one to the other in almost no time.

How could Reuben have left and allowed this to happen?

Furious, Willem stomped out of the ravine and led the stallion back down to harness with the mare and pull out the empty wagon.

"Reuben!" Willem bellowed at regular intervals.

When his team had all eight feet on level ground again and the wagon was steady, Willem heard the rustle of horse feet and spun around to find Reuben approaching. He snatched the reins out of the boy's hands.

"Get in the wagon."

Reuben's eyes widened. "What happened to the coal?"

"That's what I want to know." Willem tied Reuben's horse to the back of the wagon. "I said get in. I'm taking you home myself."

Abbie handed the pail of slop for the chickens to Levi just as she saw dust swirl up in the lane.

"It's Willem," Levi announced.

"I see that." She had not expected to see him after dispatching Reuben to assist the coal-digging effort.

"Why is Reuben riding with Willem?" Levi asked. "I thought you said he rode down to help Willem."

"He did."

Reuben sat with shoulders slumped on the bench beside Willem, arms crossed in front of him. As they got closer, Abbie realized the horse Reuben had taken was trotting behind the wagon. At least it had not gone lame. She put her hand on Levi's shoulder as Willem pulled to a stop in front of them.

"Is your father here?" Willem's gruff tone overlooked any pleasantries.

"Is everything all right?" Abbie looked from Willem to Reuben.

"I need to see your father. Reuben has something to tell him."

Abbie put her hand flat on Levi's back and urged him toward the barn. "Levi, why don't you go ask *Daed* to come?"

She could tell Levi wanted to ask questions, but he left without speaking.

"Reuben?" she said.

"I thought I saw a coyote looking down into the ravine," Reuben said. "It was a chance to see where the den might be."

"I asked him to stay with the coal." Willem jumped off the bench and paced in the dirt. "I thought he was old enough to understand what that meant."

"I am." Reuben straightened his back in protest. "Not a single person came by on the road the whole time you were gone."

Willem glared. "Obviously somebody did."

Abbie stepped into the space between Willem and Reuben. "You must both be hot and thirsty. I'm sure that after some refreshment we can have a calm conversation."

"Coyotes, Willem." Reuben set his jaw. "You know what it could mean if we could figure out where they come from. How often do we get a chance to see one in the daylight?"

"Did you find it?" Abbie asked. Never had she seen Willem so angry, and it rattled her, but she wanted to hear her brother's story.

Reuben kicked the dirt. "No. By the time I got up to my horse, it was gone. I figured it wouldn't hurt to try to track it for a few minutes. I guess I didn't realize how long I was gone."

Ananias Weaver emerged from the barn with Levi at his side.

Abbie stifled a groan. "I'll get you both something to drink."

CHAPTER 17

Did you hear?"

Ruthanna turned from the stove at the sound of her husband's voice. "Hear what?"

Eber picked up the damp rag Ruthanna had used to wipe dust from the table before setting plates out and used it to wipe his hands.

"Someone stole Willem's coal."

Ruthanna's shoulders dropped. "Surely not one of our people."

"I pray not, but we cannot be sure."

Ruthanna picked up a spoon to stir a stew of last year's paltry vegetables, which she had canned, and a rabbit Eber had trapped the day before. "I don't even want to think that one of us would do that."

"Would you rather accuse one of the fine *English* we do business with?"

"I prefer not to accuse anyone." Ruthanna tasted the stew and reached for the saltshaker.

"Of course we do not want to make false accusations."

Eber pulled a chair out from under the table, sat, and started to pull off his boots. Ruthanna wondered if he had stopped to drink anything all day. Was it her imagination that his breathing was more labored than it had been lately?

"Ruthanna, we must be very careful whom we trust."

"We trust God, do we not?"

"You know what I mean. I ran into Willem at the end of our

lane. He was on his way home from the ravine. He made the mistake of trusting Reuben Weaver to watch his load while he came home for an axe, and the boy let himself be distracted."

"He must have had a good reason. Reuben is old enough to know better."

"You would think so. But his actions illustrate that even people we trust can let us down. For right now, I think it is best if we do not trust anyone but each other."

Ruthanna laid her spoon down and took two plates from the shelf. "What are you saying, Eber? Trust no one? That's no way to live."

"I'm doing all the chores now. We don't need help anymore."

"We don't know what might happen. Caring for each other is what our people do. How can we just shut people out?"

Eber raised one foot and laid it on the opposite knee, massaging it. "I am not suggesting we be rude, only that we can be self-sufficient. We can be gracious in explaining we have no need to trouble anyone."

The baby squirmed within her, and Ruthanna rested her hand on her belly. "What about when my time comes? I will need Abbie and Esther."

He nodded. "Yes, I can see that. But we are more than two months from that day. Perhaps we will know by then who is at the root of this trouble."

Abbie waited three days. Reuben was sincerely sorry, and she believed that once Willem cooled off he would see that he had been harsh. But he did not come.

On Saturday morning she took a horse and the buggy and rode over to Willem's. It might be unseemly for her to broach the subject with him, but she could not wait any longer. Reuben was miserable, and if she could do something to alleviate his suffering, she would. She had never been afraid to speak her mind to Willem, and if she wanted to be his wife—and she did—she saw no point in cowering now.

Willem was in the pasture brushing one of his own horses.

Abbie tied her horse to a fence post near the gate and lifted the latch.

He looked up but did not greet her with a smile the way he used to. She counted her paces in her head as a way to keep calm. *One. Two. Three.* She hoped he would speak first. *Four. Five. Six.*

She stood before him, her hands crossed behind her waist. Now she counted his strokes through the horse's mane. *Seven. Eight. Nine.*

He looked up again but still did not speak.

Ten. Eleven. Twelve.

"Willem."

"Yes."

"Reuben feels terrible about your coal."

"I know."

Thirteen. Fourteen.

Abbie took a deep breath. "Of course the coal is valuable. And you worked for hours to dig it out. It was not right that someone should come along and take it."

"No, it wasn't."

Abbie moved one hand to a hip. "Must you be so unyielding?"

Fifteen. Sixteen.

Finally he let his arm drop to his side and turned to face her. "What would you like me to say, Abbie?"

"That you know Reuben is more valuable than the coal."

Willem said nothing.

"That you know coyotes have been a bigger and bigger problem. The longer the drought goes on, the more widely they will roam."

Willem sighed.

"That whatever has gone wrong between us, you know that Reuben does not deserve this punishment."

He raised an eyebrow. "Is that how you see it? That things have gone wrong between us?"

"Haven't they?"

He raised his brush again. "I suppose so, though my feelings for you have not changed."

"Nor mine for you." If he reached out with his hand, she would lay hers in it. She would not be able to help herself. Perhaps it was just as well that he made no move toward her.

"Do you still believe the church can survive?" he said.

"Have you given up trying?"

"If you mean to ask whether I am still talking to Jake Heatwole, the answer is yes. There is a difference between giving up trying and accepting reality."

"There is no reality outside God's will. We must not give up on God's will." *Twenty. Twenty-one.* "Willem?"

"Our people live a simple life," he said. "What if God's will is not as simple as we wish to think?"

"Do you doubt the teachings of the church?" A year ago Abbie would not have imagined Willem could say such a thing, but now she could hardly keep from gasping at how far he allowed himself to stray.

"I love the church, Abbie," he said. "You know that."

"Then why do you talk to Jake Heatwole and let him fill your head?" She glared.

"Because I miss the church as well. The Mennonites live plainly and speak our language and worship our God. The longer we go without our church, the harder it is to see what is so wrong with their ways."

Abbie forced herself to exhale and inhale. *Twenty-four. Twenty-five.*

"I believe even the Mennonites would agree that we are called to forgiveness."

"So we are back to Reuben."

"Yes."

Willem nodded. "I will come over later today, and Reuben and I will speak words of peace to each other."

Abbie fell into her dreams that night before the sun had been down an hour. After Willem and Reuben reconciled, her brother invited Willem to stay for supper, and after supper Levi begged their guest for a game of checkers that turned into four. Willem finally reminded the little boy that he had a cow that needed milking, and Esther affirmed Willem's departure by sending Levi to bed. Abbie cleaned up the dishes, humming to herself a favorite hymn from the *Ausbund*. By the time she finished, her mother sat at the table writing a letter and her father was nodding off in his chair with the family Bible in his lap. Drenched in gratitude for the resolution of Willem's disagreement with Reuben and the comfort of Willem's company for the evening, she went to her bed rubbery with readiness to sleep.

Shrieking hens wakened her. In the darkness, she had no idea what time it was. The thunder of footsteps in the hall told her the entire household was awake. Abbie groped for matches to light the candle at her bedside and rushed to follow her family toward the door.

"Coyotes?" Abbie's stomach hardened.

"Esther, keep Levi inside." Her father stopped for a rifle.

"I want to see." Levi pressed forward, but Esther clamped a hand on his shoulder.

Abbie trailed after her father and two brothers. Reuben held a lantern high and moved in a slow circle. Ananias put his rifle to his shoulder and fired a shot into the air. Abbie, with her candle flickering in the cooling night air, stood beside Daniel holding her breath. The torment in the henhouse had subsided.

"Abigail, did you see anything?" Ananias swept his rifle in a moonlit arc.

"No."

"Boys?"

"No, *Daed*," they answered together.

Ananias lowered the rifle. "We'd better check the hens—and figure out how a coyote got in this time."

Abbie licked her lips. A coyote needed very little room beneath a barrier to slide through. The concentration of human scent must have chased it off—that and the satisfaction of a vanquished meal. Abbie nudged Daniel forward to the henhouse and opened the door. Chickens immediately clacked and scattered. Reuben was behind her now with the lantern.

Two hens lay on the floor, lifeless. Abbie peered into every corner, counting chickens. One was missing, and she knew just which one it was.

"Three of *Mamm*'s best layers," she muttered.

Reuben grunted. "I knew there was a good reason I should track that coyote I saw from the ravine."

"You can't be sure it was the same one."

"But it could be." He knelt beside the two dead hens. "I'll take them out of here, but in the morning I am going to see if I can find any teeth marks. Then we'll know if it was a full-grown male like the one I saw."

The Sabbath passed quietly. The boys milked the cows, and Esther inspected the henhouse. Reuben studied teeth marks, though he could not be sure of a pattern. Otherwise the family ceased their labors. Levi kicked a rock around the yard. No one wanted to talk about the coyote. Abbie walked behind the barn, out of sight of the rest of her family, and permitted herself tears at another passing Sunday without a worship gathering of all the Amish families. Esther served a cold supper, and Ananias read aloud at length from an Old Testament passage about the people of Israel whining at their sufferings in the wilderness.

In the morning, as soon as breakfast was over, Abbie was surprised to see Willem's wagon approach. She met him in the yard.

"Do you feel like a trip to town? Your mother must have a good list going by now."

"Yes." She answered without hesitation. "How much do coyote traps cost?"

He stiffened. "Did you have a coyote on your land?"

She gave him the gruesome details. Some of the birds were still too frightened to lay. Even by taking what was in the pail in the kitchen, Abbie doubted she could produce enough eggs to be worth trading for traps.

"Don't worry about what they cost," Willem said. "I will figure something out that the mercantile owner will accept, and I will set those traps myself."

"We should have done it sooner."

"Don't focus on regret, Abbie. The way forward is what matters."

CHAPTER 18

"You have to take me with you." As the day ended and shadows fell, Abbie put her hand through the bridle on Willem's horse to keep him from urging the horse forward away from the Weaver house.

"It's going to get dark." Willem was on the bench already, reins in hand. "I'm just going out to listen for coyotes so I can decide where to set the traps we bought."

"I know. I want to come."

"Reuben will be jealous if you are out hunting coyotes. He thinks that's his job."

Abbie rolled her eyes. "I'm coming, Willem." She lifted the hem of her skirt and raised her leg to climb into his wagon.

"And your *daed*?"

"He knows we enjoy an evening drive and has never objected." They had not taken an evening drive for several weeks, but Abbie had kept to herself the reason she and Willem saw so little of each other now. When he came to supper the previous Saturday, his family treated him as if he still belonged among them.

Willem adjusted the lantern hanging at the front of the wagon, which they would need soon enough, but did not protest further. Abbie settled in beside him, and the horse began to move.

"Where will we go?" she asked.

"To the corner where the farms meet."

Abbie knew the spot in daylight. Willem and Rudy's farms bordered on the Weaver and Gingerich farms, and while the farms were not square as quilt patches, there was a narrow point where a person could see the back fields of all four farms. Rudy was the only one who had planted his back field, and that was last year. Otherwise the land lay fallow and neglected during this impossible summer, used as nothing more than a shortcut between farms.

"I figure to get out of the wagon and sit on the ground, perfectly still."

Abbie nodded.

"The coyotes are howling every night lately. If we listen carefully, we should be able to tell which direction the sound comes from."

"Right."

"You have to promise me you won't make any sudden movements once we're on the ground."

"I am aware of the seriousness of the situation, Willem. Some of my mother's hens still have not recovered from the fright. We all know how close that coyote was to the house."

Willem was not driving fast. Stillness cloaked their path as the sun slid behind the distant mountains and gray began to blur their sight. In the fading light, Abbie raised her eyes to the ever-present Pikes Peak. It was there any time she stepped outside, unmoving and faithful. When the Weavers arrived in Colorado and she gazed on the mountain for the first time, she had tucked away the thought that it was a symbol of what their district would someday be—a church unmoved by changing times and faithful to the Word of God.

Now, though, fear welled that her mountain of hope would crumble like so much soft lignite in Willem's hands.

Willem turned the lantern to a brighter setting. The new moon was only a few nights old and cast just a sliver of light. The lantern was all they had to see by as the horse stepped forward in a slow rhythm and the wagon swayed in response.

As they rode in near silence, Abbie choked on questions. Was Willem actively helping Jake Heatwole? What prayer was in his heart these days? Did his heart clench at the thought of a future without her, the way hers did when she tried to imagine being another man's wife? Or no one's.

"Willem." She spoke softly.

"Yes?"

"Thank you for this. For getting the traps. For trying to help us."

He turned his head to look at her, but the lantern was behind his head now and she could not make out his expression in the deepening darkness.

"Of course," he said. He reached across the bench for her hand.

She knew she ought to let go. He was going to leave the church. Leave her. She closed her eyes and prayed for God to send an Amish minister to the settlement. Soon. But she did not let go of Willem's hand.

Willem took his hand back only when he required its use in bringing the wagon to a safe stop. He unhooked the lantern, offered Abbie assistance in descending from the bench, and led her a few yards away from the wagon.

"I hope you don't mind sitting on the ground." His voice was barely audible.

She lowered herself into the dirt and pulled her knees up under her chin. Willem sat beside her, the light burning between them.

"Should we turn the light off?" Abbie whispered.

He shook his head. "I am not trying to lure the coyotes. I only want to know where they are, whose farm might be next." His voice trailed into silence.

Abbie found herself holding her breath so she would not miss a valuable sound because she was listening instead to the air flowing in and out of her lungs. Willem was still as a boulder.

The howling came, distant, mournful, insistent. Following the noise, Abbie's head turned in the direction of Rudy's farm. Allowing herself a breath, she thought of his beautiful cows. Could a coyote take down a cow? Certainly the calf was vulnerable.

She tilted her head, thinking she heard something closer. A moment later, Willem leaned in the same direction.

The crack of a rifle threw them both to the ground, Willem's weight on top of Abbie.

"You two all right?" Rudy lowered his rifle and moved toward Willem and Abbie.

At the sound of his voice, they sat up and then sprang to their feet.

"Rudy!" Abbie raised the lantern and turned it up to bring them all into its circle of light.

"You could have shot us." Willem took the light from Abbie's hand.

Rudy stood his rifle on the butt and held its slender nozzle in his hand. "Or that coyote could have pounced on you."

"We were only listening to them howl," Abbie said.

"This one wasn't howling." Rudy moved in the direction he had shot. "I saw his eyes. Bring that light and let's see if I got him."

Willem and Abbie followed Rudy's long stride.

"There." Rudy pointed with the end of his gun.

Rudy had caught the beast between the eyes. It lay sprawled as if its legs had gone out from under it in an instant.

"I don't understand," Abbie said. "I thought the scent of humans repelled coyotes."

"Usually," Willem said. "But Reuben did say he saw one in broad daylight at the ravine."

"And Ruthanna," Rudy said.

"What about Ruthanna?" Abbie stiffened.

"Didn't she tell you?" Rudy raised his eyebrows. "Right after it happened I was over at their place helping with chores. She was still rattled, but she didn't want to tell Eber. On the day of that meeting about whether Noah Chupp should be minister, a coyote approached her."

"She never said a word!"

"I guess she got it out of her system when she told me. Probably she wanted to make sure it wouldn't get back to Eber while he was so sick."

"Do you think it's been the same coyote every time?"

Even in the darkness with only the light of the lantern, Rudy saw the pale color of Abbie's face. "I expect so. He was probably hungry."

"But there are plenty of gophers and rabbits."

"That's what I'm planning to bait the traps with," Willem said.

Abbie raised a hand to her mouth, as if to banish the sickening image. She understood the realities of living on the Colorado plain, but Rudy knew her well enough to know she would recoil at innocent animals finding such a fate.

"We should all go home," Rudy said. "We can talk about this tomorrow."

"I am still going to set traps," Willem said.

Rudy nodded. "And I still think you should."

"I want to see where they are."

Two days later Willem looked up at the sound of Abbie's voice in his yard. "I didn't know you were coming by," he said.

"I wanted to be sure I caught you before you left and I wouldn't know where to find you."

She had no horse with her.

"You walked?"

"*Daed* wanted both the horses."

She must have set out the minute her mother finished serving breakfast. The sun already was rising hot in the sky. Light twisted in the braids coiled against her head and shimmered loveliness through her stature. If only she would listen to Jake Heatwole even one time. Could she not see Jake was their best hope of marrying at all?

"The traps are dangerous, Abbie." A dozen of them clanked against each other as Willem laid them in the wagon.

"I know that. I'm not foolish enough to set one off. I only want to know where they are. Levi sometimes wanders."

"He might have to reform that habit. I will speak to your father about having a stern conversation with your brother."

"If I know where they are, I can help Levi stay away from them."

"I saw how squeamish you were when I said I was going to use gophers for bait." Willem watched for change of color in her face, but she only straightened her shoulders.

"A human being could get hurt," Abbie said. "Sacrificing a few gophers is a small price to pay."

"The gophers are no friend to the farmers, either, you know."

"I know. *Daed* says they eat the wheat."

Willem tapped the side of the wagon. "Get in."

Ruthanna met Abbie's gaze later that afternoon as they sat together in the Gingerich kitchen.

"Why didn't you tell me about the coyote?" Abbie set her jaw, and Ruthanna knew she was determined to have an answer.

"*Shh.*" Ruthanna glanced toward the bedroom.

"Is Eber sleeping?" Abbie's brow furrowed.

"Just resting. I don't want him to know."

"Is it wise to keep secrets from your husband?"

"When it is for his own good. Do you realize what he would do if he knew about it?" Ruthanna fiddled with her empty coffee cup. "It was bad enough that he insisted on going to that meeting with the other men."

"Willem set traps. Some of them are on your land. You know others will look out for you if you are in danger."

Ruthanna turned her head to look out the small window in the side of the cabin. "Eber prefers to take care of us himself."

"We take care of each other. He knows that is our way."

That would involve trusting someone, and Eber had made his feelings clear on that matter. Ruthanna got up and carried her cup to the sink.

"Ruthanna, is everything all right?" Abbie scraped her chair back.

Ruthanna turned and put a hand on her back. "Of course. I'm tired, that's all. Nothing unusual for a woman in my condition."

"You still have two months." Abbie stood up and took her own cup to the sink. "You need to save your strength. I'm going to come more often to help with washing and cleaning."

"Thank you, but that's not necessary."

"But I want to."

The bedroom door opened, and Eber stepped into the main room of the cabin.

"Eber," Abbie said, "are you unwell again?"

Ruthanna's heart sank. She had hoped it was not so obvious that her husband's health was once again declining.

Abbie tugged her thread through the seam in Rudy's shirt one last time before tying off the knot. This was the fourth time she had repaired the same garment. Rudy needed at least two new shirts. At home in Ohio a man without a wife to sew for him could go to an Amish tailor when he needed new clothes. Abbie supposed Rudy had not had a single new item since he arrived in Colorado. She folded the shirt and set it on the shelf beside his bed, then gave the top quilt one last swipe to free it of wrinkles before calling her work inside complete.

She collected her cleaning rags and last week's empty bread bag and took them outside, putting them in the buggy before looking for Rudy. He was in the barn with the new calf. Abbie stood in the open barn door and marveled at his gentleness with an animal that had hesitated to cooperate with life on this side of the womb only two months ago. Well fed and lively, the calf now nudged Rudy's fingers to see what treat it might find there. Rudy spoke soothingly, more sounds than words.

Abbie stepped into the barn. "How are my favorite mother and daughter doing today?"

Rudy glanced over his shoulder and smiled. "They are very well, I am happy to say. This little one never wants to stop eating."

"Good." Abbie paced over to the stall. "Then her mother will be a wonderful milk cow once she's weaned."

"A dairy needs good milk cows."

Abbie relished hearing Rudy talk about the future—acquiring

more animals, expanding his milk and butter sales.

"You'll have a fine dairy one day." Abbie sat on a milking stool. "I'm so glad you didn't use that train ticket I caught you buying back in May."

Rudy scratched under the calf's neck. "I still have that ticket voucher."

"I would have thought you would have returned it for the cash long ago. You have wonderful land, and your animals are having young. Your milk business is growing even if your crops are not."

"You make a good argument for staying."

"I certainly hope so."

He looked at her now. "Twice you have persuaded me to stay, Abbie. I know how much it means to you, especially considering that the Chupps decided to leave the settlement."

The Chupps. Abbie tried not to think of them. They probably attended a Baptist church somewhere in Nebraska by now.

"I have to be honest with you," Rudy said. "I am still here because of you. I stay because I have a glimmer of hope that someday you might see something in me that would make you want me for more than the survival of the settlement."

"Rudy, I—"

He held up a hand. "Don't say anything. I only wanted to speak my mind. I know you don't feel that way right now. But things change."

He gave the calf a final pat and strode out of the barn.

Grateful that everyone else was out of the house for the afternoon, Abbie sat at the table with a blank sheet of paper in front of her and a black fountain pen in her hand. She wanted to write a report to the *Sugarcreek Budget*, the same Amish newspaper in which her family had first read about the wide open prospects of Colorado.

"Here we are located in the rain belt of Colorado," the glowing report had said. What it failed to note was that the yearly rainfall was half of what Amish farmers were used to in Midwestern states. Fifteen inches a year included snow in the winter. Moisture melting into the soil in the middle of January was helpful, but it did not make up for the lack of rain in the dry summer months when the settlers planted wheat and barley and rye. At least potatoes seemed to do well even with less water than the farmers wished for.

Abbie knew she could not write any of these thoughts. She wanted to say something enticing, something that would encourage other families to consider transplanting themselves to the Colorado plain. But Abbie wanted to be honest.

The majesty of Pikes Peak was always in view. She could say that honestly. And the winters were not as harsh as one might think, nothing like Ohio or Pennsylvania. Snowstorms were spaced widely apart, and in between, temperate days outnumbered cold days. All the farms were within a few miles of the ravine where coal was near the surface.

All these things were true. Somehow, though, they did not add up to the rosy account Abbie wished she could offer. What could she say that would interest someone in coming to a community that had not even had a church service in more than fourteen months, with none on the horizon?

Abbie lodged the tip of the pen in the corner of her mouth. Perhaps it would be more productive to write to a bishop, or two or three. She might be overstepping her role as a woman, but if a bishop visited, it would not matter who had invited him. A report from a bishop might encourage new settlers, or at least keep the existing settlers from giving up on their investments of money and spirit.

Abbie blew out her breath and put the pen down. No, she would not write to a bishop. *Gottes wille.* In God's time He would send a minister. It was better to pray fervently for this than to take matters into her own hands.

And writing to the *Budget* would have to wait until she had a clearer mind. Rudy's words were unexpected. She had only meant to befriend and encourage him, just as she sought to encourage all the settlers when she had opportunity or they had need. Rudy had been right about Willem's dalliance with the Mennonites. He had been right that if Willem had to choose, he would choose another church over Abbie's devotion to the Amish settlement. Willem wanted a thriving farm more than anything else.

But Abbie loved Willem Peters, something she could not honestly say about Rudy Stutzman.

"Are you sure you feel up to walking down the street?"

Ruthanna leaned on Abbie as she got out of the buggy. "I feel better if I move around. Eber will hardly let me leave the house for fear that something will happen while he is not with me, but he knows I am safe with you."

Abbie waited a moment for Ruthanna to get her feet solidly beneath her. "Ruthanna, is Eber working too much?"

Abbie lifted the basket of eggs from the buggy and they started down the street toward the Limon mercantile.

"He did not look well last week," Abbie said.

"He is tired. He festers over everything around the farm, even though we have no crop to speak of. Fences, mucking more than necessary, whatever comes into his mind."

"Eber should let someone help him."

"He won't."

"What about coal?"

"He will dig soon. Willem tells him that the *English* are all digging now. Sometimes there are thirty teams in the ravine. Eber prefers to avoid them."

"Does he let Willem help him?"

Ruthanna shook her head. "Willem tries, but Eber sends him away."

"But is he truly able to keep up?"

Ruthanna had said too much already. "Abbie, Eber would be troubled to think that you are worrying over him."

To Ruthanna's relief, Abbie let the subject go. Ruthanna looked down the street and brightened. "Look, there's Jake. Let's say hello."

"But Ruthanna—"

"He was so kind to us. I will never forget it." Ruthanna waddled forward before Abbie could pull her back.

Jake caught her eye and changed his trajectory to intersect with Ruthanna's path.

"Mrs. Gingerich, how good to see you." Jake offered a handshake, and Ruthanna accepted.

"Are you living in town now?" Ruthanna asked.

Jake nodded. "I was at the hotel for a few days, but I found furnished rooms for rent and picked up the key this morning."

"I hope you will enjoy your new home."

"There is some work to be done before I can call it a home, but I will have some help in accomplishing the tasks."

"I am glad to hear that." She wished Eber were in a position to repay Jake's kindness, but even if he were well in body Ruthanna knew that her husband's mind-set of distrust would not permit him to associate with the Mennonite minister's efforts to start a church that might tempt Amish households.

"Here comes my helper now." Jake gestured across the street.

Willem paced toward them.

Abbie gripped the egg basket with both hands. Willem had said nothing to her about helping Jake move in. But she could hardly blame him. He would have known it would upset her.

"Hello, Willem," she said. It was not like him to come into Limon without stopping by to see if the Weavers needed anything. He used to predict with impressive accuracy which days she would want to bring eggs to town to sell while they were fresh and found reasons of his own to offer to take her.

"Hello, Abbie, Ruthanna." Willem looked from the women to the minister. "I suppose Jake has told you the good news."

"Yes, he has."

Ruthanna was overeager, Abbie thought. How was it good news that Willem was helping a Mennonite minister move into town? Until a few weeks ago Jake's decision would not have mattered to Abbie one way or another. Now it threatened everything.

"Ruthanna," Abbie said, taking her friend's elbow, "we shouldn't dally. I don't want you to get too tired."

Ruthanna laughed. "I am always tired at this point."

"Still, we don't want to stand out in the hot sun for too long."

Abbie nodded at Willem and then Jake. "I wish you success in your endeavors today."

Two black hats dipped in tandem at the women.

An hour later, with their eggs traded and a few staples in the back of the buggy, Abbie helped Ruthanna back up to the bench.

"I was glad to hear the mercantile is going to carry fruit from the Ordway Amish." Ruthanna settled herself as gracefully as she could. "God has blessed them with an irrigation system that can benefit us all."

Abbie unhitched the horse and picked up the reins. Sour jealousy brooded in her spirit. The Ordway Amish, only sixty miles away, had flourishing orchards and sugar beet fields—and two ministers and a bishop. Not only did the Limon Amish struggle to grow vegetables for their families, much less cash crops, and all without a minister, but now the Mennonites were flaunting their plans in the streets of town.

Willem was serious about the Mennonites. Of all the threats that picked at Abbie's longings, this was the most persistently painful.

If she were to marry Rudy Stutzman, a bishop would have to come. He would see how desperately the families needed their church. He would do something.

Abbie blew out her breath, chastising herself for even thinking of using Rudy that way.

Still, he did care for her.

Ruthanna turned a palm up. "I feel rain."

Abbie raised her face and scanned the sky. Clouds dense with moisture moved across the sky.

"Rain, Abbie!" Ruthanna said.

Abbie moistened her lips. She ought to feel grateful. But the rain was too late. It would not save the crop. It would not save Willem.

CHAPTER 20

A week later Ruthanna went outside to check on the laundry she left on the line an hour earlier. In the midday sun she had no doubt it would be dry already, and if she left it much longer dust would whip on the wind against it and settle into the cotton weave of sheets and shirts. Eber seemed to perspire faster than Ruthanna could launder. Bending over to transfer items from the line to the basket was a task more complex by the day.

She hummed, her way of prayer, to quell her spirit restless with impatience to hold the babe in her arms and with worry that Eber would not return to himself. With a tune stuck in her head, Ruthanna almost did not hear the approaching horseman.

"Mr. Heatwole!" Ruthanna glanced toward the barn, the last place she had seen Eber.

Jake dropped his feet to the ground. "It was delightful to see you in Limon the other day."

"Yes, a pleasant surprise." Ruthanna dropped a shirt into the basket and turned to face Jake. "I will always be grateful for what you did for Eber and me."

"I would do it again if the need arises."

"Thank you." Ruthanna watched for movement from the barn, wondering if Eber could hear the voices from his workshop.

"Now, Mrs. Gingerich, I want to choose my words carefully so as not to presume or offend, but I want to make sure you understand that you would be welcome at my new church on any Sunday you choose to attend."

"Oh. Thank you—and I wish you well—but Eber and I are quite content with our Amish beliefs."

"Of course you are. I would never try to persuade you otherwise. I only mean to make sure you know you are welcome, and I would be happy to minister to you in any way that you need."

"Thank you." Ruthanna raised one hand to point casually. "Here's my husband now."

Eber came and stood close beside her. She felt the heat rise from his skin and could hardly keep from laying a hand on his forehead.

"Isn't it nice of Jake to come by?" Ruthanna said.

Jake dipped his head in greeting. "If I can ever do anything for you, please let me know."

"You have been generous enough," Eber said. "Thanks to you, we are getting along well."

"My offer stands, should you ever need something." Jake slung himself back on his horse and waved as he left.

"What did you say to him?" Eber asked.

"Nothing." Ruthanna reached for another shirt on the line. "He's getting ready to start his church."

"He seems a sincere man, and I'm grateful for what he did for me," Eber said, "but we will not be joining the Mennonites."

"I did not suppose we would."

Abbie threw down the damp rag, hardly able to believe her eyes. What was Jake Heatwole doing in Widower Samuels's barnyard? Mr. Samuels was away for the entire day. Abbie would not have Jake poking around looking for him. She strode across the small house and out the front door before Jake could even get off his horse.

"Why, Abbie, I did not expect to see you here."

"Mr. Samuels is not home."

"I see. Then perhaps I will come again another day." He started to turn his horse.

"I cannot imagine what business you have with Mr. Samuels."

Jake tipped his head up and looked at the sky for a moment. "No, I don't suppose you could."

"If you are making the rounds trying to convert our people, I would appreciate it if you would stop."

"It seems that you are imagining after all."

"Isn't it enough that you have Willem?"

"I don't 'have' Willem, Abbie. He is a good friend, and we find we have a great deal in common in the things of the Lord."

Abbie wiped her damp hands on her apron. "I am sorry if I sound rude, but surely you can see my point. We have no minister, and you are trying to start a new congregation."

"I do not see quite the conflict that you do," Jake said. "I only seek to offer ministry to a flock without a shepherd. I am not competing for anyone's soul."

Abbie crossed her arms across her chest.

"Willem cares for you very deeply." Jake stacked his hands on the saddle horn.

She said nothing. What would it matter how deeply he cared for her if Willem joined Jake Heatwole's new congregation?

For a split second, when Rudy heard the knock on the barn's doorframe, he let himself believe it would be Abbie. She had cleaned his house the week before, but bread day had come around again. If he had not frightened her off with his doubts and declarations of the previous week, more than likely she would come to visit the animals in the barn under the guise of telling him that she had left bread on the table.

But it was not Abbie.

"Hello, Jake." Rudy would have offered a handshake if his hands had not been mired in muck at the moment.

The bundle of black and white that followed Rudy around scampered to sniff Jake's hand.

"What can I do for you?" Rudy asked.

"It is I who would like to ask that question. Can I be of any help?"

Rudy surveyed the black suit Jake wore, made of a simple cut but still more fitted than an Amish suit would be. "Thank you, but I wouldn't want to ask you to soil your clothes."

Jake laughed. "Perhaps I am overdressed for the sort of calls I am making today."

"And what sort is that?"

"We don't know each other very well," Jake said. "I just stopped by to let you know that if I can help you with any spiritual concerns, I hope you will feel free to ask me. And for the record, I am always willing to take off my jacket and do whatever needs doing."

"You proved that with Ruthanna and Eber." What did Jake mean by spiritual concerns?

"You have probably heard I hope to open a new Mennonite congregation in Limon."

"Yes. God be with you." Rudy was not aware of any Mennonite families in Limon.

"I believe He is. I am not trying to pressure anyone, but I am going around to the Amish to let them know we will have our first service soon. I know some of you have been longing for plain worship."

The Stutzman family had been among the earliest to come from Europe and settle in Lancaster County, Pennsylvania, in 1737. Amish worship was in his bones. He did not see himself joining the Mennonites, but Jake was right. Rudy did long for the deep, rich worship of his people.

Willem nailed in the last of the new baseboard Jake hoped would help to keep the mice out of his furnished rooms and pushed a sofa back against the wall. The furniture had seen better days. No wonder Jake had gotten such a good price on the rooms. Even the Amish settlers who sank all their money in their land and left little for their houses had sturdier furniture. Earlier Willem had tipped the sofa over and banged a displaced crosspiece back into position and leveled the legs of the small rustic table that would serve as Jake's writing and study desk.

The doorknob turned, and Jake entered.

"How did it go?" Willem began to pick up the tools strewn around the room.

Jake shrugged. "It is difficult to tell. I can't say that anyone was surprised."

"You've made no secret of your hope to start a church, and you've always been friendly with the Amish."

"Not everyone was home, and I called on people I was sure were not interested in the Mennonites. I did not want anyone to feel left out."

"Let me guess. The Weavers, Martin Samuels, Rudy Stutzman."

"My goodness, your Abigail was quite disturbed at my presence on Widower Samuels's farm." Jake sat on the sofa.

Willem grimaced. "Did she try to throw you off the land?"

Jake chuckled. "I have a feeling she wanted to, but Amish restraint got the best of her. She seems to think I have some sort of hold on you."

Willem dropped his hammer in his open wooden toolbox. "I try to be honest with Abbie."

"She will not come to a Mennonite church of her own free will, and we cannot force her."

"There is always the Holy Ghost," Willem said. "God's will may change Abbie's will."

"Willem," Jake said, "have you thought about what it would mean if God's will does not change Abbie's will?"

Willem straightened the black hat on his head. "Abbie loves the Amish church."

"So do you."

"I do."

"And you love her."

"Yes." Willem folded himself into a small chair upholstered in a floral print, something none of the Amish would have in their homes. "But I can also see that the will of God is bigger than the Amish church. If Abbie cannot believe that with her whole heart, then she deserves a husband who will share her conviction, and I will not stand in her way."

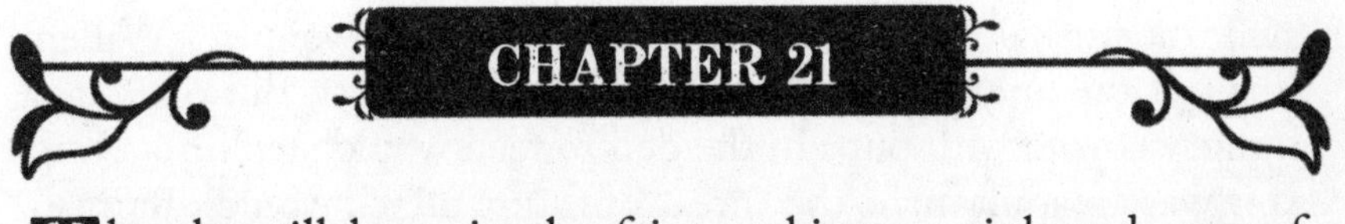

CHAPTER 21

The sky still hung in the faint ambiguous pink and gray of morning's decision to break forth again when Willem pulled on his boots and loaded his rifle. His traps were designed to kill a coyote or any other animal that found a gopher carcass attractive bait. Early every morning, before tending to farm chores or digging lignite for his *English* customers or even satisfying his own hunger with the bread that Abbie baked and brought every week, Willem made the rounds to inspect the traps. If he found an animal in one of the traps, whether predator or innocent, he would be prepared either to dispense justice or end suffering. So far, after two weeks, he had seen coyote tracks in a wide circle around a couple of traps, but none had succumbed. Today Willem took heavy gloves with him, a purchase of his last trip into Limon. If he wore them to change the bait, he hoped to minimize his own human scent on the trap.

Willem knew the coyotes were out there. He heard them every night, howling and barking whether the moon was bright or dim. Chickens were not the only targets. A coyote could kill a full-grown deer with a strategic strike to the neck. A cow would not be much different. Baby goats and calves had no defenses. The livestock of all the Amish farmers was at risk. They built their fences to keep cows and horses on their land and in pastures. Constructing a barrier that a coyote could not scale over or dig under was likely impossible, and certainly expensive beyond the means of struggling Amish settlers.

On his way out, Willem looked at his coffeepot and fleetingly longed for the sensation of thick black coffee sliding down his throat. But he did not have time for the indulgence and walked past the stove without lighting it. This might be the day that a trap held evidence of the enemy's demise.

Given the barren yield of the last two weeks in traps spread around on four farms, it was unlikely this morning would be different, but it was possible. No one purported that catching the swift nocturnal wolf-like animals was an easy venture. Willem was not the only man whose traps came up empty. But one day a hungry coyote with pups in the den to feed would step into a trap. If it was an adult male, the threat of future attack would diminish. Willem had no plans to relent on his vigilance.

Willem saddled his horse. Is that what Abbie thought—that it was possible the Amish could have a thriving congregation despite one defeat after another assaulting their efforts? Her hope kept her vigilant for the glory of God among their people. To her, it was only a matter of time and the settlement would rejoice in the triumph of worship.

He trotted the horse through his own land first, planning a wide arc.

Abbie barely slept in the two nights since Jake made his rounds welcoming any interested Amish to his Mennonite meetings. He had talked about starting a church for so long, and now he was going to do it. And he was going to take Willem away from her. The imminence of this reality dulled her appetite and robbed her sleep.

She swung her feet over the side of her bed and reached for her clothes. In a few minutes she was dressed with her hair pinned up adequately enough for the slim risk that she would see anyone on a walk at dawn. Chores during the heat of the day were inevitable, but a walk while the morning was yet cool would help her clear her mind. Abbie looked out the tiny window of her narrow bedroom and judged that the fullness of dawn was still at least thirty minutes away. But the moon had been full only a few nights before and lingered still.

As she walked, she could pray. For Willem. For Ruthanna. For Eber. For all the families. They might not be able to gather to hear sermons and take communion, but she could still pray. Even for herself, that God would quell the unrest of her spirit at the thought of losing Willem.

Abbie had traversed more than two miles on her morning quest for peace when she saw Willem on his horse silhouetted against the rising sun. Her feet stopped and she drew in a long breath. She was angry, hurt, confused, and in love. It all swirled around this man whose left shoulder sloped more severely than his right, this man who knew her heart like no other. She hated being angry with him. "Be ye angry, and sin not: let not the sun go down upon your wrath," the Bible said. And only a few verses later, "Be ye kind one to another, tenderhearted, forgiving one another, even as God for Christ's sake hath forgiven you." Ephesians 4:32 was one of the first verses Abbie's parents made her memorize before she had even learned to read it for herself. She knew it in German and in English. Sermons of her childhood had impressed on her that forgiveness was at the heart of a life obedient to Christ.

Her left foot went forward, then her right, and she counted her paces toward Willem. When she knew he had seen her, she started counting again at one.

He slid off her horse to greet her. "*Gut mariye.*"

"Good morning." Abbie hid her nervous hands in her plenteous skirt. "Are you checking traps?"

He nodded. "Are you well?"

"Very." She ran her tongue over the back side of her lips. "The Holy Ghost has convicted me that I have acted unkindly toward you and Jake. Please forgive me."

She looked into his eyes reflecting the growing light.

"Of course I forgive you, Abigail. I know that some of my choices make you unhappy. I never mean to hurt you."

"I know." She hardly heard her own voice.

"If I catch a coyote, you will be the first to know."

She smiled, wondering if he could tell how hard it was for her to do it. "Would you like to come to supper tonight? I know Levi would love to see you. We all would."

"And I would love to beat him at checkers, but I am afraid it cannot be tonight."

"Oh?"

"I have a meeting in town."

"Oh."

"It's just a meeting, Abbie."

She refused to lose her temper. "About Jake's church, I suppose." The Amish rarely held meetings in the evenings, when they preferred to be with their families. Were the Mennonites going to disparage the value of family?

"Yes."

She maintained a pleasant tone, determined not to hollow her request for forgiveness. "Another time, then."

Willem could hardly keep his eyes open when the meeting began thirteen hours after he found Abbie at the edge of the field. Other than minimal attention to farm chores that could not wait, Willem spent the day digging lignite. In mid-September residents carried out load after load of coal for cooking and heating through the winter. So far Willem's labors had yielded little coal for his own use. *English* customers with larger homes to heat were pleased with his efforts, and between cash and foodstuffs, Willem was optimistic about the coming cold season. The ravine harbored ample coal still.

The meeting was small, only Jake, Willem, and one married couple who lived in Limon. They met in Jake's sitting room.

"Thank you for coming." Jake smiled at his guests. "Tonight we remember that where two or three are, there Christ is also. Though we begin with a small group, we know the harvest is ripe. Many souls need the ministry that we begin together."

"Are you expecting many others to join the church?" James Graves put his palms on his knees as he asked the question.

"We will see how God leads," Jake answered. "At every step, we will be grateful for what God provides."

James turned to Willem. "My wife, Julia, and I have known the Mennonites before, but I am surprised to find an Amish man here for this first meeting. Are you planning to convert?"

Willem cleared his throat. "Jake and I have talked a great deal. I feel I understand the Mennonites well. We love and serve the same God."

"Do others of your people feel the same way? I've heard that you don't really have church."

"It is true that we do not have a minister," Willem said, "but we are people of deep faith."

Jake spoke. "I have been visiting Amish families. Willem is right. They have deep religious conviction, and I intend to respect them. I will not try to coerce any of the Amish to join us."

"Then why were you visiting them?" James asked.

"I want them to know they are always welcome. That's all."

Julia pressed the point. "But do you think some of them will want to join us?" She turned to Willem. "Are you going to join us, or are you merely curious?"

Willem glanced at Jake. "As Reverend Heatwole suggested, I will be waiting on God to make His will plain to me."

Jake suggested that the group take time to pray about the adventure of beginning a new church in Limon and led aloud in prayer. Then he moved the meeting on to other matters. Where would they hold services? How would they let the townspeople know of the new church? Did the Graveses have any names to suggest that Jake call on to make a personal invitation? Did any families in town have spiritual needs that a new minister might meet?

Willem said little during the course of the meeting. He had offered to make some notes of the conversation, and Jake supplied paper and a fountain pen. If James Graves tried to return to the subject of the Amish, Jake graciously redirected the conversation. Willem recorded Jake's questions and the answers that emerged from the Graveses.

By the time Jake closed the meeting in prayer, the sun was well on its way down. Willem hung two lanterns from the front of his wagon for the drive home and allowed his horse to set her own pace. He did not hear the coyotes while he was in town. Only when he was a few miles west of Limon, halfway to his own land, did he hear the mix of howling and barking.

So far Willem had not promised Jake anything, and Jake did not press for a commitment. If only Abbie would say she would come with him. But with Abbie or without her, he was not sure how much longer he could stand not to hear the Word of God preached. Even if he began with a tiny congregation, Jake planned to hold his first service within a few weeks. Willem was fairly certain he would be in the congregation that day.

CHAPTER 22

With a basket of warm muffins, Abbie walked down the lane from her home to the main road, crossed to the other side for a fifteen-minute walk, and turned down the lane to the Miller farm. She had offered to take a buggy over to fetch Ruthanna, but her friend had assured her Eber would bring her and come back for her later. When she reached the house, she found Mary and Ruthanna sitting at the table drinking coffee. Mary gestured toward a third cup, and Abbie sat in front of it.

"I just made them." Abbie unfolded the towels wrapped around the muffins and was pleased to see that the baked goods still steamed slightly.

"They smell delicious." Mary inhaled the fragrance. "Wherever did you get blueberries?"

"*Mamm* had one last jar from last year." Abbie pulled a muffin open.

"Did either of you manage to have anything to trade for Ordway fruit this year?" Mary filled Abbie's coffee cup.

Ruthanna nodded. "I don't know how he did it, but somehow Eber convinced Mr. Gates at the mercantile to give him some on credit. I'll be canning all next week."

"I'll help you," Abbie said. "We'll just have to be sure to choose a different day than when *Mamm* wants to can. She managed to coax a few more beans and squash out of her vegetable garden, and we're hoping to trade eggs for fruit."

"The rain last week must have helped," Mary said. "It wasn't much, but it was something."

"Every drop helps." Abbie flung doubt out of her tone. "We have potatoes, too. Plenty to share, I think."

"Little Abe pulled up half of what I planted." Mary stroked the head of the little boy playing with a wooden spoon at their feet. "But Albert says we'll get some produce somehow."

"We should make a canning schedule and make sure everyone's pantry is stocked." She sighed. "If only we had half the irrigation the Ordway settlement has."

"The Mullet sons went down for a month's work to harvest," Ruthanna said. "Perhaps when they return there will be extras for everyone."

"God will provide." Mary picked up her son. "He looks like he's been eating dirt." She moved to the water barrel, where she stuck the hem of her apron in to dampen it and scrubbed at Little Abe's cheek. He protested by leaning away from her at a precarious angle. When his mother set him on the floor again, he toddled away from the table.

Ruthanna felt so enormous and full of child that she could hardly imagine her waist would ever again slim down the way Mary Miller's had after Little Abe was born. Her feet swelled more every day, and the baby kept her awake at night. Life had slowed to doing only the next thing she could see that needed doing, and she hardly thought beyond the end of the day. She cleaned the cabin, made sure Eber ate and rested, and tried to rest herself in the afternoons when it seemed that the baby was less active. The heat was becoming too much. By midday the house was stifling and did not cool again until after the sun set and the evening winds blew. At home Ruthanna kept a clean, damp rag within reach to wipe across her face as often as she felt the need.

While Mary and Abbie chatted about how the settlement families would get fruits and vegetables to can for the winter, Ruthanna put a hand across her tightening belly. Against her will her entire body contracted and she found it hard to breathe.

Pain wrapped itself around her midsection, rising in her back and making her gasp before circling around to the front again. These pains were happening every day now, one every few hours or several close together.

"Ruthanna, are you all right?" Abbie's voice cut through the pain in a distant sound.

"Breathe, Ruthanna," Mary said. "Don't close your eyes. That only makes you feel the pain."

Ruthanna had not realized her eyes were closed, but she forced them open to see her two friends leaning across the small table, inspecting her. At this unnaturally close angle, their eyes seemed awkwardly wide and the furrows in their brows alarmingly deep.

"I'm fine," she managed to say.

"False labor," Mary diagnosed. "The same thing happened to me before my time."

Ruthanna nodded. "Esther tells me it is quite common." If this was false labor, she dreaded what true labor would feel like.

"How much time do you have left?"

Mary took her hand, and Ruthanna kept herself from crushing her friend's fingers as the pain finally subsided.

"Less than two months." Esther Weaver had birthed many babies besides her own, including Little Abe. Ruthanna had no one else to trust in these matters, so she repeated the calculations Esther had made long ago.

Before Ruthanna's train trip to Ohio marked off the distinction between life there and the hardship of the Colorado plain.

Before Eber got sick and exhausted the hope she had stored up for their future.

Before Jake in his kindness nevertheless made people nervous about his intentions.

"I'm all right," she said again, and Mary released her hand.

"A baby doesn't really need much." Mary took a muffin from Abbie's basket. "Whether you have a boy or a girl, the baby things don't matter. I kept Little Abe in white muslin gowns until he started to walk."

Abbie glanced at Ruthanna, hoping she was not hiding something more serious than false labor that would lead to a birth any time soon.

"The gowns are easy to make." Mary moved to the stove for the coffeepot and refilled the cups on the table. "I have a pattern. But you can use all my gowns. They are in perfect condition. Babies don't wear out their clothes."

"Thank you." Ruthanna lifted her cup and took a cautious sip of hot liquid. "Actually I've already made two from remnants of Eber's shirt fabric."

"It's generous of you to share your baby things." Abbie smiled at the toddler across the room, trying to remember how he looked when he was small enough for baby gowns. She had held him when he was new. How many months had it been now? Abbie calculated from his birthday in January and came up with twenty months.

"How is Willem?"

Abbie had been staring into her coffee and flicked her eyelids up at the sound of Mary's inquiry. "He is well."

"I know most of us don't have much crop to harvest this year," Mary said, "but that doesn't mean it cannot still be the wedding season."

Abbie felt the color drain from her cheeks. A few weeks ago she had playfully reminded Willem of the same thing. "It's hard to make plans right now."

"I suppose so. No place to read the banns. No one to perform the ceremony."

Abbie nodded politely.

"You could always go to Ordway," Mary continued. "You could get married there and stay for a few days before you came back."

Abbie put a bit of muffin in her mouth and looked around. "Where did Little Abe go?"

Mary pushed her chair back and stood up again, but she did not seem concerned. "That child. If I turn my back for half a minute, he disappears. I can hardly get anything done keeping track of him all day."

Abbie stood now. "You relax. I'll find him."

She pivoted so that most of the cabin was in sight and saw no sign of Little Abe other than a trail of small household items that served as his playthings. Abbie saw now that the Millers' front door did not catch fully when it was closed, and she pushed it open to go into the yard.

Ruthanna was relieved to see Abbie lead the small boy back into the house less than a minute later. Even if Ruthanna did feel perpetually pregnant, at least she knew her child was safe in her womb.

"You little rascal." Mary picked the boy up and put him in her lap in a wooden chair with a high carved back that must have once been a fine piece of furniture. "Ruthanna, that chest right there has all the baby things. Why don't you go through them and see what you would like to use."

Ruthanna rose from the table. By the time she reached the cedar chest, Abbie had it open and lifted out a stack of neatly folded tiny clothing items.

"The gowns are in several sizes. Little Abe was growing so fast I was sewing constantly."

"They're lovely." Ruthanna found the softness of washed and worn muslin appealing as she thought of it next to her baby's skin.

"There's a quilt, too."

"I just finished making one."

"You can always use another."

Ruthanna found nothing to disagree with in that observation and took the quilt from the chest. Tiny blue and green triangles were laid on their backs against each other. Ruthanna had made her quilt with simpler squares.

"Your quilting is beautiful," Ruthanna said.

"I wish I could say I made it. My mother sent it. She was one of the best quilters in our district at home."

Mary's innocent comment sent a sharp pang through Ruthanna, who suddenly wished that her own mother were going to be present when her baby was born. Her parents had been vague about when they might visit.

"Abbie, how is your quilt coming?" Mary asked.

"I work on it nearly every night," Abbie said.

"I can't wait to see it!" Mary picked up a tiny sweater. "Don't forget this. Little Abe was born in January. If your baby comes in November, the size should be right for the winter."

Abbie handed Ruthanna a simple black knitted sweater with an open front and one tie at the neckline.

"Do you have a cradle?"

Ruthanna shook her head. "Not yet. But Eber wants to make one, something that we can use for all our children. I think he already has the wood cut out in his workshop."

"Well then, a few burp cloths and soft towels and you'll be all set."

Ruthanna rewarded Mary's generosity with a warm smile to mask her inner sense of foreboding. She wanted Eber to return and take her in his arms and to their home.

CHAPTER 23

With the smell of fresh bread rising from behind the bench and taunting her stomach, Abbie approached Rudy's farm a few days later. As she drove the buggy past the scruffy meadow and saw both his horses grazing, she smiled. He was probably home.

At first Abbie was nervous about seeing Rudy again after his confession of two weeks ago. But they were friends and fellow settlers, and she refused to think of sacrificing either dimension of their relationship to awkwardness. The Colorado plain was too desolate and lonesome to cut herself off from anyone. When the time was right they would speak again of that day, but for now she did not want him to feel spurned because she suddenly dropped away from him.

She knocked at his door and immediately opened it to let herself in, as she did every week. If he was home during the day, he did not spend his time inside the house, so she never waited for him to answer the door.

This time, though, he sat at the rugged table that he used for meals and papers. Several envelopes lay open before him. He looked up.

"Hello."

"Hello." Abbie moved to the shelf where he stored his bread and set the flour sack she carried in with her on it. She glanced around for last week's bag.

"It's there on the back of the chair." Rudy pointed.

She picked it up and folded it neatly into a small square. "What are you reading?"

"Letters from home. I had not picked up my mail in quite some time."

"Good news, I hope."

"Amusing news."

"Oh?"

"Listen to this." He read to her from the page he held in his hand. "Your little second cousin Ezra is a mischievous fellow. Though he is only nine years old, he is the master of practical jokes. Last week he hid a barn cat in a crate and put it on a shelf in his grandmother's closet. Lest you think he was being cruel, let me assure you the creature had plenty of air and was only confined for a couple of hours. Of course the thing meowed incessantly while the boy's grandmother had her quilting group over for lunch. Afterward, when she was determined to discover why there was a cat in her house and began an earnest search, he moved the crate around to another room every twenty minutes or so. She was convinced the poor thing was trapped in a wall and was about to call someone in to open the wall when the boy confessed. Fortunately she has a good sense of humor, though she threatened retaliation when he least expects it. Now the child is suspicious of everything his grandmother does. The entire family is havihg quite a laugh."

Rudy looked up, a grin on his face. "He was such a little boy when I left. I wish I knew him now."

"They sound like lovely people."

"They are."

A lump took instant form in Abbie's throat and made her voice thick. "What other news do you hear?"

Rudy picked up another letter.

"Amos Schrock was a good friend when we were little boys. He's getting married as soon as his family's harvest is in." Wistfulness crept out of his words.

"I'm sure he would love to hear that you are well," Abbie said.

Rudy nodded slightly and picked up a note card. "This one is from my father. He is all business. How many acres he planted, how much yield he expects, how many calves have yet to be weaned."

"He wants to know you are happy." Abbie surprised herself with the sudden insight. "He wants you to write with your own news."

"I know." Rudy's gaze drifted out the window. "They all feel so far away."

Abbie did not know what to say. They *were* far away. She had come with her parents and brothers and had not often stopped to think what it must have felt like to come alone to a new state only to discover that all was not as expected.

"Speaking of calves," she managed, "how is yours doing?"

Rudy took in a deep breath and returned his gaze to Abbie's eyes. "She is well. Do you want to see her? I let her out in the fenced part of the barnyard today. She needs to get used to being away from her mother."

"You're not going to wean her yet, are you?"

Rudy tilted his head to one side. "Soon. Two months is a long time to leave a calf with its mother. I'm raising milk cows, after all. But I don't want to separate them abruptly."

He had a soft heart, Abbie thought. Many farmers she knew thought only of what they needed from their animals. Rudy remembered that his cow and calf were also mother and child.

They walked out to the barnyard together, and the calf came easily to Abbie. She scratched under its chin and looked into its huge brown eyes. In another year, this calf would be old enough for breeding and could have her own calf and begin her work of producing daily milk.

Abbie smiled at Rudy, grateful that he was not pressing her to say how she felt toward him. She did enjoy spending time with him and keeping track of his animals.

But Rudy Stutzman did not make her heart race the way Willem Peters did.

Ruthanna waddled from the house to the barn, a trek that seemed to take her longer every day. It was harder to make her legs go where she wanted them to go and keep her balance at the same time, and every day required greater effort to breathe in the thin Colorado air. She thought she had adjusted to high altitude living until she began to carry a child. Supper was ready, but Eber had not come in from the workshop all afternoon. Ruthanna was not sure how much longer she could keep the food warm without drying it out, or how much longer she could keep at bay her fear that something was wrong with Eber.

She shuffled across the dusty ground and breathed relief when she found the barn door open, uncertain that she could have managed to push it open. The heat inside the barn smacked her in the face and weakened her knees. Instant thirst made insistent demands she could not satisfy. When she did not see Eber standing in his workshop stall, Ruthanna's heart raced, and she ignored the limitations of her condition to reach as quickly as possible the place where she could look over the stall wall.

Eber lay on the stall floor.

"Eber!"

His eyes popped open.

"Are you all right?"

Sluggish, he sat up. "I'm sorry. What time is it?"

"I've had supper ready for almost half an hour."

He rubbed his eyes. "I only meant to take a quick nap."

Ruthanna hesitated to ask how long ago that had been. "It's beastly hot in here. No wonder you're sleepy."

"It's beastly hot anywhere we go, Ruthanna."

She could not argue with that.

He stood up. "Look at the cradle. I sanded everything and put it together today. I just need to put a finish on it."

Ruthanna stepped into the stall and ran her finger over the simple curved piece of each end of the cradle, then the spindles in the sides notched delicately at the centers. She pushed it gently side to side and was pleased with the way it glided.

"Thank you, Eber," she said softly. It was an exquisite gift, and Ruthanna hoped their child would one day feel as grateful as she did for the care Eber had taken.

"I told you I would have it finished before it was too late." Eber draped an arm across Ruthanna's shoulders. Though heat and dehydration would make him sleepy, she was now sure that he also had a fever.

"We still have a few weeks," she reminded him. "You don't have to make yourself ill to meet the deadline."

Abbie ignored the howling coyotes that evening. With a lantern on the table in front of her, she spread open the issue of the *Sugarcreek Budget* that she had already read three times. Beneath it were three earlier issues. As hard as she had tried to write something cheerful and encouraging to send to the *Budget*, she had instead laid her attempts in the belly of the stove and listened to them crackle into flame. If she could not be cheerful and honest at the same time, she would rather be silent. However, someone else might have written.

Most of the time the Weavers scanned the stories in the *Budget* looking for news of someone they knew. This time Abbie intended to read enough of each story to be sure she was not missing some reference to the struggling settlement, whether a comment by someone who lived within miles of the Weaver farm or someone remarking from afar on the conditions in Colorado. Two years ago a woman from Oklahoma had visited and then reported that Colorado was all right for a man who had money to spend, but a poor man had no business there. For weeks after that, a flurry of articles crisscrossed the country venturing opinions about the suitability of settlers for the demanding life on the plain.

Though she wished the woman from Oklahoma had kept her opinion to herself, Abbie understood what she meant. A settler who had sufficient money could do well carving out a life in Colorado and enjoy the beauty the state had to offer. Without money, though, the task had proven more complex than any of them expected. Most of the settlers had to just do the best they could to feed and shelter their families. Whether any of them would succeed over time remained to be seen.

Willem certainly intended to. But his terms of success would hardly attract future settlers.

Rudy aspired to a sweetness of life that was as brittle as old thread.

Abbie pored over the articles, one issue after the other. For the first time she felt the irritation of trivialities and understated criticism that wove through the articles, and the whole business struck her as an indirect way to communicate. The settlers around Limon did not have that luxury.

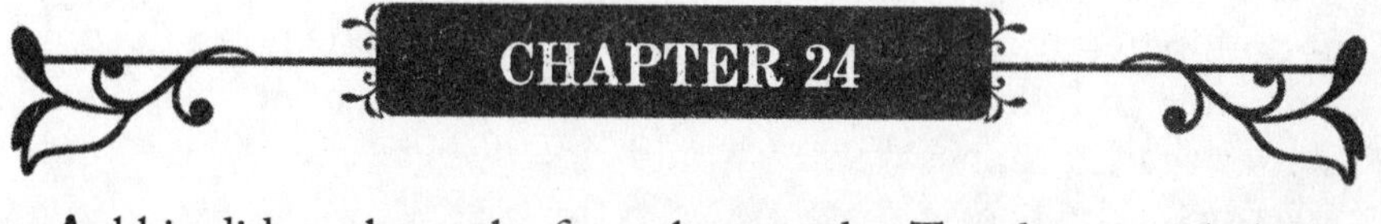

CHAPTER 24

Abbie did not leave the farm the next day. Tuesday was a baking day, and while the loaves rose through two yeasty cycles before going in the oven in twin sets, she cleaned the Weaver home. Her mother sat for much of the day in the shade cast by one side of the house or another, repositioning two chairs with the movement of the sun so she could listen to Levi read painstakingly from the family's German Bible and recite multiplication tables. Abbie took them plates of boiled eggs and cold ham at lunchtime and the first slices of fresh bread and milk for midafternoon refreshment. Levi had been grateful for both interruptions. He was a cooperative student even in midsummer, but Abbie knew he was not reading as well as many children his age. Esther Weaver was on her own to teach him.

Abbie had heard talk of the Amish families beginning their own school, even if it convened in someone's barn and the mothers rotated teaching duties. With the Chupps gone, though, Abbie supposed the energy for undertaking would dissipate. After all, the Chupps had five of the nine school-age children who would have attended. The remaining families, like hers, had only one child each between the ages of six and fourteen.

On the other hand, Abbie mused, an organized Amish school could be an attraction to families with young children. Occasionally she did Levi's lessons with him and surprised herself with her patience. Late in the afternoon, the baking finished, Abbie pondered this question as she swept a coating of flour blown astray from the mismatched pieces of linoleum that constituted the kitchen floor.

Soon it would be time to get supper on the stove. Abbie made sure that the doors at both the front and rear of the house were open to catch the breeze that the unobstructed plain often birthed in the late afternoons, just when the family was most weary from the heat. She stood for a moment looking toward Pikes Peak rising from the seemingly endless plain. It was miles and miles away. Still it dominated the view. Abbie hoped she would remember to come out later and watch the sun set behind the mountain. She knew better than to hope Willem would ride over to share this simple pleasure as he had so many times in the past.

But someone was riding in. Abbie squinted into the glaring late afternoon light to see Mary Miller urging her horse to pull the buggy faster. Mary was calling something, but Abbie could not hear her words over the clatter of the hurtling rig.

Finally Mary pulled on the reins, breathless.

"Little Abe is missing."

The instant pressure in Abbie's chest seized air from her lungs.

"Did you hear me?" Mary shrieked.

Abbie gulped, Little Abe's sweet face rising in her mind. "How long?"

Esther and Levi appeared from around the corner of the house.

"I don't even know!" Mary covered her eyes. Her shoulders rose and fell three times before she could continue. "He went down for a nap, and I sat outside to work on my mending. Then I went out to the garden to see if there was anything worth picking and started clearing weeds. When I realized how long I had been out there, I figured I should wake him up or he would never go to sleep tonight. But he was gone!"

"Ananias!" Esther hollered for her husband.

"Albert went into town and isn't back yet," Mary said. "I've looked and looked around the house and barn. I can't think where Little Abe could have gotten to."

Esther tapped Levi in the center of the back. "Find your *daed* and tell Reuben to bring the horses."

Levi lit off through the dust.

"Someone should be at the house to wait for Albert." Abbie started to hoist herself onto the buggy bench. "I'm going to take you home. We are going to turn over every stone and board of your place, and we are going to find Little Abe."

Esther nodded. "My husband and sons will not be far behind."

"What will I say to Albert?" Mary moaned. "How does a wife tell her husband that she has lost their child?"

"We're not going to worry about that." Abbie took the reins out of Mary's hands, which had gone limp. "When do you expect Albert home?"

"He's over working on Mr. Nissley's land. He said he would be home for supper."

"Then he'll be home soon, and you know he would move a mountain to find that boy."

Mary's tears gushed unrestrained now.

Abbie glanced over and saw her father, Reuben, and Daniel marching toward them in stride with each other. By God's grace they had all been together and not off in the far corner of the farm. She clicked her tongue and got the horse moving, leaving it to her mother to explain the urgency of her summons. Forcing herself to breathe as she drove, Abbie did a mental inventory of all the places a small boy might get lost on a three hundred-acre farm. But he was barely less than two years old, and she did not think he could have gotten far.

Unless he had never fallen asleep for his nap at all.

At the Miller farm, Abbie jumped out of the buggy and fell to her knees at the base of the house, looking for any space into which a small child might squirm.

"I already looked there." Mary hovered behind Abbie.

"He can't have gotten far."

"That's what I thought." Mary's tone rose in panic. "Don't you think I looked everywhere around the house and barn before I went for help?"

"The henhouse?"

"Nothing but hens."

Abbie sucked in her breath. "The outhouse?"

"We keep it latched way above his reach."

"But you looked?"

"Yes, I looked."

Abbie scrambled around the perimeter of the house and saw no sign of Little Abe's tiny footprints. She sat on her haunches and squeezed her head between her hands and closed her eyes, trying to picture where he would go. She did not know the Miller farm nearly as well as Mary did herself, but perhaps in her panic the child's mother had overlooked something obvious.

Esther arrived with Ananias and Reuben just as Abbie got to her feet.

"I left Levi with Daniel," Esther said. "Having him here would be a distraction we don't need. He's frightened as it is."

Abbie squeezed Mary's hand. "You stay here with my *mamm*. You won't be alone when Albert gets here."

"I want to keep looking." Mary lurched toward the Weaver buggy.

"You can hardly stand up," Abbie said. "You did the right thing to come and get us. Stay here and pray."

Esther took Mary's elbow and steered her back toward the door to the house. "Reuben," she said, "take one of the horses and ride for Willem as fast as you can. Then come right back."

Abbie marched toward Mary's buggy. "We can each take a direction. I am going north."

"Make sure there's a lantern in that buggy," Esther cautioned.

Mary gave a cry and balked in her progress toward the door. "It won't be dark for hours!"

Esther put her arm across Mary's back. "We will pray."

Abbie covered her mouth with her hand at the thought that they might not find the little boy well before dark. Surely they would find him playing in the dirt or he would look up and realize he could not see his mother and his cry would give him away. Convinced they would be passing him around a crowded room well before dark, nevertheless Abbie rummaged under the buggy bench to make sure there was a working lantern before she seated herself and picked up the reins.

The longer Abbie searched, the more her chest clamped down on her breath. If anyone else had found Little Abe, someone would have ridden to the north acres to let her know. By now, well past suppertime, surely Albert had come home to find his wife a frantic puddle of anxiety and disbelief, and he would have taken his other horse out. Reuben would have returned from Willem's farm hours ago, and the two of them must be searching.

Hours.

Hours since Mary's buggy rattled onto Weaver land, and perhaps hours more since Little Abe slipped out of the Miller house undetected.

Abbie's thickened throat scarcely allowed air to pass.

Her first impulse had been to give the horse its head and hurtle toward Little Abe, scanning the countryside. But he was so small. It would be too easy to gallop past him if he had fallen asleep in a ragged field or lay frightened in the shade of a ball of thistle. Instead, Abbie mentally divided the land north of the Miller's home into calculated sections and set out to cover every square yard in a systematic manner. But when she had taken the buggy through every acre without finding him, and still no one galloped toward her with the news of a rescue, she started over, widening the perimeter of her search and slowing her pace even further.

"God," she said aloud at regular intervals, "I cannot understand Your will in this. He is an innocent child."

The horse grew sluggish, and Abbie urged it on. Periodically she slid out of the buggy and walked widening concentric circles around the horse before returning to ride to another sector. Finally she admitted she could no longer see well enough in the descending gray to trust her eyes, and she stopped long enough to fish the lantern out from under the seat and shield the wick from the rising wind long enough to light it. She heard only her own breath, a desperate, shallow, tattered effort to suppress the visions that roared through her mind.

"Little Abe!" she called out, over and over.

She listened for the slightest rustle of small feet, the faintest cry of a small boy's voice, or the gathering approach of a rider with good news. None of these sounds met her ears.

Abbie stepped farther away from the buggy in full darkness.

The only vibration to break the silence was the distant howl of a coyote.

CHAPTER 25

Standing in deepening gloom, Abbie held the lantern high, sweeping slowly from side to side in a field of dry, half-grown wheat that would probably not be worth the price of having it milled.

"Little Abe, where are you?" she said softly.

When Abbie raised her eyes to consider where she would move next, she gazed into the shadowy distance, wondering where the other searchers were. She blinked twice at a shifting shape before she realized it was Willem astride his horse.

"Willem!"

He gave no sign of having heard her shout, instead holding his pose in the pale light cast from the moon in its last quarter. Abbie could barely make him out. If it had been anyone else she might have told herself her eyes were transforming a large thistle ball into something she wished were there. But the slope of his shoulders, one raised higher than the other in his characteristic posture, made her certain.

"Willem!" Abbie swung her light from left to right hoping he would see it and be curious enough to investigate.

He shifted this time, but away from her. Willem moved slowly, no doubt for the same reasons Abbie did—to look and listen carefully for any sign of Little Abe. His horse made a full quarter turn now and began a slow pace. Abbie kicked at a small loose stone and heard it thwack a stalk of wheat six feet away. With equal desire she wanted to find Little Abe or to hear the thunder of a horse whose rider came to tell her he was found. Willem's concentration in the search told her the boy was almost certainly still missing. Willem eased out of her sight, and Abbie's heart fractured.

Keep the boy safe till we find him. She blew out her breath heavily as she pondered whether God was listening to her prayers.

The coyote's howl once again dominated the night and seemed to echo gusting in the wind. Night breezes often cooled the temperature considerably, but tonight Abbie perspired as much from anxiety as heat. Not wanting to wander too far from the buggy, she began a path that would take her in a straight line to where the horse and buggy stood at the center of her wide circles.

"Little Abe!" she called out once again, forcing conviction into her tone.

She gasped and held still. A tiny sound. Holding her breath, she listened for any swish in the wheat or footstep in the narrows rows between planting. Had it only been a noise carried on the wind?

"Little Abe!"

A cry. A child's cry, this time full and fearful and angry. Abbie turned around and hustled back through the wheat, swinging the lantern as she ran beyond the circle she had just abandoned and toward the cry.

"Little Abe! I'm coming!"

She found him face down in the ground trying to push himself up. Abbie set the lantern on the ground and knelt to fold him into her arms. Partially upright, Little Abe clung to her neck with grubby hands, his small shoulders heaving with shallow breaths and his plump cheeks smeared with dirt and tears. Abbie ran her hands over his arms and torso and legs, looking for injury. Where his right knee should have been, her hand hit earth, and she grabbed the lantern to pull it closer.

Little Abe's chubby leg was stuck in a gopher hole. Despite the warnings Abbie had heard Mary give her son time and again, the little boy remained fascinated by gophers and giggled every time he saw a round, brown face with tiny ears peek out of a hole or dash across the ground. He was too little to understand the risk of a gopher hole and just little enough for an appendage to fit into one. Abbie clasped him tight, waiting for both their hearts to calm.

Little Abe did not want to let go of her as Abbie tried to settle him in the mound of dirt that would have warned an adult that the hole was nearby.

"I'm not going to leave," she said with more calm than she felt. "We have to get your leg out, Little Abe."

He whimpered and tightened his grip on her neck.

On her knees, Abbie pried his hands off her skin and moved them to her skirt. "Here. Hold on to my dress."

She kissed his forehead, and his wide, frightened eyes stared at her, but he made no more effort to grab her neck.

The dry earth was unyielding to her fingers, and Abbie did not want to cause further injury. The boy might have hurt his ankle when he felt into the hole. Abbie banished from her mind the thought that gophers underground could have nibbled on his toes. If only she had a table knife or a spoon or anything to dig with. She felt around on the ground until she came up with a stone hardly bigger than a coin. One stroke at a time, she began chipping away at the edge of the hole to widen it just enough to pull Little Abe's leg out.

She drove with the child in her lap, his face buried against her chest and his arms wrapped around her waist. His heart beat wildly against her body, a testimony to his hours of fear, but he did not cry.

Abbie dipped her head to speak into his ear. "We'll get you home to your *mamm* and *daed*. You'll go to sleep in your own bed."

He nodded and dug his head against her as if he wanted to burrow a tunnel straight through her like a gopher. His skull against her breastbone was uncomfortable, but Abbie would tolerate whatever comforted Little Abe. When they got out of the dismal wheat field and onto the road that cut through the Miller farm, Abbie urged the horse a little faster, and faster still as the house came into view. By now Abbie drove with one hand around the reins and the other around Little Abe's tense back.

The front door stood wide open, and the light of half a dozen small oil lamps emanated out of the structure.

"We're almost there," she murmured to the boy.

"*Mamm.*" This was the first word he had spoken during the ride, though Abbie was sure he knew several dozen words.

"Yes, your *mamm* is waiting. She will be so glad to see you."

"Home." Little Abe sat up and twisted around toward the light-warmed house.

"That's right!"

A figure appeared in the doorframe, and Little Abe pointed. "*Mamm. Mamm.*"

A grin of relief split Abbie's face. She tightened her grip on Abe before he could get any ideas about getting down from the bench before the buggy stopped.

Mary rushed to the buggy and swept her child out of Abbie's lap and squeezed. Her chest heaved in sobs of relief.

"Be careful of his leg. I'm not sure if he got hurt." Abbie's own legs were melting rubber by the time her feet hit solid ground.

"Where did you find him?" Mary inspected the boy, running a hand over every inch of him.

Abbie explained the gopher hole.

Mary exhaled. "Albert has been trying to get rid of the gophers because he thinks they eat the wheat. But it is hard to find all the holes."

Abbie put an arm around Mary's shoulders, and they stepped into the house.

Esther looked up from the stove. "I'm heating water."

Mary nodded. "He needs a bath."

Abbie glanced around and settled her eyes on two tea cups. "Everyone else is still out looking?"

"The bell." Mary looked out through the open front door. "We need to ring the bell and call everyone in."

"I'll do it."

At the corner of the house, Abbie tugged on the bell and kept it clanging until she heard horse hooves beating from every direction.

At dawn Rudy stood at the corner of his barn and whistled for his dog, Rug. Though the small dog often wandered the acres late at night, it was unusual for him not to scratch to be let in at some point. Rudy had long ago become accustomed to opening the door at two in the morning and falling immediately back into sleep as if he had not been interrupted at all. Waking and finding the spot at the foot of his bed empty was disconcerting.

At his whistle, several cows mooed, a horse neighed, and chickens fluttered in the henhouse, but no dog appeared. Rudy paced around the outside of the barn to satisfy himself that the dog was not sleeping so comfortably under an eave that he could not bother to respond to a breakfast summons. Then he ventured to the farthest point in the barnyard and the spot in the fence where the dog was most likely to appear. Still not seeing the animal, Rudy hoisted himself over the fence and whistled again.

His whistle died half formed when he saw Rug—or the carcass that had been the dog. The teeth marks of a full-grown male coyote told the story, first clamping into the dog's neck then ripping open the abdomen.

Rudy turned around and retched. He had worked with animals long enough to see bloodier visages than this one. But the dog had been a companion in the wilderness. Rudy wiped his mouth, straightened, and went to the barn for a shovel.

Abbie's eyes widened as she forced down the knot in her throat. "I'm so sorry, Rudy. How awful for you."

"I thought you would want to know before you came over with bread and wondered where he was." Rudy sat astride his horse in the Weaver barnyard looking as dismal as Abbie had ever seen him.

Abbie nodded. She would have wondered. The dog consistently greeted her, and she reciprocated by scratching under his chin.

"Rudy," she said, "I have something to tell you as well. Little Abe Miller went missing last night."

His eyes widened.

"He's all right. He wandered off while Mary worked in the garden, but we found him after a few hours."

"God be praised."

"Yes. God is good. We all worry about our animals because we know what a coyote can do. But I can't help wondering what would have happened if that coyote had found a helpless child instead of your dog."

"The human scent would have turned the beast away."

"Would it? The coyotes seem to come closer and closer."

"Perhaps it is best if you do not mention my dog to anyone." Rudy wrapped the reins around his hand. "No point in putting a distressful notion in people's minds. But I hope Mary Miller will keep her boy close."

CHAPTER 26

A meal?"

Millie Nissley looked up from the beans in her garden. She had been more ambitious than most in what she planted, but it seemed to Abbie that her yield was as halfhearted as anyone else's vegetable patch. At mid-September, most gardens had finished for the season and Amish women were already canning.

"Nothing fancy," Abbie said. "Mary Miller and I would love to have everyone together to share our gratitude to God for Little Abe's safety." As she had already four times that morning, Abbie told an abbreviated version of the drama of Little Abe's rescue and was careful to give thanks to God for answered prayer.

"All of the families?" Millie looked dubious.

"I will invite everyone. Wouldn't it be lovely if everyone came? It would almost be like having church."

"We have no one to preach." Millie dropped a handful of beans into a basket.

"I know." Abbie was undeterred. "We can still sing and pray and be grateful."

"It's been a hard summer to think about being grateful."

Abbie nodded. "But Little Abe is safe. That matters more than anything else that has happened."

"What about food?"

"We have plenty of potatoes to roast and share. A couple of families have said they can spare a meat chicken or two. The Mullet sons have returned from Ordway with fruit. I made extra bread yesterday. Everyone will share as they are able."

"You seem to have thought of everything."

"Come at suppertime." Abbie stepped away from the garden and toward the buggy she had parked a few yards away. "We still have some light in the evenings."

Millie nodded without promising the family's attendance. As Abbie climbed into the buggy, she reviewed her mental list. She had visited five farms, and of course Mary and Esther knew the plans already. With the Chupps gone, that left Rudy, Willem, Martin Samuels, and the Troyers. She glanced at the sun approaching its zenith and judged that she still had time to talk to Mrs. Troyer, make her bread rounds, and clean Willem's house before it was time to start the potatoes roasting.

Willem sank into a chair as Abbie readied her cleaning supplies. "What awful news about Rudy's dog."

"I hope I didn't sound unsympathetic when he told me." Abbie dampened a rag. "All I could think about was, what if it had been Little Abe?"

"But it wasn't."

"But it could have been."

"You must not let your mind dwell there," Willem said.

Abbie shrugged. "I'm trying not to. I'm trying to be grateful. In fact, Mary asked me to invite everyone for a meal tonight. She and Albert want to give thanks for Little Abe's safety by being with all the families."

"Everyone?"

Abbie began to wipe off the stove. "I drove around half of creation this morning making sure everyone is invited. I hope they will come." She paused to look at him. "I hope you will come."

Willem wiped crumbs from the table and into one hand but then was not sure what to do with them. "It is a good thing to be grateful."

"It will be almost like having a church service. We might have to sit on the ground, but we can be together. We can pray. We will share our food, just like we used to do after church. We can even sing our hymns. It will cheer everyone's hearts to hear the harmonies and ponder the words of God's greatness."

When she put it so simply, Willem could hardly argue. He often hummed from the *Ausbund* as he worked, and his ears ached to hear surrounding voices fill in melody and harmonies. The gathering itself was not what caused him to hesitate. Rather, it was that the common meal would feed Abbie's hope for a true Amish church when the likelihood had become all but impossible. And Willem's presence, in particular, might stir a hope that they once again were of one heart.

Abbie rinsed out the rag and started on the table, scrubbing in preparation for polishing. As rugged as his table was, she was persistent in coaxing out the best sheen it could offer. She wanted to wheedle the best of out everything. It was one of the reasons he loved her, but every day brought reasons to reconcile reality with hope. The table would never be what she wanted it to be, and neither would the church.

Willem stood up and dropped the crumbs in his hand into the slop bucket that would go to the chickens.

Abbie stopped scrubbing and turned her pleading brown eyes to him. "Please come."

Willem gave a one-sided smile, still unable to resist that expression even when he knew their future was in doubt. "A man has to eat."

With her unfolding fingers buried in the yardage of her dress, Ruthanna ticked off the weeks. She had only seen the doctor in Limon once, preferring to let Esther Weaver monitor her pregnancy. As long as there were no unusual symptoms, Esther said, Ruthanna had no reason not to expect a healthy delivery. The child turned and kicked and rested at intervals that assured Ruthanna all was well. By her best count, she had six more weeks.

At least the sun was not quite as scorching as it had been a few weeks ago. While the days still elongated in summer fashion, the height of the afternoon temperatures dropped a degree or two each day. Still, it was hot, and Ruthanna was tired of being hot, tired of lumbering around in a body that was less recognizable by the day, tired of not sleeping because she could not find a comfortable position, tired of fearing her restlessness would disturb Eber.

Abbie made sure Ruthanna had a chair and a plate of food. Two or three families had loaded benches into their buggies and arrived ready to share seating. Several of the families did not see each other often, and the shared meal on the Miller farm sparked conversation to catch up on family news while children and young people relished being with people their own age.

Not everyone came, though, and Ruthanna saw the disappointment written on Abbie's face.

"I notice that the Yutzys have not come." Millie Nissley glanced around as she settled on the bench next to Abbie. "I didn't think they would."

"Why shouldn't they?" Abbie's voice carried a note of stubbornness Ruthanna knew well. "Perhaps they are simply delayed."

"I don't think we'll see too much more of them." Mrs. Nissley pushed a fork through a potato.

"Why would you say that?" Abbie demanded.

"Amelia Yutzy never wanted to come in the first place. Her children are not much older than Little Abe. She worries about them night and day out in this wilderness."

"It's not really a wilderness," Ruthanna offered. "We're all still getting our feet under us. Even farming in Ohio is not without challenges."

Mrs. Nissley swallowed a bite and stabbed another. "She wants to go home. I think her husband is going to agree very soon."

Ruthanna flicked her eyes toward Abbie, who paled just as Ruthanna expected.

"I think perhaps I should be going." Ruthanna balanced her plate in one hand and stood up.

"But you hardly touched your food," Abbie said, "and we haven't started singing yet."

"I know. But I don't like leaving Eber."

"I'm sorry he didn't feel well enough to come. I'll fix a plate of food for you to take him and get Reuben to drive you home. I don't want Eber to feel left out."

Ruthanna nodded, grateful for the detail of Abbie's ministrations. For now it was easiest to let others think Eber was simply tired and that a woman in her condition would be more comfortable at home.

Abbie waved good-bye to Ruthanna as Reuben pulled the Weaver buggy away from the other buggies and wagons lined up along the fence. She wanted to hold this vision as long as she could. They could have gathered like this long ago, buggies and horses announcing they were one body and children's voices lifting toward a future when every other Sunday morning would bring the families together. There was no reason to wait for a crisis like Monday night before being grateful and enjoying true Christian fellowship.

Esther and Mary were collecting plates to carry into the house to wash. Albert sat on a bench, leaning forward on his knees watching his son play in the dirt. Abbie spied Daniel pairing off with Lizzie Mullet to stroll outside the circle.

Abbie sat in the empty spot between Willem and Rudy on a bench. She nudged each of them with one elbow. "In church one of the men always starts the singing. It wouldn't be proper for me to do it."

Rudy gestured that Willem should begin, and Willem deferred to Rudy.

Abbie exhaled. "I know it shows humility when the men suggest another should go first, but please, you both have beautiful voices, so couldn't one of you just start singing?"

Willem cleared his throat. He had only sung a few bars when Rudy joined. The swell of eager voices rolled over the gathering in cool refreshment. Even after all this time without regular church services, the words welled with confidence. Abbie joined, though the knot of gratitude in her throat produced a scratchy sound. Around her the harmonies fell into place.

Where shall I go? I am so ignorant. Only to God can I go, because

God alone will be my helper. I trust in You, God, in all my distress. You will not forsake me. You will stand with me, even in death. I have committed myself to Your Word. That is why I have lost favor in all places. By losing the world's favor, I gained Yours. Therefore I say to the world: Away with you! I will follow Christ.

The wind flapped the hem of Abbie's skirt and caused her to reach for her prayer *kapp* and make sure it was secure. She kept singing, but she saw the glances around the circle. The wind abruptly became fierce and dumped its chill over the gathering. The temperature plummeted in an instant. Women dashed to keep food from blowing over and reached for hands of small children. Men hastily loaded benches.

Abbie had hoped for more than one hymn. The plain had stolen the moment. Next time, she thought, she would arrange for the shared meal to be held inside someone's barn. Rudy's was the largest. There *would* be a next time.

CHAPTER 27

As soon as Rudy milked his last cow in the morning, he harnessed a horse to the buggy and trotted toward Martin Samuels's farm. Over a plate of roasted potatoes and boiled green beans with a chunk of salted pork at the Millers' gathering, Martin had asked Rudy to come look at a cow that was behaving poorly. Rudy liked to evaluate cows early in the day, after the night had dissipated body heat and before the animals had time to take on a new day's fever.

Wind had howled overnight, drowning out even the coyotes, and Rudy saw the effects. Loose thistle huddled against every fence he passed. Even weeds that withstood summer's blasts now bent in disarray. As soon as he finished with Martin's cow, Rudy planned to climb on his own roof and make sure his shingles remained secure.

Rudy turned on the road that would take him to Martin's land and began to watch for the collection of outbuildings. The house itself was small, but Martin had a good-sized barn and a shed he had built only last year out of odds and ends of lumber. Rudy slowed as he approached the compound, confused at the absence of the shed. Where it should have stood, he saw an exposed pile of lignite beside an open wagon.

Then Martin charged out of his barn with a shovel, not bothering to lift his eyes, and attacked the pile. With the shovel's point, he alternated between transferring coal to the wagon and knocking aside the splinters that had been his shed only the night before.

Rudy slowed his horse and narrowed his eyes. When he was close enough, he spoke.

"Martin."

Widower Samuels snapped his head up.

"I'm sorry about your shed." Rudy surveyed the scattered remnants. "That wind was mighty fierce."

"Yes, it was." Martin threw another shovelful of coal into the wagon.

And then the inconsistency rolling around in Rudy's mind fell into place. "Where did the coal come from, Martin?"

"The ravine, of course."

"Directly?"

"What is that supposed to mean?"

Rudy tightened the reins to keep his horse from drifting. "I thought you had not dug any coal yet."

"How else would I get it?" Martin stopped shoveling, but neither would he meet Rudy's eye.

"Thirty men a day dig in the ravine. Even the *English* remarked they have not seen you. We have been concerned you might not be prepared for the winter."

"As you can see, I have a good start on what I need." Martin adjusted the hat on his head.

Rudy moistened his lips, wishing a conclusion made sense other than the one foremost in his mind. "Martin, is that Willem Peters's missing coal?"

Martin dropped the shovel. "I appreciate that you came to see my cow. I'll show you where she is."

There were no elders to consult, no bishop to report to. Rudy had his doubts about whether Willem was doing right by Abbie, but he deserved to know what happened to a day's hard labor.

"I'd better come back another time." Rudy started to turn his rig around.

"My cow could go down if you don't help."

"I suspect I'll be back soon enough. In the meantime, make sure she's taking enough water."

Martin kicked his boot at the coal. Rudy did not look back.

Willem nodded his thanks as Abbie set a plate of hearty breakfast in front of him. Three biscuits, four scrambled eggs, and chopped fried potatoes mirrored the plate in front of Reuben. When she asked, Willem said he already had his breakfast, as Reuben did when the family had breakfast together, but neither declined her offer of another plate of food before they left the farm together to dig coal. Though she would pack food for them to take, she doubted either would stop to eat again until supper. Willem and Reuben paused for silent prayer, and Abbie held still as well. When Willem opened his eyes, he smiled at her.

"*Kaffi?*" she said.

"Please."

She had a hard time not meeting his green eyes. A few weeks ago they would have had an entire conversation in a room full of people just with chaste glances and turns of the head. Now she guarded her hope, and it was all because of Jake Heatwole. In her mind, Abbie turned the question in every direction but refused to be the one to give voice to the heaviness between them. If she asked about Jake and Willem's intention, and he said only what he had said in the past, her heart would sink yet again. And if he leaned more distinctly toward Jake, she would have to run from the room. When Willem made up his mind, he would tell her, and she would either shed her tears or let her heart burst in rejoicing.

She poured coffee for both Willem and Reuben and nudged a small pitcher of cream toward Willem, knowing he would pour generously from it.

The knock on the front door startled her. She paced through the house and returned a moment later with Rudy behind her.

"I believe I have found your coal," Rudy said.

Willem took the time to unhitch his wagon only because he wanted to cut across the network of Amish farms in a direct route to Martin Samuels's house as close to a gallop as possible. The wagon would only slow him down.

"Wait." Abbie pulled at his elbow as he unfastened the hitch.

"Maybe there is an explanation. Give Martin a chance."

Willem sighed and stared into her dark eyes. At times her perpetual optimism was beyond his words. "Abigail, you heard what Rudy just said."

"Don't go in anger. Cool down first."

"And by that time will there be any evidence on the widower Samuels's farm of that coal?" He pulled out of her grasp and saddled his stallion. By now the entire Weaver family stood with Rudy in the yard. Willem did not look back at any of them as he pressed his heels into the stallion's sides.

Martin Samuels was stacking broken slats of wood along the side of the barn when Willem reined up beside him.

"I see Rudy wasted no time." Martin dropped another slat onto the pile.

"I see Rudy was right," Willem countered. A load of coal, a quantity that would have fit nicely in his wagon, was divided between a pile on the ground and the bed of Martin's wagon. "No one ever saw you digging, Martin. Not a single time."

"We still have long hours of light. No one could be at the ravine every moment of every day." Martin closed the gap between the barn and the coal.

Still on his horse, Willem followed Martin. "You have been a subject of much conversation. We were all concerned. Even Eber tried to dig before he fell ill again. But no one ever saw you."

"Perhaps I bought it from someone digging for profit. You are not the only one who does so."

Willem shook his head. "A man digging for you would have mentioned it amid our concern. And you led Rudy to believe you had been digging yourself."

"I will run my business, and you will run yours."

"Martin," Willem said, his jaw tight, "if you needed help, all you had to do was ask. You know that. You did not have to steal my coal."

"All coal looks alike." Martin turned his back to Willem. "You cannot possibly prove that this coal is yours."

"Why should I have to?" Willem's tone took on an edge. "Confession and forgiveness would be a more peaceable way to resolve matters."

"I do not owe you an explanation."

"It is no coincidence that the collapse of your shed in a windstorm is the first anyone knows of your coal supply."

"Can't you go any faster?" Abbie gripped the bench of Rudy's buggy.

"This gelding is as old as the hills," Rudy said, "and I've already pushed the poor animal to race from Martin's place to yours. I thought I was just going to look at a sick cow or I would have brought a team."

Abbie exhaled and let her shoulders slump.

"Don't worry," Rudy said. "Willem is not going to hurt Martin."

Abbie remembered the look in Willem's face the day he dragged Reuben home after the coal went missing. If he had been that angry with Reuben, he would be much more angry with the culprit of the crime. *Crime.* She hated to even think of using that word in connection with any of the Amish settlers.

"Don't you know a shortcut?" Abbie kept her eyes straight ahead, watching for any turnoff that might speed their journey.

"I said I would take you." Rudy glanced at her. "But if you want to do something helpful, I suggest prayer for a demonstration of love and forgiveness."

Abbie nodded. "In my distress I cried unto the Lord, and he heard me. Deliver my soul, O Lord, from lying lips, and from a deceitful tongue." She murmured the words of Psalm 120.

When they finally pulled into the widower Samuels's yard, Abbie was relieved to see both Willem and Martin standing upright, though Martin had his feet spread and his hands on his hips as he glared at Willem. The buggy swayed to a stop beside them.

Rudy closed a hand gently around her wrist. "Stay here."

Abbie did not protest as Rudy slid his hand down and encircled her fingers, but she did not take her eyes off of Willem.

"Can you stand before God and declare that you did not take my coal?" Willem said.

Abbie sucked in her breath.

Martin crossed his wrists behind his back. "A few minutes ago you were suggesting confession and forgiveness. Now you sound like an *English* court."

Willem stepped toward Martin. "The way of confession is always open. This has been a difficult year for all of us. We must try to understand and encourage each other."

Martin picked up a piece of coal and threw it into his wagon. "I will drive the coal to your farm. You can follow me to make sure I don't take off with it."

Abbie looked from Willem to Martin, who still had not admitted wrongdoing.

"Keep the coal," Willem said, "but come with Reuben and me to the ravine today to dig. Three men will make the work go faster than two, and you will still have your coal."

"I have a sick cow to tend to." Martin's voice had dropped to a mutter.

"No one wants your cow to go down." Rudy jumped down out of the buggy. "I'll see to your cow now, Martin."

Abbie let her breath out.

CHAPTER 28

I heard." Ruthanna gestured that Abbie should follow her away from the house and into the open yard. "News like that gets around fast."

"I didn't think you had left your farm since supper at the Millers'."

"I haven't." Ruthanna's pace felt like a sluggish elephant even to her.

"Rudy?"

Ruthanna nodded. "I don't think he meant to gossip. By the time he stopped by I don't think it was a secret anymore. He wanted to know how we are for coal."

Abbie turned the old yard chair around and indicated that Ruthanna should sit. "I know Eber hasn't been up to digging."

"I have enough to cook with, and the nights aren't cold yet." Ruthanna tried to get comfortable in the chair, a task growing in difficulty with every inch of her waistline.

Abbie stood behind Ruthanna and began to rub her shoulders. "I'll talk to *Daed* and my *bruder*. They can make sure you have what you need."

"Rudy has already offered."

Abbie pressed into her shoulder, and Ruthanna gave a sigh of bliss. "You have strong fingers. Eber cannot even rub my sore feet these days."

"He seems quite ill again, Ruthanna."

Ruthanna forced herself to breathe. "He is."

"I can take a buggy to Limon and get the doctor."

"He was here three days ago. He never has anything new to say. It might be an ulcer, and Eber needs to rest, or it might be something worse. The pain in his stomach comes and goes."

"Maybe we can get a doctor to come from Colorado Springs, or take Eber there. They will have a hospital. The trains go every day."

"He won't go. He says that if it is God's will for him to die, then he will go to his Savior gladly."

Abbie's hands ceased their comforting motion as she swung around to crouch in front of Ruthanna and look her in the face. "Did he really say such a thing?"

Ruthanna nodded.

"But our people have no objection to medical care. Where did he get such a notion?"

"*Gottes wille.*"

"Both of you should go to Colorado Springs and stay. Eber could see a specialist, and you could have the baby there."

"The child is not due for more than a month. We have no money. Where would we stay? How would we buy food? Who would look after our animals?"

"You know that the men would look after the farm. We could take up a collection for your other needs. That is our way."

Ruthanna shook her head slowly. "Abbie, no one has any cash to speak of. Everyone gets by with trading. Besides, Eber will not agree."

"This is no time for him to be proud. You should at least talk to him. We'll figure out a way."

Ruthanna changed the subject. "Rudy said the Nissleys want to have a meeting about what happened with the coal. Do you plan to go?"

Abbie lifted her shoulders and let them drop slowly as she stood up. "I suppose. It's tomorrow. Pray for us all."

"If it is true, then Martin is accountable to all of us." Adam Nissley opened his blue eyes wide, creating ridges in his forehead. "Even without a minister, we all know that what he did was wrong."

Abbie stood in the back of the crowded room. Not many of the other women were present, but no one had told her she could not be present. Millie Nissley poured coffee and handed cups around the ragged circle in her sitting room. Abbie watched as Willem took his cup and characteristically blew across the surface of the hot liquid before sipping. She wished she had thought to bring a coffee cake or rolls to share, though it hardly felt like a casual social occasion. Men either sat stiffly in their chairs or leaned forward on their knees.

Other than Eber, the one man missing was Martin Samuels, and Abbie wondered whether he had declined to attend or they had intentionally left him out. It seemed to her that he ought to have the opportunity to speak to his own people in a matter that so obviously concerned him.

"It is true," Willem said softly.

"Is he willing to confess?" Adam said.

"You will have to ask him that question." Willem sipped his coffee.

Abbie crossed her arms and clasped her elbows. Despite his rush to justice on the day Rudy discovered the coal, Willem had mustered surprising calm. But Abbie saw the way his fingers wrapped around his coffee cup, indignation swelling in his clenched joints. What was happening to him? He never used to let troubles disturb him to this extent.

Albert Miller spoke up. "I would never have imagined Martin was capable of this. If we cannot trust each other, then who can we trust?"

"We will all have to look out for each other," Moses Troyer said, "to make sure this does not happen again. If any of us sees another falling into sin, let him speak up."

Abbie swallowed her thought. The point of trust was not checking up on each other. Whether or not they all trusted one another, they could trust God to care for them. Willem had been offended, but he had not truly suffered. She watched his face now, but he simply caught Millie Nissley's eye and she brought the coffeepot to refill his cup.

When the knock on the door disrupted the tone in the room and all heads turned, Abbie was closest to the door.

She pulled it open to find Jake Heatwole standing on the other side.

Willem immediately stood. Color rose through Abbie's cheeks as she tensed every muscle in her face. Willem forced himself to look away from her and meet Jake's eyes.

"I don't mean to barge in," Jake said, "but I heard about the disappointment you have all endured in the last couple of days."

Willem nodded. Jake was not so distanced from the Amish that he did not understand that what wounded one of them wounded all of them.

Adam Nissley rose. "This is a private meeting, Mr. Heatwole."

Willem resisted the urge to sigh audibly. If the Amish families would listen to Jake's kindness, they would see that he meant no harm.

"I only wanted to see if there might be something I could do to help." Jake glanced around the room, unperturbed.

"I think we have the matter well in hand." Eli Yoder held his stiff-seated pose. "We will decide for ourselves what is fair."

"I did not suppose you required any assistance with that determination." Jake had not stepped any farther into the room than Abbie initially allowed. "You are all people of conscience. I suspect even Martin Samuels's transgression is a lapse due to more general difficulties."

"Are you excusing him, then?" Eli Yoder shuffled his feet slightly.

"Not at all," Jake said. "In fact, I make no judgment about the matter at all. I merely came to minister if there might be any need that I might fill."

No one spoke. Abbie still stood at the door, one hand grasping the thick panel of wood.

"Would you like some *kaffi*?" Millie asked.

Willem heard the reluctance in her voice and saw the relief in her face when Jake shook his head.

"I will not intrude further," Jake said. "But if you don't mind, Mr. Nissley, I would like to remain outside for a few minutes. Then if anyone feels the need to talk, I will not be far away."

Adam pressed his lips together, but he nodded. Jake stepped outside the door, and Abbie closed it behind him and leaned against it.

Willem swallowed his second cup of coffee in one gulp. "Thank you, Mrs. Nissley, for your kind refreshment." He nodded at the men around the room and the women on the periphery. Abbie's eyes widened, but he knew she would not speak or try to stop him in a room full of people. Willem brushed a hand against hers on his way out.

Jake stood a few yards from the house stroking the slender nose of his horse. "Hello, Willem."

Willem patted the horse's rump. "Forgiveness has a hard edge, Jake. I need prayer if I am going to face Martin Samuels with love in my heart once again."

The house quieted soon after sunset. Hours later, Abbie turned up the wick in the oil lamp that illumined her quilt square. Triangles of blue and green and purple and brown and crimson and black and white blurred together in her wearied eyes. The trunk of this family's tree—the Yutzys, in Abbie's mind—was stitched with precision, and she had started adding colors alternating with white to form the leaves of the tree. After the meeting earlier in the day, Abbie was more determined than ever to finish the quilt before further division could set in among the Amish families. Six of twelve blocks were finished, and she would not let up on the impeccable quality she chased. She had ripped out entire rows already, and she would do it again if she had to. The finished quilt must be a testament of enduring beauty, because it would represent the growth and spread of the settlement.

Abbie murmured prayers for every household in the settlement, even the long-gone Chupps, whenever she stitched. Twice she had stayed up all night, only realizing dawn would soon invade the sky when her mother shuffled into the kitchen to light the stove and start breakfast. She knew the names of every child in the settlement, though their precise ages often escaped her and she would have to calculate based on what she knew about the rest of the family. She knew whose wheat had suffered most in the June hailstorm and whose vegetables had flourished most in the July heat. She knew who might yet eke out a bit of cash from a second planting and who had given up trying. And she prayed for them all.

For Eber in his prolonged illness, that he might yet find hope.

For Willem in his temptation to leave the church.

For Rudy in his fragile dreams.

For Ruthanna and her tension-filled muscles.

For her parents and Daniel, Reuben, and Levi.

For Little Abe's safety and his parents' nerves.

For Martin Samuels and the stress that would make him do the unthinkable.

For all of them. Every leaf of every tree of life in her quilt and the prosperous future her heart ached for.

CHAPTER 29

For as far back as she could remember, humming an *Ausbund* tune had soothed Abbie's mind. She used to hum as she walked to the rural school where she studied in the early grades when she was nervous the *English* teacher might not understand her words through the thick Pennsylvania Dutch accent. She hummed when one of the farm animals was giving birth or gasping in the moments before death. She hummed as she concentrated on making bread that would meet her mother's standard.

And she hummed now as she prepared to clean Martin Samuels's house. It was his regular day. Abbie could hardly tell him that because he had stolen Willem's coal she would no longer bring him bread or sweep his floor. For nearly a week now she had hummed her way through disappointment at what he had done and the tension brooding in every conversation she overheard between men. The women were not any less suspicious. Abbie was nearly as disappointed in the shroud of distrust that fell over the families as she was in Martin. If she raised the question of forgiveness, someone was sure to point out that the widower Samuels had yet to express any convincing remorse.

Abbie had not spoken to Willem since he stepped past her with clear intent to converse with Jake Heatwole about the events rattling the Amish settlement. She should not have been surprised, but his wordless steps had settled into place the wall rising, brick by brick, between them for weeks. And that was perhaps the greatest disappointment. When she left this week's bread, she did not allow herself to look around and wonder if he might spot her and offer a greeting.

Out of courtesy, she knocked, but as usual did not wait for a response. The only time she had found Martin in his house on one of her weekly visits was when he was ill. That was more than a year and a half ago. Abbie set her bucket of brushes and sponges in the middle of his sitting room and inspected her surroundings. She could see straight through to his lean-to kitchen and the crusted dishes stacked to one side of the washtub. The disarray was notably worse than usual, which Abbie credited to the turmoil in his spirit. There was no point in taking his bread loaves into the kitchen until she had cleared a place to put them. Instead she set them on the small desk that had been in his wife's family for sixty years before her death. Abbie nudged aside a spread of paper. Once she had emptied her arms, she attempted to stack them with better order.

Abbie's eyes fell on an open letter, and the words sprang up before she could chastise herself for reading sentences not meant for her. Blinking, she picked up the two sheets of paper filled with tiny script. The more she read, the more tightly she held a hand over her mouth. She nearly tripped over her bucket in her haste to reach her buggy and turn the horse toward home.

"So it's true?" Abbie's jaw dropped as she stared at her father in the sitting room where he sat with the family Bible open in his lap. Since there was no harvest, he had taken to filling hours he used to spend on farm work by reading the German tome.

Ananias tipped his face forward so he could look at her over the tops of his round reading glasses. "Yes, what you read is true. But you should not have been reading Martin's papers."

"I told you, I didn't mean to. I was so shocked that I couldn't stop."

"That is a failure of your self-control, Abigail. What you have learned was not supposed to go beyond a private council meeting with the bishop."

Abbie flopped into a chair across from Ananias. "But that meeting was fifteen months ago. Were you really never going to tell anyone what happened there?"

Ananias nodded. "That was our intent."

"But *Daed*, don't you see? If this has been dividing us all this time, how could we ever hope for a successful settlement?" Abbie quelled the urge to stand up and stomp around the room.

"We believed it was our only hope for what we all wanted."

Abbie reached up with both hands and pulled on the strings of her prayer *kapp*. "But how could that be? If the visiting bishop would not even stay to give us communion because of your argument, how could you hope to heal such a deep spiritual divide by ignoring it?"

"*Argument* is an indelicate word, Abigail."

She put her head back on the top of the chair and stared at the ceiling. How could her *daed* remain unflustered? Abbie calmed her breath and returned her gaze to her father.

"The bishop you met with must have talked to other bishops in Kansas and Nebraska. There must be a reason they stopped visiting."

"I have no way to know what the bishops say to each other."

"Please talk to me, *Daed*. I want to understand."

"You already understand the essence. The council was not of one mind about whether there is true salvation outside the Amish church."

"That question has always been part of our history. I suspect that if you convened a meeting of all the Amish bishops and ministers, they would not all agree either."

"And you would be right." Ananias smoothed a hand across the open Bible in his lap. "But each district must decide what it will teach. Because we have families here who came from several different districts, the disparity of thought is more pronounced than it might be elsewhere."

The back door swung open and Levi charged into the house. "Aren't we going to have lunch?"

"In a little while," Abbie said.

"*Daed*, Reuben wants to know if you are going to dig coal this afternoon."

"I have not decided," Ananias said.

"If you do, can I go with you?" Levi draped himself across an end of the sofa.

"It's dangerous for a little boy," Ananias said.

"But I'm not so little anymore. I want to!"

Abbie rolled her eyes. "Levi, please, *Daed* and I are talking."

"When are you going to be finished talking?"

"Levi!" Abbie stood up, pulled the boy to his feet, and pointed him back out the door with a firm shove.

When Levi was gone, her father raised an eyebrow. "Might you have been harsh?"

"I'm sorry. I'll apologize to Levi later for my impatience." Abbie sat down again and smoothed her skirt. "I wanted to be sure we finish our conversation."

"There is not much more to say."

"Why don't the bishops visit anymore, even just a few times a year?"

"Part of the reason bishops visited was to decide whether they would want to move here. They have seen for themselves what a challenge it would be, even apart from the spiritual question."

Abbie could not dispute this observation. Even bishops had to be able to support their families. She shifted in her chair. "And what do you think on the spiritual question?"

"Abigail."

"Tell me, *Daed*."

"I am not interested in stirring up conflict."

"The conflict is already there, *Daed*. It runs under everything that happens. If we could only worship together, so many things could be better."

Ananias closed the Bible and stacked his hands on top of it.

"*Daed*, please. I am not asking out of disrespect or lack of submission, only lack of understanding."

He stood up and put the Bible on its carved stand. "My conscience tells me that I must interpret the Word of God to mean that there is no salvation outside the church."

"Outside the Amish church. Is that what you mean?"

He nodded.

Abbie sank against the back of her chair, her shoulders sagging. "So the Chupps?"

"If they have left the church, I believe they have turned their backs on the Lord's gift of salvation."

Abbie crossed her ankles and quickly uncrossed them. She could not think what to do with her feet or her hands or her face. If her father was right, Willem was in grave danger. *"Come with me,"* he had said to her on the day of their doomed picnic. She did not want him to go to the Mennonites at all, and she could not imagine going with him. As badly as he wanted his farm to succeed, even more Abbie wanted their church to succeed. But questioning Willem's salvation—or even Jake's?

"Abigail?"

She snapped her head up and found her father's gray eyes peering at her.

"Have I answered all your questions?"

"Yes, *Daed*."

"And do you now understand why I hesitated to do so?"

She nodded.

"You must not speak of this to anyone."

"But *Daed*—"

"Not anyone."

Every sway and bump in the road seemed to punch Ruthanna in the back and steal her breath. Frightened beyond imagination, she had left Eber alone in the bed clutching his stomach. All day long she had tried to ease his pain and usher in a period of rest. It had been bad enough when he was feverish and exhausted. Watching his pain contort him sliced through her. Finally she knew she did not want to be alone when the end came, and if she did not get help, the end would come soon. It had taken her a long time to climb into the buggy unassisted. Now she was driving so fast, with both hands clenched around the reins, that she could not even raise a palm to wipe away the tears that blurred her vision. She rumbled into the Weaver yard and screamed the names of every member of the family.

Abigail rushed toward the buggy. "Are you in labor?"

"No."

"You're sure?"

"Yes."

"Eber?"

Ruthanna nodded.

Abbie spun around in a circle, her gaze sweeping the property.

"Is your *mamm* here?" Panic struck Ruthanna. Esther was Eber's best hope for relief.

"She's here somewhere."

"Please, Abbie, you have to find her."

Ananias emerged from the house with Levi on his heels.

"We need *Mamm*," Abbie said. "Right now."

"She walked over to visit with Mary Miller," Ananias said.

Ruthanna did not recognize the sound that pulled at her depths.

Abbie climbed into the wagon. "It's Eber."

"I will go for the doctor myself." Ananias slapped the haunch of Ruthanna's horse, then pivoted and started for the Weaver buggy.

Ruthanna surrendered the reins to Abbie, closed her eyes, and trusted that the Holy Ghost would translate her fear into prayer.

CHAPTER 30

With Ruthanna leaning against her for the short distance between where she parked the buggy and the door to the Gingerich house, Abbie focused through the quiver in her knees and her stampeding heart.

Ruthanna groaned and put her open hand against her back.

"Do you feel all right?" Abbie asked.

"Eber is what matters now." Ruthanna turned the doorknob, and they stepped inside the house before she paused to catch her breath. "He's in the bedroom."

Abbie rolled in her bottom lip and bit gently, going ahead of Ruthanna toward the bedroom. The stench made her turn her head before she got there. She indulged the rise of bile from her own stomach for only a second before swallowing it and forcing firm steps. Eber lay tangled in sweat-drenched bedding with one arm draped around a smell metal pail. Abbie did not have to look to know its contents were viscous green fluid and blood. She paced around the bed in the cramped room, picking up a towel from the dresser on her way and used it to wipe Eber's pallid face. The bed creaked as Ruthanna lowered herself onto the other side and took Eber's head in her lap.

"When did this start?" Abbie asked softly. She lifted a bowl of water and judged it had already been used several times to rinse soiled cloths.

"A few hours."

Limon was eight miles. Even if Ananias Weaver found the

doctor quickly, eight miles back would seem like a trek through the Rockies. "The doctor is coming," she said.

Ruthanna stroked Eber's matted hair and beard. "I know this is the end, Abbie."

"Reuben will find my *mamm*. She'll be here soon." Abbie turned away to cover her nose and mouth for a moment, trying to find even a minute stream of air that did not taste rancid. Taking small breaths, she turned around. "Shall we try to make him more comfortable? Clean things up?"

Ruthanna kissed Eber's sweat-caked forehead. "The spare sheets are in the bottom drawer."

Abbie pulled the drawer open and lifted the sheets and set them on the dresser. She had once seen a nurse in a hospital change the sheets under a patient who could not get out of bed. Gingerly she pulled back the sheet covering Eber. His skeletal condition, garbed only in undergarments, shocked her, but she pressed her lips together and tossed the soiled top sheet to the floor. Starting gently with one corner of the bottom sheet, she began inching it out from under Eber. Ruthanna stood to help and they managed to change the sheets and Eber's undershirt.

Abbie bundled the sheets in her arms and picked up the revolting pail. "I'll get some fresh water from the well and put these to soak."

Ruthanna pushed the window open before returning to her vigil post on the bed beside Eber. She picked up another small pail and set it within reach. Not once had Eber opened his eyes while Ruthanna and Abbie cleaned up around him, and now Ruthanna wondered if she would ever see the blazing blue of his eyes again. Had she known that his last gaze would be the last, she would have fallen into the pleading pools of his eyes to soak up one final memory of his face.

She picked up a limp hand and held it between both of hers. "Does it feel better to be cleaned up? I'm sorry I couldn't manage to do that on my own."

Eber took a ragged breath, his chest barely lifting, and Ruthanna stilled her movements to see if he would exhale. Five seconds passed, then ten. She counted almost to twenty before the air moved out of him.

"I hope you know how much I love you," she whispered. "God smiled on me the day we met. I could not have hoped for God's will to be more gracious toward me."

He inhaled with a rasp, his mouth opening slightly.

Ruthanna cupped her hand around his face. "I would take away every throb of your pain if only I could."

His exhale was the faintest she had ever heard.

Ruthanna winced, moved a hand to the side of her protruding abdomen, and forced herself to exhale. The pain was longer than usual, the hardening beneath her hand more persistent. False labor pains had been striking at unpredictable intervals for weeks. Esther reminded her every time they spoke that she would know real labor when it began. That was still weeks away by Ruthanna's reckoning.

A sob clenched her chest as the vice around her middle released its grip. Her child would not know the light of its father's eyes, or the cradle of his arms, or the beat of his heart as he held the babe to his chest. Ruthanna slid down in the bed, reaching her arms around her own midsection to grasp her husband's thin form.

It seemed like Abbie had to let the bucket down a long way before she heard it splash against the surface of the well's water. It was no different on her own family's farm. Normally she was careful not to use more water than she needed, but today was no time to conserve. She dumped the water into a tub she had found outside Ruthanna's front door that now held the soiled sheets then let the bucket down again. Soaking out the stains would take plenty of cold water.

When she heard the horse's hooves she paused to look up. "Willem!"

He seemed surprised to see her. Then his eyes dropped to the tub. "The baby?"

"Eber."

When the bucket came to the top of the well again, Willem grabbed it and emptied it into the tub. "What happened?"

Abbie scratched at the back of one hand. "It's time."

Willem's eyes widened. "Time for what? I just came to see what chores needed doing."

Abbie's stomach rolled, and she wondered how many times she would have to voice these words. "I should have insisted they both go to Colorado Springs or Denver. Another doctor might have made a difference. The *English* have specialists."

Willem grasped her fidgeting wrist. "Abigail, say what you must."

"When is the last time you saw Eber?"

"A few days ago. A week."

"I would have come sooner if I had any idea." She ran her tongue over her lips and looked up at his eyes. "Eber will leave this world today."

Willem started and his eyes snapped toward the house.

"*Daed* has already gone to Limon for the doctor," Abbie said, "but it will not matter now."

"You can't be sure of that."

Abbie pushed his hand off her wrist and gestured toward the tub. "I've been in there, Willem. I've seen him. He's been a lot sicker than he let any of us believe."

Willem held a hand over both eyes.

Abbie trembled through her core. "I should go back in. Ruthanna should not be alone." She turned to go.

Willem stopped her and wrapped his arms around her. Despite her resolve, Abbie melted against him and buried her head in his chest while he stroked the back of her neck. Neither his firm hold nor solid stance quelled the dread rising from a foreign space at the pit of her stomach. She circled his waist with her arms, and still she shook.

"I have to go in," she said hoarsely.

"We'll go together." Willem unfolded the embrace and steered Abbie toward the house.

Eber's stomach had retched several times in a vain attempt to empty, but unconscious he could not lift his head to the pail. Ruthanna did her best to turn him on his side with a towel under his face so she could lie beside him and wipe the blood that dribbled between his parched lips. Relief rushed through Ruthanna when she saw Willem and Abbie come through the door together.

"Thank you," Ruthanna murmured. "Thank you both."

Abbie picked up the washbasin from the dresser and the two rags draped across its rim. "I'll get some fresh water."

"The barrel in the kitchen is almost empty."

"I can fill it," Willem said.

Ruthanna nodded, her hand once again going to the pain in her abdomen. Abbie left with the washbasin. Ruthanna listened to the familiar sounds of throwing the reddish brown water out the back door and swishing water in the basin to rinse it clean before filling it afresh. Abbie's skirts rustled with the normal movements of simple housekeeping. Ruthanna could tell Abbie had paused to pull a rag across the kitchen table and push the canisters of flour and sugar to one side.

Ruthanna groaned and tried to shift her weight.

"Are you all right?" Willem asked.

"I think I need to sit up for a while," she said. Her back ached violently as the now familiar roll of pain began a fresh circuit. She put a hand out, and Willem grasped her arm all the way to the elbow as she righted herself. Beside her, Eber's breath leaked out of him, and Ruthanna once again counted the seconds and waited for his lungs to move. The number was higher with each interval. She lost track of whether she was measuring Eber's breath or her own pain.

The front door opened, and a moment later Esther Weaver's form blocked the light coming from the main room.

"Reuben brought me," Esther said. She immediately moved to Ruthanna and laid a hand on her midsection.

"Thank you for coming."

"Are you in labor?" Esther asked quietly.

"The false pains." Ruthanna grimaced.

"They are not always false," Esther said, "not at this stage."

Ruthanna shook her head. "It's too soon." She turned her head back to Eber, trying to remember where she left off counting before Esther came in and unsure whether she had missed a breath cycle.

She did not think so.

Esther rounded the bed for a closer look at Eber. Ruthanna knew better than to seek a glimmer of hope.

Eber's chest did not move. Ruthanna wiped his mouth again and laid her ear against his mouth even as her abdomen squeezed with fresh fury.

Esther lifted Ruthanna's hand, drawing Ruthanna's gaze up.

"I'm concerned, Ruthanna," Esther whispered. "This is a terrible moment for you, but we must think of the baby."

Ruthanna exhaled sharply and sucked in three quick breaths. Still she counted. Still Eber's chest did not move.

She felt the trickle of fluid between her legs.

CHAPTER 31

Eber's chest lifted. Or perhaps Ruthanna only thought it had. "Ruthanna."

She looked up at Esther's face.

Esther pointed to the puddle forming on the floor beneath Ruthanna's feet.

Ruthanna nodded in answer to Esther's unspoken question. Her waters had broken.

Esther glanced at Eber, before turning toward the door and softly calling Abbie's name.

Abbie entered the bedroom with the basin of fresh water, her eyes immediately going to Eber. Willem shuffled toward her and took the basin. Abbie sat on the edge of the bed with her arms around Ruthanna.

Ruthanna grimaced and grunted with the next pain.

"It's only been a couple of minutes since the last one," Esther observed. "Your baby is coming, Ruthanna."

"But Eber." Ruthanna huffed out her strained breath.

Abbie stood up and pulled Ruthanna to her feet as well. She held Ruthanna's face in both hands. "Eber is gone, Ruthanna. But his child will soon be in your arms."

Ruthanna wailed for the first time. Whether in pain or grief she was not sure and it did not matter. Eber had left her for the arms of the Savior.

"But what about Eber?" Ruthanna asked when the contraction subsided.

Abbie pulled the sheet up over Eber's face. "We'll take care of him, too. But we have to get you comfortable."

"Where? I can't give birth in the bed now."

Abbie looked at Willem. "Bring some hay from the barn, Willem. We'll make a pallet."

Willem nodded and left. Ruthanna gripped Abbie's hand as she led her to a chair in the main room. Eber always said that as soon as they got a bit of money they would get some decent chairs, or he would learn to make a glider for her. For now, all she had to sit on was the straight-back padless chair Eber had used when he sat outside. As she sat, she turned the chair toward the bedroom and fastened her eyes again on the shape on the bed. Esther was tucking the white sheet around Eber's form.

The next pain seized her.

Abbie was scrambling around the stove, trying to stoke the fire and looking for a pot.

"The big one is on the back porch." Ruthanna forced the words out between gritted teeth.

"You're going to be all right, Ruthanna." Abbie touched Ruthanna's shoulder before stepping out the back door.

The room suddenly went frosty. Ruthanna began to shiver. Her husband was wrapped in a sheet, and her baby was coming a month early. How could she have a baby without Eber?

She leaned forward and keened.

As soon as he dragged half a bale of hay through the back door and Abbie spread the most tattered quilt she could find over it, Willem excused himself. He paused only for a scant look at Eber before dragging the now empty water barrel out of the kitchen and toward the well. The cows would need to be milked before long, and he wondered when the last time was that Ruthanna took a slop bucket out to the chickens. Eber's horse was still hitched to the buggy Ruthanna had taken to the Weavers.

Willem was glad for the chores. He could stay near without feeling in the way of the birthing work. He stood the barrel on end next to the well and began to fill it one bucket at a time.

Rudy galloped into the yard. "I ran into Ananias on his way for the doctor."

"It's too late." Willem sighed and dumped another bucket.

Rudy slung out of his saddle and folded his long form as if he had been kicked in the stomach. "God's will is surely mysterious sometimes."

Willem nodded. "There's no way to get word to the doctor that he need not come."

Rudy let out one long, slow breath. "Perhaps he will have a potion for Ruthanna. She must be frantic, but she will need to rest."

"I'm afraid it is too late for her to rest as well, although she might yet have need of the good doctor's expertise before the night is over. I assume he knows how to deliver a baby."

Rudy stopped Willem's cranking motion with one long hand. "Ruthanna is birthing her child now? With Eber just gone?"

"What we really need," Willem said, "is an undertaker. I know we usually bury our dead within a day or so, but Ruthanna will be in no condition. And she will insist on being there."

"She should be there. Eber will only have one funeral."

"Eber will have to be embalmed to give her some time to recover from the birth. A few days, at least. We could try to buy some ice to put under him, but the days are still warm. It will be difficult to cover the smell."

"You are right that he should be embalmed." Rudy released his hold, and Willem resumed cranking up the bucket. "But an *English* undertaker will want a fee."

"Yes, I suppose he will. We'll have to sort that out later."

"Maybe he would like free eggs and fresh milk for a few weeks." Rudy turned back to his horse and prepared to mount. "I will go to Limon and see what arrangement I can make."

Abbie knelt at Ruthanna's head and let her friend dig her fingernails into her arm with neither flinch nor protest. When she was not grunting against pain, Ruthanna sobbed and cried her husband's name. On the stove, the soup pot of water seemed to refuse to boil, and when Willem returned with the barrel, Abbie wanted to start another pot.

Abbie reminded herself that her mother had been an unofficial but experienced midwife at dozens of births, but still she admired the quiet calm Esther exuded as she went about getting Ruthanna comfortable on the pallet of hay with her knees up and inspecting to see how far labor had progressed.

"Try to relax between contractions," Esther said with one hand on Ruthanna's abdomen. "I do not think it will be long before it's time to push."

"It was not supposed to be like this." Ruthanna's voice was at near-shriek pitch. "Eber wanted a child even more than I did. God waited years before giving us one."

"*Shh.*" Esther patted Ruthanna's arm. "The hardest part is ahead of you. You must save your strength."

Ruthanna flopped her head back on the hay. "My strength died with my husband."

Esther positioned herself where she could look Ruthanna in the eye. "You still have a baby coming. Nothing is going to change that. You must focus on what you have to do."

Ruthanna's head swung widely from side to side. "What does it matter without Eber?"

"This child is a gift from God," Esther said softly but firmly. "When he is in your arms, you will treasure him. You will see Eber in his face every day. Right now you must birth him, nothing else."

Ruthanna's cry settled into a whimper, but when the next contraction came, she was ready.

Abbie squeezed her hand. Many Amish women her age had several children of their own, but Abbie had never before been present at a birth. It was wonderful and terrible at the same time. Her mother seemed to know just what to do. Abbie tried to imagine what it would be like when she had a child. Would her mother be able to remain calm when her own daughter travailed?

"Abbie," Esther said, "we are going to need string and a clean pair of scissors or a knife."

Abbie looked around.

"In the basket on the top shelf." Ruthanna's voice was flat but her instructions accurate.

Abbie could see the basket now, the one Ruthanna had used as she worked on her baby's quilt. When she pulled it off the shelf, Abbie could see the small quilt neatly folded in the flat woven bottom.

"The cradle," Ruthanna croaked. "It's still in the barn, but I think Eber finished it."

"There's plenty of time for that." Esther pushed Ruthanna's knees apart. "When the next contraction begins, you can bear down."

The water had barely reached boiling when Eber and Ruthanna's daughter slid into the world. Esther laid the baby on a clean towel and then tied off the cord and cut it. Just as the child let out her first wail, Esther turned her toward Ruthanna and Abbie.

Abbie gasped. "She is beautiful, Ruthanna. So beautiful!"

Esther wrapped the baby in the towel and handed the bundle to Abbie. "Don't spend too much time admiring her. She'll want her mother soon enough."

Ruthanna smiled through the streaks of grimy tears on her face. "And her mother wants her."

Marveling, Abbie released the baby into Ruthanna's waiting arms and then settled in again as together they counted fingers and toes.

"She's perfect. Her father would have—" Ruthanna's voice broke.

Abbie leaned her head against Ruthanna's. She had no words for the moment.

"Poor Willem," Ruthanna said, "waiting outside all this time. You'd better go tell him."

Abbie wiped her eyes with the back of one hand and nodded.

Outside, a moment later, she stopped to gaze at Willem in the fractured instant before he sensed her presence. This was the man she had imagined having children with. The thought that they might have no future triggered tears.

Willem spotted her from where he sat on the ground with his elbows propped on his knees and his head hanging between his dangling hands. He jumped to his feet. "The baby?"

"A girl. They're both fine."

A grin cracked Willem's face. "A girl. I hope she is as lovely as her mother."

"Every bit." Abbie's throat was too thick to say more.

Willem opened his arms, and Abbie went into them for the second time that day. She breathed in the sweaty scent of a man unafraid of hard work—and a man whose salvation her own father would question if he knew what Willem contemplated. Abbie banished the thought.

"I guess my *daed* could not find the doctor," Abbie said. "He never came."

Willem kissed the top of her head. "Rudy was here. He went for an undertaker."

CHAPTER 32

The weather was not cold and dreary, as Ruthanna had supposed it would be. She had not imagined the day she buried her husband could be warm, sunny, and inviting. It was the sort of day that beckoned giggles and bare feet in a creek, picking wild sunflowers and naming clouds.

Those were the wishes of girlhood, not the order of a funeral.

Standing behind her home, Ruthanna pulled the baby's quilt away from her face and stroked a silken cheek. She had barely discovered how to feed the child comfortably, much less face the fatherless years that stretched ahead. Someday this innocent little girl would hear the story of her father's death on the day of her birth. Ruthanna would avoid the topic for as many years as she could. No child should have to learn to mingle grief with rejoicing, missing a man she never knew simply because of a coincidence of dates.

Not coincidence, Ruthanna reminded herself. *Gottes wille.* Was not everything that happened God's will and meant to teach her something? Ruthanna could not see the lesson in tragedy. She saw no hope in devastation, no justice for a little girl with no *daed.*

The back door opened. Abbie's face looked as drawn and pale as Ruthanna supposed her own was.

"Is it time?" Ruthanna asked.

"The first buggies are here."

Ruthanna adjusted her daughter's slight weight in her arms and followed Abbie into the house, where Abbie and Esther had prepared the humble home for the service. The undertaker's black wagon had come early in the morning to return Eber to his bedroom, this time embalmed and laid in an unlined coffin on a wide plank balanced over a bench. The crisp white sheet would come off soon. All other furniture in the room had been removed to the barn, save one chair for Ruthanna. Esther had insisted it was too soon to expect Ruthanna to stand to greet the Amish families who would come to see Eber. Dark cloths covered the windows, casting the room into unfamiliar midday gray shadows.

"Do you want to see him before the others come in?" Abbie asked.

Ruthanna nodded, the knot in her throat too big for speech.

Abbie stepped quietly across the room, which now felt cavernous to Ruthanna, to lift the sheet and gently fold it into a tight, small rectangle.

Ruthanna's heart pounded. Eber lay in the same unadorned white shirt and dark trousers that had been his wedding suit, with his arms folded across his chest. The undertaker had made Eber look healthier than he had been in the last few weeks, the fullness of his cheeks unlike the gaunt outline Ruthanna had become accustomed to.

Oh Eber.

They all came, even Widower Samuels. Tears burned behind Abbie's eyes.

Her memory of the last time the Amish had gathered for a worship service had grown fuzzy around the edges, and she could not be sure every family had been there. As desperately as she wanted them to be a church together, she hated the occasion that summoned them on this day. A few *English* families arrived as well, tentative about the procedure but earnest in their intention. They understood few truths about the Amish, but they understood loss. Of this Abbie had no doubt.

Abbie rotated between greeting people at the door, checking to see if Ruthanna needed anything, and helping her mother organize the steadily widening array of food the visitors carried in. Her father and brothers had gathered every bench and stool from the surrounding farms, and still children would have to sit on the floor and some of the men stand. The Gingerich home simply was not spacious enough to bring comfort to a gathering fraught with distress. No one's home would have been. They had all built quickly, eager to have shelter and begin farming and expecting to expand soon.

But soon had not come for any of them. While they might have held a Sunday service in a barn, tradition demanded Eber be laid out in his home with his wife and daughter beside him. From the kitchen, where she found space on the crowded counter for yet another plate of food, Abbie could look into the bedroom and see Ruthanna cradling her four-day-old daughter. Families entered for the viewing. Some murmured to Ruthanna words that Abbie could not hear but could suppose.

"It's God's will."

"You must trust."

"We will pray for you."

Abbie believed those affirmations, yet they sounded hollow even in her own mind on this day. She picked up an empty milking stool, before someone else would discover its unoccupied state, and carried it into the bedroom to sit beside Ruthanna. In a moment, Jake Heatwole would come through the front door. Abbie had seen him trot his horse into the yard.

Jake.

When Willem suggested asking him to lead the service, even Abbie could not dispute the wisdom. The Ordway settlement was a day and a half of travel in each direction, and no one could be sure a minister would come. Even if one had, he would have been a stranger. Jake knew Eber, and Ruthanna trusted him.

If her father was right, though, and the latent fissure under the Amish settlement was a pressured crack about the salvation of a man like Jake Heatwole, Abbie could not help wondering what this moment of trying to do right by Eber would mean.

She put out her arms and offered to take the baby, but Ruthanna only ran a single finger down the tiny curve of the infant's nose.

Life unto death. This was the theme of Jake's sermon, as well it should be. Willem listened to Jake's voice rise and fall, rise and fall, in somber waves expounding the truth of John 5. The Father has given the Son authority to judge, and all people should be ready for the moment of their deaths. Jake believed that Eber had been ready. When the Book of Life was opened at the Great White Throne of Revelation 20, Eber Gingerich's name would appear on its pages.

As Willem had expected he would, Jake stood in the crowded house for nearly an hour and preached with an open Bible. He paused several times to look over the heads of the assembly and into the bedroom where Ruthanna and Abbie sat. Willem was sure they heard Jake's words, including the kind comfort he offered the grieving widow at regular intervals. With his back to the bedroom, Willem could not see Ruthanna's face. But he had seen it before the service. He had seen it many times over the last four days and could not imagine that it had gained any cheer or color.

Jake was right. Eber had been ready. Though the bishops might say that no one could be certain of another's salvation at the time of death, Willem had no doubt about Eber. He had not been a perfect man. No man was. But his heart belonged to the Lord.

Jake closed his Bible and let silence shroud the room before intoning, "Eber Gingerich was twenty-seven years old."

The *English* would have read a long eulogy, but the Amish congregation recognized this simple statement as their cue to kneel for Jake's prayer. Shuffling boots and scraping benches filled the room for a few minutes. It was not easy for Willem to unfold his lanky form and find space for his knees on the floor, but Jake waited until everyone had settled. His prayer was brief, sincere, comforting. At his "Amen" the congregation once against shifted, this time to stand for the benediction. Willem used the opportunity to look over the heads of his fellow settlers into the bedroom in time to see Ruthanna shudder.

The moment the last nail went into the coffin, obscuring Eber's face until eternity, had nearly undone Rudy. A shriek had escaped Ruthanna's control. But now Rudy gripped his corner of the coffin and nodded to Willem and the two other pallbearers that he was ready. With the ponderous dignity the task evoked, they carried the coffin to Willem's open wagon and set it in the empty bed. Reuben, Daniel, and Levi Weaver had hitched all the horses and turned the buggies around while everyone else attending the funeral shared a meal and said their final farewells to Eber. Now it was time for the entire community to process and lay him to rest. The spot Ruthanna picked out was beyond the horse pasture, closer to the bedraggled wheat field than the house, because she believed Eber would want to be there. Rudy had helped to dig the grave yesterday, mourning with each slam of the shovel into the earth. Eventually, he supposed, there would be a flat stone bearing Eber's name.

The pallbearers released their hold on the coffin almost simultaneously. Rudy could feel the tremor of regret in the movement of their hands. Regret that they had not realized sooner how serious Eber's illness was. Regret that his life had ended too soon. Regret that they did not know the words to speak to his widow.

Rudy got in his own buggy and waited for his turn to click his tongue and lift his reins to put his horse into motion. Mourners passed the field where Eber's animals grazed and the field he would never harvest and tied their horses to the fence he had built.

Abbie sat stiffly on the edge of her bed that night and watched Ruthanna sleep. She lay in the bed with her eyes closed, anyway. Abbie was not sure for a long time that Ruthanna truly was sleeping.

After Eber's death and the baby's birth, Abbie had spent two days and nights at Ruthanna's home. She cleaned up after the undertaker came for his sober task and nourished and cared for Ruthanna's physical needs. On the day before the funeral, Ruthanna moved to the Weavers' house. Abbie was more than glad to share the bed in her narrow room. Eber's cradle sat on the floor beside the bed. The baby was snuggled in a cotton sack that tied at the neck. Abbie had found it among the baby things Mary Miller had given Ruthanna.

Abbie had stroked Ruthanna's back until her friend stopped fidgeting and breathed in a deep, regular rhythm, perhaps for the first time in weeks. Now she slowly lifted her hand but was afraid that getting in the bed would wake Ruthanna, and Abbie was not willing to take that risk. If she had to, she would sit up all night.

The baby whimpered. Abbie knew she had been fed and changed only an hour ago. At the second whimper, Abbie eased off the bed, bent over, picked up the child, and slipped out of the room.

She inhaled the infant's sweetness and prayed for her mother.

CHAPTER 33

I could come with you," Ruthanna said a week later.

Abbie set a basket of food in the Weaver buggy. "You would get some notion in your head about helping."

"It's my farm. I should help."

"You have other things on your mind." Abbie laid a hand on the baby's head as she slept in her mother's arms.

Ruthanna blew out her breath. "Going to talk to the banker in Limon last Friday did not help matters."

"This is a new day, a new week. God will make His provision clear."

Ruthanna looked less sure than Abbie's words sounded.

"In the meantime," Abbie said, "I'm just taking lunch to Willem and Rudy. I hope to bring you word that the barn has been mucked."

Abbie kissed her friend's cheek and the baby's head before getting in the buggy. She had been going to the Gingerich farm every day since the funeral to check. Reuben's offer to bring the animals to the Weaver farm so it would be easier to care for them met with Ruthanna's resistance. It was too much trouble, she said, when she would be going home any day now.

At Ruthanna's farm, Abbie saw Willem's stallion and Rudy's gelding grazing aimlessly alongside Ruthanna's two horses. She tied her horse to the fence, leaving it hitched, and retrieved a quilt and the lunch basket of salt pork, cheese, bread, and apple cake. As she crossed the yard toward the barn, Willem emerged with a wheelbarrow. He grinned, and she could not help but smile back.

"Rudy," Willem called over his shoulder, "Abbie is here."

Rudy emerged wiping his hands on a rag.

"I hope you're both hungry," Abbie said.

Rudy's blue eyes greeted her gaze. "Just give us a moment to clean up."

Willem followed Rudy to the well, where they dumped water into their hands and rubbed them together. When she saw them splashing their faces and drinking from cupped hands, Abbie looked around for a patch of shade against the side of the barn and spread the quilt. Ruthanna's house had been put to right after the funeral and scrubbed clean. Abbie thought she ought to find it just that way when she was ready to come home. Surely Willem and Rudy would continue to help with chores until Ruthanna could pay for some help.

The men returned and dropped onto the quilt. Abbie unpacked the basket.

"We heard about what happened in Limon on Friday," Willem said.

"Something will work out," Abbie said. It seemed to her that the banker's conversation with Ruthanna should have been confidential.

"It sounds as if Ruthanna had no idea how much debt Eber took on to keep the place running." Rudy wrapped a chunk of pork in a soft slice of bread.

"They lived so frugally," Abbie said. "I can't imagine where the money went."

"Buying hay because they couldn't grow it. Lumber for fence posts. Turning the shack that was on the land into something they could live in. Building a decent barn." Willem ticked off his points on his fingers.

Abbie sighed. "I know. But so much money! No wonder Eber would never agree to a hired hand even when he was so ill."

"Ruthanna will have some decisions to make," Rudy said.

"She can sell some of the land." Abbie poured water from a jug into a tin cup and sipped it. "She does not have to farm. There are other ways to make a living."

A strange horse trotted into the yard with an *English* astride. "Ruthanna Gingerich?"

"She's not here." Abbie untucked her legs and stood up. "She's staying at my family's home right now. Can I help you?"

He pulled an envelope out of a saddlebag. "She got a telegram. Will you sign for it and take it to her?"

Ruthanna lifted her squirming daughter from the cradle, carried her down to the Weaver kitchen, and took her place at the table. She held the baby upright over her shoulder during the silent prayer before the evening meal. Every day she learned something new about what would soothe the child or what the pitch of her cry might mean, and today's lesson in mothering had been the discovery that her baby would rather be upright and patted on the back than cradled in the arms and swayed. Ruthanna closed her eyes for a moment in a posture of gratitude she did not feel. But perhaps if she cultivated her habit of giving thanks she might one day feel grateful again.

Ananias intoned, "Amen," and the family began to pass serving dishes. Beside Levi, Esther closely supervised his portions, insisting that he should put more on his plate than the skinny boy was inclined to do. No matter how many times his family assured him they were not going to starve, Levi tried to conserve food. Abbie had expressed exasperation about this to Ruthanna more than once.

With her free hand, Ruthanna took a bowl of green beans from Daniel and set it next to her plate so she could use the spoon to serve herself. Esther had wrung the neck of a chicken a few hours ago, and Ruthanna took a thigh from the platter and put it next to the beans.

Around her the clatter of passing dishes morphed into the scrape of forks against plates, but Ruthanna did not eat. She patted her baby's back and jiggled her gently.

Esther caught her eye and said, "Abbie says you received a telegram today. Not bad news from home, I hope."

"It was from my parents," Ruthanna said. "They feel terrible that they could not get here for Eber's funeral, but my mother is coming now."

Across the table, Abbie smiled. "I'll be so glad to see her! And it will be wonderful for you to have help for a while."

"She will arrive on Thursday on a midmorning train."

"We'll be delighted to have her stay here with us at first," Esther said. "I don't want you to feel rushed to go back to your home before you are ready."

Ruthanna took a deep breath, hating that the words she prepared to speak would crush her best friend.

"I don't think I will go back to the house at all."

Forks stopped in midair. Around the table, eyes lifted toward Ruthanna.

"My mother wants me to come home with her. And I want to go."

Abbie set her fork down gently. "Of course a visit with your family would do you good. The farm will be here when you get back."

Tears burned in Ruthanna's eyes. "I hope someday I will come back to visit you and find a thriving Amish settlement. But I think it's best if I list the farm with a broker and move back to my parents' home. We'll leave on Friday."

Abbie washed the platter, the last of the supper dishes. She dried it slowly, listening to Ruthanna's murmuring to her baby in the next room. Abbie slid the platter into its place on the shelf and hung the damp towel over the back of a chair. On her way into the main room, she paused for a moment to lean against the doorframe and twiddle her prayer *kapp* strings while she watched Ruthanna. Despite her tragic start to motherhood, she was learning to know her infant well and responded to the child's fussing with calm and cooing. Finally, Abbie chose a seat where she could see her friend's face clearly.

"I know you are not happy with my decision," Ruthanna said softly. "It breaks what is left of my heart to think of leaving you, but it is right that I go."

Abbie tucked her hands under her thighs to keep from appearing as agitated as she felt. "Your whole life has changed in ten days. Maybe this is not the time to make such a major decision. You still have the farm and people who care for you."

"You didn't hear for yourself what the banker said." Ruthanna adjusted the baby on her lap so she could look into her eyes and hold both tiny hands. "After so much drought and soil erosion from the wind, the land is barely worth what we paid for it. Eber borrowed against our equity money several times. The last time he tried, the bank turned him down."

"I'm so sorry. But the rest of the settlers will not let you suffer. You can stay here all winter, if you like. Your animals can stay in our barn. In the spring, Willem and Rudy and my brothers will put your crop in. It won't always be like this."

Silence descended. Abbie held her breath.

"My husband died," Ruthanna finally said, her voice a whisper. "I have a newborn. I have overwhelming debt I knew nothing about. I cannot struggle against reality right now, Abbie. Even if I can sell the farm to get out from under the debt, I will have no money. Please try to understand. My daughter deserves a better start, and I can give her that if I go home."

"This is home."

"I certainly hoped it would be. When she is older, I will bring my daughter back and show her Eber's grave. Promise me you will make sure the marker is laid as soon as it is ready."

"Of course I will. But you could stay at least long enough to see to that."

"It would be too hard. The mound would still be fresh and would cut my heart open all over again."

Abbie's shoulders sank in defeat. "I'm sorry. I have no idea what it must be like to lose a husband."

Ruthanna gave a wan smile. "You will have a wonderful life here, Abbie. You want a church here more than anyone else. We all know that and admire it in you."

Abbie swallowed hard. "It won't be the same without you."

"Willem loves you. I hope you know that."

Abbie nodded. She did know. But did he love her enough?

Ruthanna was up with the baby for a long stretch in the middle of the night. Abbie heard her get out of bed several times and saw her pacing the room with the baby on her shoulder, illumined by the moon. It was no surprise when Ruthanna did not get up for breakfast. Abbie crept out of the room as quietly as she could, pulling her dress and *kapp* off the hook on her way out. She dressed quickly in Levi's already empty room and went down the narrow stairs to the kitchen. Esther was heating the stove. A bowl of eggs shed of their shells sat on the table. Ananias's glasses were balanced at the end of his nose as he studied some papers.

Abbie took a large fork from a drawer and began to beat the eggs. "I wish Ruthanna would change her mind," she blurted.

"I know how much you will miss her," Esther said.

"She should not make a decision when she is under so much stress."

"She has to do what she believes is right. It is not for us to judge." Esther dropped a generous pat of butter into a frying pan, which sizzled immediately.

Ananias cleared his throat. "She made the right decision, Abigail."

"How can you say that, *Daed*? She hasn't given the church a chance to help her."

"We are not much of a church, Abbie. We are barely a settlement."

"But we can be if it is what we all want."

Ananias stood and tapped his fingers on the papers on the table. "I have made a decision as well. We will return to Ohio. We will go before the end of the month, before the winter turns harsh."

"*Daed!*"

Esther dumped the bowl of eggs into the sputtering pan.

CHAPTER 34

Abbie's brain tied itself in a knot, incapacitating her tongue. Her mother, silent, stirred the eggs.

"I am responsible for the family's welfare, Abigail." Ananias picked up his papers and tapped them against the table to straighten the bottom edge of the pile. "I do not come to this decision easily, but it is in the best interest of all of us if we return to Ohio."

Abbie bit her bottom lip, choosing her words carefully. "All the reasons we left Ohio are still there. Land is expensive. The county is getting crowded."

"That is true. But the reasons we came to Colorado are no longer here. The opportunities have not proven fruitful. I cannot afford to give my sons land here, either. If I cannot succeed at farming, neither will they."

"The winter could bring blizzards of snow to end the drought," Abbie said. "We could have two good harvests next year."

Esther took plates off the shelf and put them on the table.

"We also hoped more families would come," Ananias said. "Daniel is of marriageable age, but we have no young unmarried women."

"He seems partial to Lizzie Mullet."

"She is not suitable."

Ananias's clipped tone bore growing impatience, but Abbie pushed on. "Why not? She's seventeen and comports herself well."

"Her father and I are not of like mind."

The sentence punched the air out of her. "You mean about

whether there is true salvation outside our church?"

"Abigail!" Ananias thumped the table.

Esther stirred the eggs but turned her head over one shoulder. "What is she talking about, Ananias?"

"We will not speak further on that question."

"Daniel is still young," Abbie said quietly. She did not need Lizzie Mullet to make her point. "Many of our men wait a few more years to marry."

"They wait so they can become established financially. There is no hope for that here."

"There is always hope, surely. *Gottes wille.*" Dread gushed through Abbie's veins on the way back to her heart and lungs. "We may not get any new families now. It is too close to winter. But in the spring—"

"Abigail."

She pressed her lips together to make herself stop talking.

"Reuben is not far beyond Daniel," Ananias said. "And what about you?"

Her eyes widened.

"I mean no insult. You are my precious daughter. But I regret that I did not insist that you marry before we left Ohio. You have limited prospects here as well."

"I do not worry about my future, *Daed.*"

Esther stepped to the bottom of the stairs and called the names of her three sons to summon them to breakfast. To Abbie her voice sounded mist-like, insubstantial.

"Your Willem seems to be in no hurry," Ananias said.

"Neither am I."

Ananias cleared his throat. "I may not be able to give my blessing to your union."

"I thought you liked Willem." Abbie swallowed back her own reservations about Willem's forthcoming decisions.

"I do."

"Then?"

"I have heard that he may not be a true believer. I would want you to be wed to a man who believes in the true church. But you and I agreed we would not speak of this matter at the risk of spreading more division. Leave the family out of it, please."

The boys thundered down the stairs seeking morning nourishment.

"*Shh!*" Esther said. "Have you forgotten a baby sleeps upstairs?"

"Isn't Ruthanna getting up for breakfast?" Levi slid into his usual chair.

"She can sleep as long as the child sleeps."

Esther gestured that her daughter should sit down, and Abbie complied although the thought of eating at that moment caused her stomach to revolt. She spent the moments of silent prayer trying to quell quivering nerves. The family ate, and Ananias quoted in German from memory a passage in Deuteronomy about teaching children to follow the ways of the Lord. Abbie could barely meet his eyes when the meal was over.

As soon as her father left the table, with her brothers right behind, Abbie stood to scrape dishes. There was not much to scrape. The family had long ago learned to eat every morsel of nourishment at a meal. Even Levi had stopped claiming that he was not hungry.

Esther began to fill the sink with water.

"*Mamm?*"

"Yes."

"Did you know about this?"

"Your father is the head of the family, Abigail."

"I understand that he makes these decisions, but did you know?"

Esther dipped a plate in water and rubbed three fingers around the rim. "No."

"Do you want to go back to Ohio?"

Esther wrapped her hands in a towel and said, "Why do you ask these questions, Abbie?"

"I'm just trying to make sense of it all."

"I have always trusted your father's decisions. I will not stop now."

"But do you want to go back to Ohio?"

Esther sighed. "I have rather come to love living in Colorado. The color of the sky is like nothing I have seen anywhere. The way the mountain breaks the sunset, the peculiar vegetation, even the sound of coyotes. It all has a beauty of its own."

"I know what you mean." Abbie put her arms around her mother and whispered, "What if I don't want to go?"

"You know our way of submission. *Demut.*" Esther gently released herself from Abbie's embrace and turned back to the dishes. "If you were to marry, it would be different."

Abbie moistened her lips in thought. As an unmarried woman, did she have any choice but to obey her father? On the other hand, he was right in pointing out that she was past the age when most of her friends had married. She would not be making a girlish decision. Colorado had stolen her heart, and she still believed someday there would be a flourishing church.

"What if I said I want to stay here?" Abbie finally said.

"Stay where?" Levi shuffled in from the back porch.

"I think I'll go for a walk," Abbie said.

"I thought you wanted to stay." Levi wrinkled his face.

"I was talking about something else. I do want to go for a walk—if it's all right with you, *Mamm.*"

Esther nodded.

"I want to go, too." Levi widened his eyes in hope.

"I just want to do some thinking, Levi. It won't be very fun."

"Please?"

"He's been squirming the last few days," Esther said. "It would do him good for you to wear him out."

Abbie knew Levi would pepper her with a thousand questions, but she nodded.

"Where are we going to walk?" Levi followed her out the back door.

"We'll just walk and see where we end up."

"I want to walk in the fields."

"I guess we can do that." Abbie adjusted her direction to cut across the yard away from the barn and toward the path that would take them past the pasture to the forgotten wheat fields. "There won't be much to look at. You know we have no crop."

"There's still a lot to look at. I can catch some bugs for my collection."

Insects would abound, feasting unimpeded on the parched,

stunted stalks of the crop that might have persuaded her father to make a different decision.

"What did you really mean when you said you want to stay?" Levi concentrated on making his stride match hers.

Abbie put a hand on the back of his head. It would be *Daed*'s decision what to tell his sons and when. "Never mind. It's nothing you have to worry about."

"I'm not worried. I used to be worried that we would run out of food, but I'm not worried anymore."

"I'm glad to hear that. What changed your mind?"

"*Daed* takes care of the family, and God takes care of *Daed*. Right?"

"Right."

"Then God takes care of the family. That's what I decided. It's better than worrying."

"Good thinking."

"Can you give me my lessons from now on?"

"Don't you like studying with *Mamm*?"

"I like to study with you. When you give me my lessons, I always think you are a good teacher."

"Thank you." She scratched the middle of his back. "I'll think about it."

"I want to race. Do you want to race?"

She shook her head. "No. But I'd love to watch you run."

Fourteen hours later Abbie spread her tree of life quilt out on the kitchen table. She had little progress to show for the last two weeks. Eber's death had stymied her aspirations. The baby's early birth and the funeral plans had banished ordinary routines. Ruthanna's presence in the house with the baby meant there always seemed to be something Abbie felt she ought to be doing to make Ruthanna's life easier.

But nothing would bring Eber back, and now Ruthanna had decided to make her own life easier by returning to her family.

Abbie's vision glazed over as she stared at the tiny triangles that made up the finished portions of the quilt. Instead of the quilt, she saw the lush greens of the Ohio countryside, where there were lakes and dependable rainfall and proper houses and worship services every other Sunday. Her father had not yet said where in Ohio he planned to take the family. Perhaps the Weavers would end up in eastern Ohio not far from Ruthanna's family, and Abbie could see her friend across the Pennsylvania border frequently. She imagined now what Eber and Ruthanna's little girl would look like when she was two or seven or ten years old. Maybe she would have Eber's dark hair. She already had his long nose.

Abbie left the quilt on the table and stepped out the back door to listen to the rapid chatter of the magpies, the chirping crickets, the whispering sibilants of the wind. She disagreed with her mother on the beauty of the coyotes howling, still unable to banish the mental image of what might have happened to Little Abe Miller. But the rest of it buoyed her spirit regardless of the crumbling financial realities.

With a sigh she wondered if she were the only one with blinders on, or the only one still clinging to the vision that had drawn them all out here. She glanced back inside at the quilt spread in the lamp's light and pondered how many of the families she prayed for would still be here when she finished the quilt.

CHAPTER 35

"I suppose you heard about my *daed*'s decision." Abbie laid the sack of bread on Willem's table and stood with her hands on the three mounds.

Willem nodded from his chair across the table. "He surprised us all. He went around yesterday because he wanted all the settlers to hear it from him."

Abbie absently picked up last week's bread sack and folded in half, then quarters, then eighths.

"He is doing what he thinks is best," Willem said.

"I know." Abbie did not know where to settle her blurry eyes. "He has never been one to do anything on a lark."

"Your *daed* is a good man, Abbie."

"I believe he would say the same about you." She set the flat flour sack on the corner of the table.

"We understand each other."

A gasp escaped Abbie's lips. "Not entirely."

Willem tilted his chair back and scratched under his chin. "What's on your mind?"

Abbie reached into her bucket for a clean rag and turned to Willem's water barrel to drench it. Without speaking she began to wipe off the table.

His chair hit the floor, and his hand reached across the planks to stop her motion. "You don't have to do that now."

"It is what I am here for, is it not?"

"Is it?"

She met his green eyes now. If Willem went to the Mennonites, his action would cause more division than any words her father did not want her to speak. "Before Eber. . .before the baby. . .I found out something."

"Yes?"

"My *daed* does not believe there is salvation outside the Amish church."

"I see."

Did he? What if her *daed* was right? "It seems the men in the settlement do not agree on this doctrine."

Willem shifted in his chair, turning to one side. "Obviously I am in no position to dispute that statement."

"What am I to think, Willem? If you go to the Mennonites, and if I do as you suggest and go with you—"

"Then you fear we would be condemning ourselves."

Abbie started wiping the table again. "Do you believe I should turn my back on what my father believes?"

"Whatever you believe, you father would want your faith to be based on your own conviction."

"He does not think you are serious about me."

"Ah, well. I have not confided in him as I have in you."

She said nothing.

"Come with me, Abbie. Come with me."

"So you have made up your mind?" She turned to the sink to twist the moisture out of the rag and kept her back to him.

Willem knew what she wanted to hear, but hypocrisy would be unbearable.

"Will you go with your parents?"

He saw her shoulders lift then fall, but she did not turn to face him.

"Will I have a choice?" she said at last.

"You are a grown woman."

"A grown *unmarried* woman."

"Our women sometimes find another calling."

She slapped the rag against the sink and spun around. "A

calling to keep house for a relative, for instance? I don't have any relatives around here. I have no place to go if my parents leave and you won't have me."

"I will always have you, Abbie." Willem stood now and walked around the table to stand before her and cradle both her elbows in his hands.

She wriggled against him at first, then her hands settled on his forearms. Her touch was light, hesitant, tentative. But she did not move.

After a long moment, he leaned in to kiss her. If his words failed to stir her, perhaps his lips would. The softness of her mouth welcomed him, and she made no move to break away.

When he raised his head again, he moved one hand to her cheek. "Come with me."

She stepped to the side. "You're confusing me."

"Am I?"

"Yes."

He returned to his side of the table. "At least take some time to consider your circumstances. I was in Limon the other day and saw a posting at the mercantile."

"What sort of posting?" She was listening and had not resumed scrubbing.

"A position. An *English* family I know is looking for a woman to be a companion to their young son. I believe he is recovering from some sort of respiratory illness and needs to be kept still, but they want to be sure his education continues."

"A teacher?"

He shrugged. "Of sorts. You help with Levi's lessons. This boy is about that age."

"But I have no formal qualifications."

"Perhaps that does not worry them right now. The man in the mercantile said they were more concerned to find someone temperamentally suited to being with him for a few hours a day. With the right conversation, the education would take care of itself."

"I don't know, Willem. I have never worked for an *English* family."

"They are nice people, and it's only for a few months while he recuperates."

She pressed her lips together, and he wondered if she still tasted him.

"I understand why your father wants to leave," he said, "but I also understand why you want to stay."

Rudy nodded to confirm to Abbie that he had heard the Weaver family news. They stood side by side along the fence around his pasture. He could see the sack of bread on the bench of her buggy, but she seemed in no hurry to deliver it to the house.

"The calf is doing well," she murmured as she folded her arms across the top of the wooden fence and set her chin in the crook of one elbow.

"She is fully weaned, though I find I cannot leave her in the same field with her mother or she tries to suckle still."

"She's a beautiful animal."

"You see beauty where everyone else sees potential for profit."

"Not everyone, surely."

"Just about. Even Amish cats have to earn their keep by keeping mice out of the barn."

"We used to have a dog in Ohio," Abbie said, "but he had to be able to herd. When he got too old, *Daed* shot him."

Rudy gazed at her face. Her eyes watched the calf but seemed to see right through the animal and fix on a point on the horizon. He leaned on the fence next to her. The thought that Abbie would leave the settlement sliced through him. She was the one who stopped him from selling his cows and getting on a train months ago. Without her he would have no reason to stay after all.

Wordless, he reached over and folded his fingers around her hand. The reluctance he expected did not come. Instead she turned her palm up and laced her fingers through his. In the end, he was the one to break the grasp without knowing what it meant.

Ruthanna's pulse quickened more than she had expected it would. She rode between Ananias and Abbie, who held the baby, on the way to Limon to meet her mother's train. They would be absurdly early, but Ruthanna had not wanted to risk any delay. A neighbor's wagon blocking the road, a cracked harness, a loose wheel—a dozen small incidents could cause them to be late. Even now Ruthanna prayed silently that an axle would not break or the horse would not step in a hole and go lame, as she mentally checked off the landmarks that meant they were approaching the outskirts of Limon.

When they pulled up to the depot, Ananias nodded toward the clock that hung on the outside wall.

"Thank you for indulging me," Ruthanna said. "I just couldn't bear to think of not being here the minute she gets off the train."

"Will you be all right here, then? Abbie can wait with you."

"Yes, fine."

"Do you have to rush off, *Daed*?" Abbie asked.

"We are very early for the train. I figure to see the land agent as long as I am in town," Ananias said. "I'd like to know what he thinks he can get for the property and how long he thinks it will take to find a buyer."

Ruthanna saw the droop in Abbie's face at her father's unvarnished account of his intent.

"No point in wasting time," Ananias said.

Ananias lowered himself from the bench and then offered assistance to Ruthanna. She reached for her daughter, but Abbie held the child securely with one arm and with the other braced herself to step down. Ruthanna did not object. Soon enough they would stand on this platform and bid each other farewell. She would not deny Abbie the pleasure of holding the baby now. They walked over to a vacant bench while Ananias took his seat in the buggy and urged the horse forward again.

Abbie adjusted the baby on her lap, and Ruthanna looped an arm through Abbie's elbow. "Maybe we'll see each other in Pennsylvania or Ohio someday," she said.

"Maybe." Abbie raised her eyes to Pikes Peak in the distance. "I love you, Ruthanna, but it breaks my heart to think of your leaving this place. Being here without you seems unimaginable."

"What about the job that Willem told you about?"

"Shall I consider it?"

"If it meant you could stay, wouldn't that be reason enough? No one is suggesting you become *English*." Ruthanna used the hem of her shawl to wipe her daughter's drool.

Abbie breathed in deeply and out heavily. "I am not sure how to make my *daed* understand. He would not see how working a few months for an *English* family would solve anything."

"What would he think if you said you wanted to marry?"

Abbie rolled her eyes. "I've told you about Willem. You know how he feels about Jake and the new church."

"I wasn't thinking of Willem."

"Then who?"

"Are you so blind that you do not see how Rudy feels about you? Now more than ever."

"Rudy is very sweet," Abbie said. "A tender soul."

"And he would jump at the chance to be your faithful, loving husband."

"But how could I encourage him when he knows how I feel about Willem?"

"Centuries of strong Amish marriages have been built on something other than those kinds of feelings."

Abbie twisted her neck and looked at Ruthanna with furrowed brow. "I know you married Eber because you loved him."

"He was the desire of my heart. I was blessed that God gave him to me."

"Don't I deserve that?" Abbie said hoarsely.

Ruthanna stroked her friend's arm. "I know you thought you would marry Willem, but if his choice takes him away, perhaps Rudy is God's way to give you the desire of your heart in the settlement."

A whistle blew, and a train barreled toward them.

CHAPTER 36

Words formed in Abbie's mind the next morning but tangled themselves up between her tongue and her lips. She held Ruthanna's daughter and watched Willem load Ruthanna's trunk and the small bag her mother had traveled with. Ruthanna had come to Colorado with few possessions and left with fewer. She had packed only the few baby clothes she had stitched, the quilt she had made before her wedding to Eber, his Bible, and a change of clothes in case the baby spit up on her on the train. In a separate crate, packed in straw, was the cradle Eber made.

"Are they almost ready?" Willem asked as he checked the harness that strapped Ruthanna's buggy to the horse.

A nod was all Abbie could manage. She checked the knot of ribbon at the baby's neck.

"She'll write," Willem said.

Abbie nodded again and failed to resist the shiver that traveled up her spine.

"And you'll write," Willem said. "You'll still be friends."

It took three attempts before Abbie could push air through her throat. "I don't understand what the hurry is. Her mother could stay a while and see what Ruthanna's life was like out here."

"It's not that kind of a visit. Ruthanna may as well go and get settled."

"Get on with her life. That's what you mean."

"Yes. I suppose that is what I mean. Eber is gone. She can't save the farm. Raising a child alone must be frightening. Her parents want to help."

Abbie grazed one hand over the fuzz on the baby's head. It looked like it would grow in to yellow blond hair like her mother's, but it was impossible to be sure.

"I can't imagine not being able to ride over and see her. We didn't meet each other until we came here, but she is the closest thing I've known to a sister."

Willem lifted his chin toward the opening door of the Weaver house. Ruthanna and her mother, arm in arm, walked toward the buggy.

"Let me help you up with the baby."

Willem offered his hand, and Abbie took it.

"It was nice of you to buy her rig." She settled into the rear bench of Ruthanna's buggy.

"I'll send her what it's really worth when I can, but at least she has a bit of traveling money. Something to get situated with."

The buggy rocked as Ruthanna climbed in and sat next to Abbie. Her mother took the seat beside Willem.

Abbie forced a smile. Speech had evaporated once again.

At the train station, Willem and Ruthanna's mother hung back. Ruthanna clung to Abbie, who clung to the baby. She pulled a slip of paper out of the sleeve of her dress and tucked it into Abbie's.

"My address," Ruthanna said. "I want you to write to me as soon as you've made up your mind what to do."

Abbie's head bobbed.

Not once had Ruthanna doubted that she was making the right decision for her child. If she had been on her own, even without Eber, she might have borrowed Abbie's persistence. She had thought she would, in those final weeks when she had to admit that life was ebbing out of her husband. But the babe in her arms, rather than her womb, changed everything.

"You are the truest friend I have ever known," Ruthanna whispered.

She felt the soundless sob in her friend's chest.

"I pray you will not feel abandoned for long," Ruthanna said.

"Don't be so stubborn that you end up alone."

Abbie dipped her head to kiss the baby one last time before transferring the tight bundle into Ruthanna's arms. "Wherever I end up, I want you to write to me about everything she does. When she smiles for the first time, when she cuts her first tooth, when she starts to crawl. Everything."

"I promise." Ruthanna put the baby upright over her shoulder and the child burped.

Abbie giggled. "I guess she wanted to say good-bye, too."

Willem and Ruthanna's mother approached.

"I suppose we should get on the train," Ruthanna said. "Thank you, Willem. For everything."

"I counted Eber a good friend," he said.

"Look after his grave for me. Don't let it grow over."

"I won't."

Ruthanna handed the baby to her mother and opened her arms once again to the friend who had never let her down, regretting that her decision could not but disappoint the settler with the greatest enthusiasm for the venture they had all undertaken. But her daughter needed to be enfolded into dozens of faithful waiting arms, not to grow up with a mother too burdened by farm chores to look after her properly.

When she kissed Abbie's cheek, she tasted the salt of tears.

Willem did not rush Abbie. They watched the train chug out of sight, and still he held his pose and awaited her readiness to turn toward the buggy. If they had been alone, rather than standing on a public railroad platform, he would have wrapped his arms around her and welcomed a release of her grief. Only when an oncoming whistle announced the next impending shuffle of passengers did she pivot and march to the buggy.

Willem helped her up to the bench, unhitched the horse, and took up the reins. She sat beside him silent and straight backed, staring straight ahead. Willem navigated away from the bustle of the train station and through the streets of Limon to the road that would gradually narrow into the route that led to the Amish farms. He drove for several miles, occasionally glancing at her unyielding posture.

"I want you to meet someone," he said at last. "It's on the way home."

"I've just said good-bye to my best friend." Abbie's tone snapped, but she did not turn her head.

"I know. But soon enough you'll have to make your own decision, and this could help."

"You mean you think I should get on with my life, too."

"I mean," he said carefully, "that you should know what choices you have."

"Is this about that *English* job?"

He nodded.

"I'm not ready."

"Your father listed his property with a land agent yesterday and has already struck a deal for his cows. If you have any hope of deciding for yourself, rather than letting circumstances dictate, you should let me introduce you to this family."

"Whatever happens will be God's will. If I wait and the job is gone, it will still be God's will." Not only did Abbie refuse to look at him, but she turned her head with deliberation in the opposite direction.

Willem slowed the horse so there would be more time to talk before the turnoff. "And if you meet the family today and you like them, that would also be God's will. Wouldn't you agree?"

He saw the twitch in her shoulders and knew she was softening.

"I'll just introduce you," he said. "If you don't want to do more than say hello, look at me and blink twice. I will politely excuse us, and we will be on our way."

She whirled on him. "You have this all figured out, don't you?"

He cranked his head away and allowed himself a quick smile. When the lane came up on the left, he made the turn.

When Abbie agreed to go inside the house with Mrs. Wood, Willem waited outside. Abbie was not sure whether to be furious or relieved. The kindness in Louise Wood's face had undone her. Willem must have known it would. Apparently the moment had passed to blink twice and be whisked out of a circumstance she felt ill equipped to meet.

The ranch house sprawled more than any of the Amish homes, but Abbie supposed the ranch itself also was better established. From the outside, even her untrained eye could discern the outline of the original house and the slight change in the width of the siding where a wing was added to one side. Inside, one foot now detected a slight ridge in the flooring under a long runner carpet as Mrs. Wood led Abbie to a comfortable sitting room. The original parlor had been converted to a music room featuring a grand piano. Otherwise, though, the house was modestly furnished, and Mrs. Wood's high-necked dress was made of a muted green calico that had seen regular washings for at least two years.

"May I make you a cup of tea?" Louise gestured for Abbie to take a seat.

"I don't want to be any bother."

"It's no bother. I was about to have some anyway. The kettle is already on."

Abbie smiled. "Then I would love some."

"I'll see if I can rustle up some cookies as well. I won't be but a minute."

When Louise left the room, Abbie leaned forward in her chair to see if she could see out the window across the room. Willem had his back to the house while he ran his hand down the horse's long nose. For better or for worse, she was inside now and he was out of blinking range. She looked around the room, and her eyes settled on a photograph of a stiff trio. Between a man and a woman sat a little boy. Abbie peered at the picture for clues as to its age. But she was unfamiliar with photographs in general. The Amish avoided them. She did not actually know anyone who had ever sat for a photograph.

Apparently now she did, because the woman in the picture clearly was Louise Wood.

"Here we are." Louise returned with a tray bearing a plate of sugar cookies and two tea cups. She set it on a table beside Abbie.

"I'm so glad Willem introduced us. We're sure to have a delightful chat."

The warmth in her tone melted Abbie.

Louise handed her a cup. "Willem tells me you have a little brother about my son's age."

"Yes. Levi is eight." Abbie did her best not to jiggle the cup.

"Now that's a nice strong biblical name. Of course, Abigail was quite a woman of courage in the Bible. I'm sure you're well named."

Abbie took a sip of tea. "What is your son's name?"

Louise laughed. "I'm afraid it's Melton Finley Wood IV. Much too much name for a little boy, but you can see the strength of the family tradition. We call him Fin."

"I like that."

"He's not a difficult child. Quite sweet in temperament, actually. But he is a bit rambunctious and used to life on the ranch. The doctor says we must keep him quiet for at least three more months."

"What does he enjoy?"

"He doesn't seem to like to read on his own, but he does like to be read to."

As Louise launched into describing her son, her eyes lit and her cheeks softened. Within a few minutes Abbie was eager to meet Fin for herself, already sure she would like him.

Keeping a recuperating *English* child entertained by feeding his mind was not so different than Noah Chupp's making shoes for *English* children. Abbie was certain she could do a good job. Still, staying behind when her family returned to Ohio for a reason other than marriage was a drastic decision.

CHAPTER 37

By late morning on Monday, Abbie had scrubbed two piles of clothing against the washboard on the back porch and hung pants and shirts on the line strung between metal poles behind the house. In the middle of October, with temperatures more bearable than July, August, or even September, most days were still cloudless and the air free of any whisper of moisture. The clothes would dry and she would be back in the yard to collect them as soon as the lunch dishes were cleared.

Unless the train had run into trouble, Ruthanna was home by now.

Home.

Could Pennsylvania feel like home again after the substance of Ruthanna's married life had unfolded in Colorado? Abbie turned the question over in her mind as she carried the thickly woven basket, now empty, to the back porch. Even though she had not married, Abbie had fallen in love in this drought-ridden state. Even if she could not marry Willem, he held her heart. Would any other place ever feel like home?

She missed Ruthanna. Mary Miller was a good friend, but the bond Abbie shared with Mary was thin and crackly compared to Ruthanna's intimacy with the desires that lined the corners of Abbie's heart. Her eyes warmed with sudden tears, and Abbie wanted to be alone. Instead of pulling open the back door and going inside to help with lunch, she strode across the yard to the barn. It would have to do for now, just long enough to corral the emotions that threatened to spill through her day. Inside the barn, Abbie reached for a horse blanket on a shelf before marching to the empty stall at the back of the structure. The straw in this unused retreat was not fresh, but it was reasonably clean. She spread the blanket, sat, pulled her knees up, wrapped her arms around them, and buried her face in the folds of her skirt. Breathing with deliberation, she tried to form her thoughts into prayer. The words wriggled away without taking shape.

Abbie lifted her head when she heard the voices approaching. One was *Daed*'s. The other she did not recognize. They spoke English, not Pennsylvania Dutch. Abbie crawled across the straw and peered around the opening of the stall.

"The barn seems solidly built." The strange man knocked on the barn wall. "That will help us set the highest price we can hope for."

"Of course I want to get a good price," Ananias said. "But I also want to sell quickly. I believe I have a realistic expectation of the market in the price I seek."

"Yes, there are several similar properties available right now—as you well know, since some of them were Amish farms. In any event, I think we can present your land in an attractive way."

"Do you have the papers you wish me to sign?"

"Right here in my satchel."

Abbie sat back on her haunches and let her shoulders sag. The land agent.

"I have spoken to a few people about equipment and animals," her father said. "I thought selling those items separately would be my best hope for cash to move my family."

"That is wise, I'm sure. I don't believe any buyers would assume the sale of anything but the land and the house and barn. But if you have difficulty, let me know. We might hasten a sale by enhancing what we include in the price."

"I am anxious to raise enough cash for train tickets. I want to be home before winter."

Home. There was that word again, coming from her own father's mouth. Even Ananias Weaver did not think of his Colorado land as home. Abbie pressed the heels of her hands against her eyes and waited for the men to withdraw through the barn door.

The day was one of the longest Abbie could remember. She managed pleasantries with her family over lunch, folded the laundry, sat with Levi as he practiced his reading, cleaned the chicken coop, and mopped the kitchen floor. Supper was somber. By then the entire family, including Levi, knew that Ananias had reached an agreement with the land agent. It was hard for Abbie to know what any of her brothers thought. If Reuben or Daniel disagreed with their father, they hid it well. Neither did they avow support for the plan to return to Ohio. Levi remembered little about living anywhere but Colorado, but in time he would likely have only vague memories of his childhood here.

After supper, Abbie spread her quilt on the table. If the house were larger, she would have wished for a proper quilting frame where she could pull the project taut and be more confident in the straightness of her stitches. But with care and persistence, she had developed a system of rolling out of the way the parts of the quilt she was not working on. While she could not see the entire quilt, she focused on the square that represented each household as she crafted the angled stitching.

Twice Abbie turned up the lamp. The sounds of the family shifted from chores and conversation in the other room to bidding each other good night and shuffling steps on the stairs rising from the kitchen. Still Abbie stitched and prayed and ached to see the quilt complete.

"Abigail."

Stilling the needle between her fingers, Abbie looked up. In his nightshirt, her father stood on the bottom step. "Yes, *Daed*?"

"Are you aware of the time?"

She glanced out the window into the blackness but admitted she did not know the time.

"It is after one in the morning," Ananias said.

"I didn't realize." Abbie finished a stitch and stuck her needle through the fabric to secure it.

"I hope you will put as much determination into packing for

the move," Ananias said.

Abbie said nothing.

"I find the land agent a trustworthy man," her father said. "So as soon as I can raise enough cash for train tickets and shipping a few crates, we will go. It is better that none of us is caught by surprise when the time comes."

"I understand." Abbie folded her project down to its smallest size, which still covered much of the table.

"Good. I will set the boys to building some crates tomorrow. Good night."

"Good night, *Daed*."

Ananias turned and went up the stairs he had just descended. Abbie sat at the table with both hands resting on her folded quilt. Mrs. Wood had not sent word yet about the position. Her husband had not been available during Abbie's visit three days ago, but Louise felt sure he would give his approval, and as soon as he did she would send one of the ranch hands with a note.

And then Abbie would face a decision full on. Abbie put out the lamp but made no move to climb the stairs.

Rudy brimmed with resolve one moment and surrendered to reticence the next. This wretched cycle had been going on for days. Weeks. Perhaps months. Tuesday afternoon was no different.

He bore no ill will toward Willem Peters, but it seemed to Rudy that Willem had set his course long ago. Not all of the settlers knew Willem as well as Rudy did. They were two unmarried men on adjoining farms who shouldered together for tasks that required the strength of more than one man, and between them they had made sure Eber Gingerich lacked for nothing either. Their conversations rarely strayed from the work before them, and they made no pretense of having similar temperament, but Rudy felt he knew Willem's drive and intentions.

It didn't seem possible that Abbie did not also know.

Rudy went to the trough his horses drank from and splashed water on his face. With his eyes closed and the chill of well water tingling in his pores, he made up his mind. He had one clean shirt. Now was the time to put it on.

The back door opened and Levi stood bursting with his announcement. "Rudy is here. He says he wants to talk to you."

Abbie pulled her hands out of the dish water, where she had been wiping the last of Tuesday's supper dishes. "Then ask him to come in. Where are your manners?"

"He said would I please ask you to come outside." Levi raised both hands to scratch the back of his neck.

"Oh. All right, then. *Danki.*"

Abbie put the last plate in the rack and dried her hands. She tugged on both strings to be sure her *kapp* sat on her head evenly and went out the back door into the gray, dusky air. Sunset came so much earlier now than it did during the long, hot summer.

"Hello, Rudy. What a nice surprise to see you."

Rudy dipped his hat slightly. "I thought you might enjoy an evening stroll. We have some time before it's dark, I think."

Abbie looked to the west, where the orange fingers of the descending sun spread their grasp. "A stroll would be lovely."

They turned and fell into an unhurried pace together. Rudy had both thumbs hooked under his suspenders. Abbie twiddled one tie of her *kapp* between two fingers.

"I imagine you miss Ruthanna fiercely," Rudy said.

Tension cascaded out of Abbie's shoulders. "I hardly had a chance to get used to the idea that she would go, and then she was gone."

"I still have the urge to go by the farm and see if they need something."

Abbie smiled. "You are a good man, Rudy Stutzman." And he was.

"We were all stunned about your father's decision. It must weigh heavy on you."

Abbie's throat thickened. What a refreshing sensation it was to hear from another's mouth such truth about her own spirit.

"Will you go with them?" Rudy asked.

Abbie blew out her breath. "My *daed* certainly thinks I will."

"But you—what do you want to do?"

Abbie raised a hand toward the distant mountain. "On some days this feels like the most forlorn place on earth. But other days I can scarcely breathe for how lovely it is."

"And the church?"

Abbie stopped and turned toward Rudy. For the first time, she saw that he was perspiring, even though the evening was not overly warm. "So many questions, Rudy."

He took one of her hands, and she heard the shallowness of his breath.

"If you were to marry, your parents could not object to your remaining here."

"No, I suppose not."

"Why should you pine for Willem?" he said softly. "He will go to the Mennonites."

"I know." Her words were more a movement of her mouth than sound.

"If you were to marry me," Rudy said, "we could be the first of the settlers to marry. Surely a minister would come from Ordway for such an event. It would be a great encouragement to the others to see that we want to pledge our futures to this place."

"Is that what you want, Rudy? Truly?"

"If I can be with you, I can be happy anywhere."

Abbie's hand trembled, and she could not stop it. "I need some time, Rudy."

"I'll wait."

CHAPTER 38

"Daed!" Abbie called over her shoulder two days later and then returned her gaze to the view out the front window. "An *English* is here with a wagon."

Ananias snapped shut the accounts book in his lap. "He's here for the hay."

"You're getting rid of the hay?"

"Did you think I would crate it up to ship to Ohio?"

Abbie blinked three times at the man who patted his horse's rump on his way to the Weaver front door. "I hadn't thought about the hay."

Ananias crossed the room. "You were here the day I took delivery on hay because we had so little from our own fields. What's left is still worth something. We must use every asset."

"But the animals," Abbie said.

"The cows will be gone before the day is over. The horses can make do with grazing and straw until I sort out what to do with them."

Ananias left Abbie standing in the front room of the house and strode across the yard to greet the *English*. He gestured toward the barn and the man nodded and returned to his rig. Abbie backed away from the window as her mouth soured. Hearing her *daed* say that he wanted to leave before the end of the month was hard enough. Visible progress in his effort to raise train fare sucked breath from her chest in a way she was unprepared for. He would sell the coal, too, she realized. Though lignite was plentiful, the savings in labor would be worth something to a family who had sufficient cash. And the chickens. Either they would go to a nearby farm, or her mother would pluck and cook one every day until they were gone.

Abbie suddenly wanted to bury her face in the neck of one of the cows that had kept the Weavers in milk, cheese, and butter all this time. As the *English* man turned his wagon around and lined it up alongside the barn, Abbie strode in the opposite direction out to the pasture where the cows spent their days, hoping that her father had at least tried to find the animals a home with another Amish family. She opened the gate, entered the field, and closed the gate behind her. The ground was weedy rubble in clumps but mostly hard-packed barren earth that could not sustain the cows that swished tails against flies. Abbie tried not to look toward the barn, but when she heard the rattle of a wagon and knew it could not yet be filled with hay, she relented and turned around.

It was Willem's wagon she heard.

Willem spotted Abbie in the field with relief. He would not have to contrive some awkward reason to see her out of hearing distance of her family. He looped the reins around the top of the fence and then climbed over. The slump in her shoulders bore witness to the disappointment she carried within herself, and Willem hoped the errand that brought him to her would transform both her posture and her mood.

He strode across the grassless pasture. "I stopped by the Woods'. Mrs. Wood has sent a note."

Her spine straightened and her eyebrows rose.

Willem offered her the cream-colored envelope elegantly addressed to Miss Abigail Weaver.

"What was her decision?" Abbie tentatively fingered one edge of the envelope.

"She didn't say. You'll have to read the note."

Abbie slid one finger under the sealed flap and pulled out the note. Willem watched her eyes go back and forth as she absorbed the words.

"Well?" he said.

Abbie smiled. "The position is mine if I choose to take it."

He reached for her hand. "I knew the two of you would like each other."

"Her husband has given his approval, and she hopes it will be convenient for me to start very soon. She would like me to come for tea on Friday and meet the boy."

"And will you?"

Abbie took her hand from his and raised it to her cheek. "I was not certain until this moment what I would do, but I believe I will gladly accept her kind offer."

"So you won't leave with your family."

She turned her head toward the activity around the barn. Reuben, Daniel, her father, and the *English* man had created an efficient system for transferring the hay.

Willem followed her gaze. "I see your *daed* is following through on his decision."

She nodded.

"We all understand his choice," Willem said.

"I don't. I wish he would at least wait to see what moisture the winter brings, but he seems intent on making sure he can't change his mind."

Willem let the silence drape the space between them for a moment, knowing the comfort of his arms would only add to her confusion.

"I could carry a note back to Mrs. Wood, if you like," he finally said.

"I have nothing to write on. I'll have to go to the house and see if I can find a suitable scrap of paper." Abbie lifted a hand to control a sniffle.

"She won't expect anything fancy. She does not share our ways, but she understands them."

Thirty minutes later Abbie handed Willem the note and waved as he scrambled up to the bench of his wagon in three practiced motions.

The *English* wagon was about as full as it could be, bales carefully stacked and balanced to withstand the sway of the ride to their new home. Abbie did not know the man, nor how he had heard about the Weaver hay. Reuben and Daniel lifted the last bale into place and the *English* shook Ananias's hand. Abbie turned her head as the cash passed between them. She glanced into the field and wondered how many more hours—or perhaps only minutes—would pass before the cows would take a final nibble of Weaver land before being roped and led behind a horse or a wagon.

She resolved not to watch. There were half a dozen ways to make herself useful for the rest of the day without listening for the sound of dread to fill her spirit.

Ananias approached. "Did you see that the boys put your trunk in your room?"

"Yes." How could she miss a trunk that sat where Eber's cradle had stood only a few days ago? Abbie measured her steps toward the house so as not to seem eager to escape her father's eye.

"Let me know when you've packed it. The boys can carry it out to the barn for a few days."

"A few days?"

Ananias nodded. "Once the cows are gone I should have what I need for the train tickets."

"So soon?" Her heart pounded.

"Abigail," he said, "we've already talked about this. We may as well be expedient."

"I know." She tried to stride ahead of her father, but he kept pace.

"You can take your hope chest, too, of course. I know you've prepared those items with care for your marriage, and there is no reason they should go to waste."

Abbie struck the ground with the heel of her right foot and rolled it forward for balance, but she did not pick it up again. "*Daed*."

"Yes?" He halted beside her.

"I have decided I want to stay." She scoured his face for a reaction and did not have to wait long.

Ananias's jaw tensed as he spread his feet under his shoulders, knees locked. "Has Willem finally chosen to take a wife?"

"Not so far as I know."

Ananias waited for more.

"I do not wish to disrespect you, *Daed*," Abbie said, "but my calling is here."

"Your calling is to your husband, though I am somewhat relieved that you and Willem realize your differences. Rudy is much more suited to you. He is less likely to wander from the true faith."

Abbie flushed. Had Rudy spoken to her father? Until now, she had not thought so.

"I have made no decision about a husband." Abbie cradled her own elbows. "I have accepted a position with an *English* family."

Ananias raised two fingers to one temple. "Perhaps I have misjudged you as well."

"No, *Daed*. My heart belongs to our people. But it also belongs here in Colorado."

"I do not hear you asking for my consent."

She paused. "May I have your blessing?"

Ananias resumed walking toward the house. Abbie trembled.

Abbie did not have one dress that was better than another. She had three, and all of them lacked in some way. One had frayed cuffs, another faded color, and the third mended seams. This had never mattered to her before, but somehow in Louise Wood's home, Abbie felt self-conscious. Perhaps it was the china arranged on the table for tea or the damask tablecloth or the wave of Louise's sweeping golden hair held in place with a pearl-ridged comb. Louise's dress was a muted solid color, but Abbie suspected it was what the *English* called Sunday best.

"Everything looks lovely," Abbie said, because it did.

"Don't mind the fuss." Louise gestured to a chair at the end of the dining room table. "Every now and again I like to give Fin a chance to practice his manners."

"I'm anxious to meet him." Abbie arranged herself in the chair.

"Excuse me while I call Fin."

Louise stepped from the room, and Abbie allowed herself to absorb the room in more detail. Yellow chintz curtains draped from three matching windows against a pale green wallpaper print. In spite of the china and tablecloth, the tea offering was fairly simple: rolls in a bread warmer, a tea pot in a cozy, a few slices of cheese, and a bowl of red grapes. When Abbie heard the shuffle of feet in the next room, she wondered if Fin was as nervous as she was. A moment later, Louise appeared in the wide doorframe that separated the dining room from the front parlor with her hand on her son's shoulder.

"Fin, this is Miss Weaver," Louise said.

Fin folded one arm across his stomach and bowed. "I am very pleased to meet you."

"And I you," Abbie said.

The boy approached her and offered a handshake, which Abbie accepted immediately.

"I hope you will feel comfortable in our home," he said.

Abbie smiled. The child was adorable in his navy blue suit and collared white shirt with his brown hair carefully parted and slicked down. She knew a boy who enjoyed being active on a ranch would not dress this way often, but he was making every effort to please his mother, just as Levi would have done.

They were going to get along just fine.

CHAPTER 39

Outside the bank on Thursday morning, Willem straightened his suit and double-checked that the seam at the top of his shirt Abbie had mended a month ago still held. An oversized envelope contained assorted papers that may or may not be relevant to the day's quest. He wanted to be prepared for any question.

Inside the bank, Willem surveyed the lobby. A half-dozen people stood in lines to see the three tellers on duty, and around the perimeter of the room were several imposing desks occupied by men with stern faces and airs of authority. Willem had an appointment with one of them, the chief loan officer. He caught the man's eye and smiled as he crossed the lobby.

"Hello, Mr. Peters. Thank you for coming in this morning. I trust things are well on your farm."

"Well enough, considering the challenges all the farms have faced this year." Willem was determined not to sound pitiful. It would only impede progress toward his goal. "I have been a conscientious steward of my resources."

The banker gestured to a chair opposite the desk. "What can I do for you today?"

Willem sat up straight with his papers in his lap. "You may be aware that several properties near mine have become available."

"I have heard this, though I am not familiar with the particulars." The banker adjusted his rimless glasses.

"Eber Gingerich passed away, and his widow decided to sell the land. And now Ananias Weaver has decided to return to Pennsylvania."

"I'm sorry to hear that." The loan officer thrummed the edge of his desk.

Willem resisted the urge to look to one side and kept his gaze fixed on the banker's face. "Both of these farms abut my property, which has caused me to wonder if this might be the time to enlarge my acreage. In the future, a larger farm would yield greater profit."

The banker leaned back in his chair. "Profitability in farming is subject to many circumstances. Number of acres is only one of them."

"I believe it to be a solid starting point. I would like to look into buying one of these farms, or at least some portion of the acres. To do so, I would need a higher line of credit."

"Mr. Peters, even the *English* farmers are having a tough go right now. The ranchers are doing a little better, but the drought has been difficult for everyone."

Willem did not move, lest any gesture suggest a crack in confidence. "Farming requires taking the long view, does it not? If we do not make plans during the difficult years, we will not be prepared for the opportunity of abundance in the future."

"Well, now, I suppose there is nothing to disagree with there, Mr. Peters. But this is a bank. I am a loan officer. Our decisions come down to taking acceptable risks."

"I don't believe I have given you any reason to regard me as an unacceptable risk."

"No, not so far. But how would you make the increased payments that would come with a new loan when your farm has yielded so little in the last two years?"

"I've brought some papers that will demonstrate my assets beyond the value of my mortgaged land." Willem slid the documents out of the envelope and laid them on the desk.

The loan officer leaned forward and began studying the papers. He flipped over several of them and looked up at Willem. "I grant you that you present a more encouraging picture than I had supposed, but it would still seem inadvisable for you to take on more debt."

"If I failed to make my payments, the land would belong to the bank."

"And it might be worth even less than it is now if drought and soil erosion continue. We would require a substantial down payment to hedge against that possibility."

"How much?"

The banker named a figure.

"If I could come up with that amount," Willem said, "would you consider my application?"

The banker cleared his throat. "I would agree to take the matter to the full loan committee, but I make no promise of the result you desire."

"Fair enough."

Willem collected his papers and returned to his wagon down the street. At the familiar lilt of a laugh, he turned his head.

"Willem!" Abbie said.

Beside her stood Rudy.

"We didn't know you were coming into town," Abbie said. "We could have all come together."

We. Willem was not sure he had ever heard Abbie use that word to describe Rudy and herself. And he was equally uncertain he could remember a time when Abbie had come to Limon with Rudy. Abbie had not laughed since before Eber died. What had Rudy said to raise her mood? Willem reminded himself he had no right to be jealous as he looked from Abbie to Rudy and observed that they stood close together.

"Have you just come from the bank?" Rudy's blue eyes met Willem's evenly.

"Yes. I had some financial business to attend to." Willem dropped his envelope of papers onto the floor of the wagon.

Rudy pushed the fingertips of both hands together. "Perhaps it is no coincidence that you see the banker just as the farms around yours become available at an attractive price."

"Rudy!" Abbie took a step away.

"Am I mistaken?" Rudy said.

Willem spread his feet in a solid stance. "Nothing in *Ordnung* prohibits a man from making a wise business transaction."

Abbie's mouth dropped open. "Would you really try to profit from Ruthanna's loss? From my father's concern for his sons?"

Her tone stabbed him, and he hoisted himself into his wagon without answering.

Abbie held still during the silent prayer before her family's evening meal. Behind her closed eyes, while she smelled the roasted chicken whose neck her mother had twisted a few hours ago, Abbie saw Willem driving off in his wagon. She had expected him to deny Rudy's accusation, but he had not. How was it possible that Rudy seemed to know Willem better than she did?

Her father murmured his "Amen," and the family began to pass dishes around the table. Looking at chicken for the fourth night in a row, Abbie's calculation of how many were left in the coop obstructed her gratitude. Esther could have sold her chickens, especially the ones that were laying consistently, but she seemed to have chosen to feed her family with them. Green beans from the plentitude of the Ordway Amish, potatoes Abbie had dug last week, and bread filled out the meal.

"Eat." Esther urged Levi, who had passed the potatoes to Reuben without serving himself.

"I'm only a little bit hungry."

Abbie heard the scuffling sound that meant Levi had hooked his ankles behind the front legs of his chair. He had been doing so well with eating until the last few days. She laid a piece of bread on his plate without asking if he wanted it. Levi tore off a corner and put it in his mouth.

"I have urged all of you to pack your things." Ananias sliced off a piece of chicken breast. "If you have not done so, please do so soon. We leave on Monday."

Abbie caught her fork just before it slipped from her grasp.

Ananias pulled a neat stack of small papers from his lap and spread them on the table beside his plate. Levi leaned over to examine them.

"Are those train tickets?" Levi asked.

Ananias nodded.

"But they didn't give you enough. There are only five, and there are six of us."

Abbie dropped her eyes to her plate and carefully set her fork down.

"Abigail has decided to remain here." Ananias took a bite of potato. "And I have decided not to quarrel with her about it."

Levi knocked the train tickets to the floor.

"Levi!" Esther pointed at the papers. "Pick those up right now."

Despite the reluctance in his face and shoulders, Levi complied. "Why don't you want to come with us, Abbie?"

"My heart would remain here." Abbie reached to stroke Levi's head, but he ducked away from her touch.

"Don't you love us?"

"Of course I do."

"Then why aren't you coming?"

"Love is complicated sometimes."

Levi kicked the table leg.

"Levi, behave." Ananias's words stilled Levi's agitation but not the sulk on his face.

Abbie glanced at Daniel and Reuben, neither of whom had stopped eating with their father's announcements.

"It will likely take some time for the farm to sell," Ananias said. "Abbie can remain in the house until then. She has found a job for the time being. We'll leave enough furniture for her to get by. She can keep the buggy, since no one but an Amish family would want it and none of them can afford it. Once the land sells, she will be on her own, since that is what she has chosen."

Abbie looked at her *daed*, but he did not meet her eyes.

"Who do you think will come?" Willem passed Jake a bowl of boiled eggs and then picked up a slice of Abbie's bread.

Across the table in Willem's kitchen, Jake cracked the shell and began to peel an egg for the simple breakfast they shared Friday morning.

"I don't know," Jake said. "I've spoken to a lot of families. People are polite, but that does not mean they will come. Perhaps we'll have half a dozen for our first Sunday morning worship service. Even if it is just you and me, Christ will be present and glorified."

"Are you sure you wouldn't like to wait until you're certain more people will come?" Willem slathered butter on his bread.

"It's time," Jake said. "Mennonites have been scattered in the area for five years. And all the ministers agree it is time for a mission to the Amish around Limon, since you do not have a minister of your own. In a few weeks, I will be ordained as a bishop. When people see that this is not a passing desire on my part, they will give more serious consideration."

Willem reached behind to the stove and brought the coffeepot to the table. "I'm serious, Jake. I hope you know that."

"I do. I know it may cost you dearly."

Willem filled his coffee cup. "Abbie has decided to stay when her family leaves."

Jake gave a half smile. "So there is hope for the two of you?"

Willem shrugged, thinking of the way Abbie and Rudy had stood together at the edge of the street. "I don't think that's the reason she is staying, but I hold hope in my heart. All things are possible with God."

CHAPTER 40

Willem lingered over his sparse Sunday breakfast. He could have managed more than coffee and a thick slice of bread, which he did not even bother to butter, but his mind was hours ahead of a dawn meal. Morning farm chores did not pause for the Sabbath. Willem had always found it humorous that while God decreed in Deuteronomy that livestock should have a Sabbath from their labors, God did not spare their owners the chores of caring for the animals. One morning a week that did not start with milking would have satisfied Willem.

He swallowed the last of his coffee, pushed his chair back from the table, and paced to the stove. If he stoked it now, when he came back from the barn it would be hot enough to boil water and he could clean up properly for church.

Church.

Willem spoke the word aloud to savor the sensation on his tongue. *Church.* Far too many months had passed since he last indulged in the anticipation of worship with others who believed. Occasionally he joined the Weavers for their somber family worship. Most Sunday mornings, after the chores, he sat alone with his Bible on his knees reading a favorite passage and trying to remember a sermon that taught him what it meant. Now he thought that if he had known he would be so long without preaching he would have listened more carefully when he had the opportunity.

But today would be different. Today he would ride in his new buggy to Limon, to Jake's humble rooms, and pray for the others whom God would send to the gathering. Together they would pray for future worshippers who had not yet heard the call but would heed it in the months ahead. Willem would feel the Spirit move in his heart telling him the hymn they should sing, and he would intone the opening notes as the words rose from his throat. When he returned to his farm and sat at the table again, it would be with the drenching satisfaction of worship washing over his soul.

Abbie crossed her wrists and laid them in her lap, her head as still as a tongue settled into a groove at the back of a cedar chest.

Reuben and Daniel betrayed no emotion about this last Sunday as a complete family. Levi had refused to meet her eye all morning, and her mother's face was drawn with unspoken resignation. When Abbie decided to stay in Colorado, she had not thought of this moment, this ache of the last.

The last full day they would have together.

The last time they would sit in the circle of their front room to hear her *daed* lead them in family worship.

She had missed the last smile on Levi's face because she had not known it would be the last. Now she doubted he would relent. The sagging disappointment in his young face told her he knew she would not relent, either.

Her father had chosen to read from the sixth chapter of Deuteronomy, where God warned the people of Israel against the sin of disobedience.

"Beware lest thou forget the Lord," he read. And a few verses later, "Ye shall not go after other gods."

And then, "Ye shall not tempt the Lord your God."

Is that what *Daed* thought she was doing? Chasing after other gods? Testing the Lord?

Perhaps he meant it as a warning against following Willem to the Mennonites.

A Mennonite church would never be the church of Abbie's heart, but surely it did not have to mean that Willem did not love the one true God.

Rudy thought Willem was trying to serve two masters. Why else would he be trying to buy the Weavers' farm, or Ruthanna's land? Willem said all the right words about loving God, Rudy had observed, but he also did not want to pass up an opportunity to increase his worldly wealth at the expense of people he was supposed to care for.

Willem was with the Mennonites that morning. He had given up trying to be discreet about his intentions. All the Amish families knew this was the day Jake Heatwole had chosen to hold his first pubic worship service. Abbie supposed next Willem would be actively recruiting Amish families to join him.

Abbie allowed herself a slight shift in position. Why should she not tell Rudy she would marry him? He was right. They were well suited to each other in ways she had not realized until a few weeks ago. Together they could coax a living from the land and with their union announce that the core of Amish families did not have to dwindle away. It *was* still possible to think of a future. If she married, her father would not object—even in the guise of a family sermon—to her choice to remain in Colorado.

Yes. Rudy was right. Willem had staked his future in his decision to worship with the Mennonites, and now it was time for her to stake hers.

Eight.

That was how many people entered Jake's sitting room for a worship service.

Jake, Willem, and James and Julia, the Limon couple who had attended an organizing meeting because they once had Mennonite neighbors they liked well.

Theresa Sutton, an unmarried middle-aged woman who took in sewing and who had mended two of Jake's shirts.

And Albert, Mary, and Little Abe Miller.

When the family of three slipped in the door just before Jake's opening prayer, Willem forgot to blink as he watched them settle. Little Abe, still several months shy of two, was born on the

Colorado plain and could not have any memory of a church service, let alone the self-discipline Amish children learned about sitting still during ponderous twelve-stanza hymns and two sermons. The seating arrangement was informal. Albert and Mary tucked their son between them on a small sofa and both kept a hand on one knee. Gratitude for their presence tingled out of the pores of Willem's skin.

He was not the only one, not the only Amish to accept Jake's invitation.

What Abbie would think when she heard what her friends had done Willem hated to consider. Abruptly aware that he was staring at the Millers, he moved his eyes to Jake. A holy hush fluttered through the room as Jake prayed.

Willem began a hymn. Within a few notes everyone but Little Abe was singing. *Where shall I go? I am so ignorant. Only to God can I go, because God alone will be my helper. I trust in You, God, in all my distress.* The small boy forgot his squirming and put one finger in his mouth while he watched the phenomenon. When Willem paused to breathe between phrases, he smiled at Abraham, who buried his face in his mother's shoulder.

Jake stood up and opened his Bible. He took his text from Colossians 3 and gently reminded the assembly that they were God's children and called to clothe themselves with compassion, kindness, humility, meekness, patience, and forgiveness.

And love. Above all love.

Jake was a gracious preacher, Willem decided. His words, his posture, his tone of voice, the way he looked each person in the eye—he showed himself to be a shepherd who would leave no sheep out of the fold.

He would be everything Abbie could hope for in a minister. So much had changed in her life in the last few weeks. She needed what Jake could give as much as he did. He could ask her one more time. The worst that could happen was she would say no.

Abbie sat up in bed and felt around the base of the candle for the box of matches. The first match lit on one strike, and she held its flame carefully against the wick until the candle caught. She had been in bed for two hours and unable to keep her eyes closed for more than half a minute at a time. Whether wide eyed in the dark or tight eyed in bursts of determination to sleep, her mind conjured the image of her quilt, its desperate squares yearning for completion and the unity of finding their formation with each other.

Outside Abbie's curtainless window, the moon was new and dark. The candle could not find even a shadow of light to cast against and only fluttered in the breeze her own movement caused as Abbie pushed back the bed covers and felt the cool wood beneath her bare feet. If she could not sleep and could not relax and could not even pray, she may as well get up and quilt even though it was the middle of the night. She picked up her candle and crept down the stairs into the kitchen. There she lit the lamp on the table and took her quilt from the laundry basket that had becomes its home.

Abbie spread the quilt and fingered the square she had thought of as belonging to the Weaver household. She had prayed so many hours for the trees of life of the other settler families. Now she wondered if she had failed to pray enough for her own.

"I'll be sorry to miss your wedding."

Abbie gasped and turned toward her mother's face still hidden in darkness. "*Mamm!* I thought you went to bed hours ago." Abbie moved the lamp to light Esther's form sitting upright in one of the few wooden chairs left in the front room.

Esther shook her head. "I never went up. Somehow I couldn't bring myself to waste my last night here sleeping. I've been listening to the coyotes."

Abbie held still for a moment and listened as well. "Why did you say that about my wedding?"

"Maybe it won't be Willem," Esther said. "But I hope there will be someone for you. I hate to think of leaving you here all alone."

Abbie smoothed a hand across Willem's finished square. "No, I don't think it will be Willem after all."

"I've been saving some blue yardage for your wedding dress. I always hoped we would make your dress together. I'll give it to you in the morning with a prayer that you will yet use it."

"Thank you, *Mamm.*" Abbie's throat swelled in an instant, and she swallowed back the knot. "Do you really think I could be happy with someone else?"

"I think we all can choose to be happy by receiving God's blessing. I hope God will bless you, and I hope you will recognize it when He does."

Abbie stood, picked up her chair, and carried it to the space beside her mother. Sitting again, she leaned her head on Esther's shoulder and said, "I have something to tell you. I've made a decision."

CHAPTER 41

Dawn pinked the Monday sky and slithered through the windows, but Willem was already awake, dressed, and ready to dispense with the morning chores. This was not a morning to be late. He downed the reheated coffee, collected the eggs, made the rounds in the barn, let the animals into the pasture, and hitched a team to the wagon. The weight his wagon would carry that day—in one direction—warranted the extra horse.

By the time he pulled into the Weaver farm, which had a quieted, desolate appearance, the sky was bright with October brilliance. The bottom trunk in the stack outside the front door sagged under the weight it bore, but the precision of the arrangement suggested Ananias's work. Perhaps the trunks had been outside all night awaiting conveyance to the train station in Limon. The door opened, and Levi came out and leaned against the pile to fidget with his shoes. Wearing them likely was an unaccustomed sensation for a child with toughened bare soles, but riding the train was not the same as running free on the farm. He would have to wear shoes all the way to Ohio, where it could already be cool enough that Levi would have to resign himself to shoes for the winter.

Abbie was next to emerge from the house. "*Gut mariye,* Willem. I didn't expect to see you."

"I offered to take your family to the train." Willem let himself down from the bench and approached the trunks. "Your *daed* agreed my wagon would accommodate the trunks and passengers more comfortably than your buggy."

"We would have managed."

She looked over his shoulder at nothing in particular, as if she did not want to meet his eyes.

"This must be a difficult day for you." Willem stepped into her line of sight. "It seemed only right for me to help."

Abbie wrapped her shawl around her shoulders more tightly and turned to look over her shoulder at the open door, though no one appeared.

Willem slapped a trunk. "Levi, do you want to help me start loading?"

Levi banged a hand against the side of one shoe. "I suppose so. But I'm not very strong."

"Even a small bit of help makes the job easier."

"You could wait for Daniel or Reuben." Abbie spoke but still looked away.

She knew he had been to the Mennonite service, Willem realized, and today she was bidding her family farewell. Still, her mood was off. There was something she did not want him to see in her face.

At the train station, Abbie reached for Levi's hand, and to her relief he did not resist the gesture. He stood with her while Willem helped the rest of her family check their baggage with the porter.

"You're not going to love that *English* boy instead of me, are you?" Levi looked at his shoes as he asked the question.

"He's a sweet child," Abbie said, "but he is not my little *bruder*."

"I still wish you would come."

She stroked the back of his head now. He was getting so tall. "I know."

"You can visit. I'll ask *Daed* to send you the money for a train ticket."

Abbie doubted very much her father would consent to the request, but she held back from twisting Levi's earnest hope. "We can write letters."

"I won't know your address when you move."

"Silly. I'll send it to you."

"You don't know our address. We don't have one yet."

"*Mamm* will send it to me. And I know the addresses of our grandparents and all our aunts and uncles. They will always know where to find you."

Levi shrugged, unconvinced.

Abbie glanced at their family. Willem was shaking hands with them one at a time. *Mamm. Daed.* Daniel. Reuben. Then he hung back. Abbie realized she was holding her breath. She raised her eyes toward Pikes Peak, seeking a prayerful reminder of why she had chosen a path that would separate her from the people she could barely imagine living without.

What would happen if she watched the train pull away and changed her mind? She had a few chickens and Rudy's assurance he would keep her in milk and cheese. Louise would pay her in cash, but only twice a month.

She sniffed back the drip easing out of her nose as Esther opened her arms. When her mother's embrace closed around her, Abbie caught a sob before it left her chest. She kissed both her mother's cheeks and tasted the tears she had not seen. Daniel and Reuben nodded stiffly when she caught their eyes over Esther's shoulder.

Ananias shuffled toward her. "Abigail, I pray you find God's peace in your decision."

"*Danki, Daed.*" Thank you. She looked into his eyes and dared to hope.

Ananias put one hand to her cheek. "Good-bye, daughter."

He broke the gaze before Abbie could manage words again and pivoted toward the waiting train.

"Come, Levi. It's time to go."

Abbie constrained her emotions and watched her family file up the steps into the train. Glare on the wide windows of the passenger car sliced them from her sight as soon as the last one—her father—turned toward the bank of seats. Nevertheless, Abbie stood on the platform and waited for the whistle, followed by the roar of the engine devouring fuel and the thud of doors slamming shut as railroad employees secured one set after another. Finally the great wheels began to turn. Abbie's shoulders heaved in rhythm as the train gained steam and chugged out of the station.

She paused for a moment to compose herself before turning to face Willem. The moment would have been easier if others had come to see her family off, but she was fairly certain her father had spurned the notion of a fussy farewell. From the day he announced the family would leave, Ananias had been sparse with his social gestures and reluctant to allow distraction from his methodical march toward departure. Now she might not be able to hide the disappointment that shuddered through her from this man who knew her so well.

Abbie smelled the scent of Willem. He had left his discreet post and now stood behind her. She pivoted slowly.

"We should be on our way home." Abbie hoped Willem was not planning on errands.

"I'll take you right now."

She walked beside him to the wagon but declined his assistance getting up to the bench.

"Are you sure you want to go straight home?" Willem released the brake and raised the reins. "The house. . .well, it will seem empty, will it not?"

"I have to face it. There's no point putting it off."

"Abbie," he said, "if there's anything I can do to help, you know I will do it."

She craned her gaze away. "There's not much to manage. *Daed* disposed of nearly everything."

Willem nudged the team into the road.

"Are you really going to try to buy our land?" Abbie gripped the bench with both hands.

Willem waved the reins gently. "I'd like to buy some of it. The bank officers may not agree."

"*Gottes wille.*"

"Yes. God's will." He looked at her. "I don't want you to be angry with me."

"How can I be angry with God's will?"

"It will help your family if I can buy some of the acres. I would pay as fair a price as anyone."

Abbie pressed her lips together. Did he think she did not

understand that the price considered fair had dropped considerably in recent months?

"Abbie, something else is bothering you. We know each other too well for me not to notice."

She permitted herself a glance at his face but looked away quickly. Even her mother had promised not to tell her father of Abbie's decision until the train had crossed into Nebraska. Rudy deserved to hear the news that she would accept his proposal before Willem did.

"I've changed my mind," she said. "I'd like you to take me to Rudy's farm."

"Of course. We'll stop by there first. Then I'll make sure you get home all right."

"There's no need for you to wait for me."

"Abbie—"

"Please, Willem. Just take me to Rudy's."

"May I kiss you?" Rudy's face glowed in relief as he gripped both her hands.

Abbie nodded. Now that the moment had come, she wanted him to. His lips were dry, but softer than she had imagined lips so thin could be. He lingered only a few nervous seconds. Before he could pull back, Abbie leaned in with firmer pressure. Rudy's arms encircled her now. This is what the embrace of her husband would feel like, the man she would lie beside and rise beside.

"I was so sure you were going to turn me down," Rudy whispered into her ear. "I didn't even speak to your father."

"Then why did you ask me?"

"I had nothing to lose."

"Well, I didn't turn you down. So we'll have some plans to make."

He released her. "We'll do whatever you want to the house. I'll find a way. You'll see. This place can be a home."

"I know it can. It will be *our* home."

"Your family is gone. I hate to think of you alone in that house."

Abbie could not remember a time she had ever been alone in

the house for an entire night.

"When. . .how soon. . .?"

Rudy twisted his lips in calculation. "A month? We'll have to wait until the harvest is over in Ordway before we could hope a minister would come."

"Of course."

"Will you finish your quilt in time? Will it be ready to use as our wedding quilt?"

Abbie swallowed hard. When she started the quilt, she imagined it in Willem's house, not Rudy's. But she had nothing else to offer.

"It's almost finished," she said.

"Good. I don't want you to be discouraged because some families have left. I want you to look at your quilt and believe that more will come."

"You are very sweet, Rudy Stutzman."

He kissed her again.

CHAPTER 42

Can't we sit on the sun porch?" Eight-year-old Fin Wood's eyes pleaded with Abbie. "Just one more chapter?"

She nodded. "But you have to read aloud this time."

"I like listening to you read."

"I know, but we have to be sure you can read for yourself. We'll take turns with every paragraph. How would that be?"

Fin made a slow pivot and led her toward the sun porch. Once winter gusted in, the porch would be too cold. For now waning October days offered appeal. They settled in together on a brown wicker loveseat cushioned in a red-and-blue floral chintz. As she tucked her skirt, Abbie felt the smooth crispness of the fabric and noticed the bits of green and yellow at the edges of the flowers. Her fingers lingered on the curve of a broad leaf.

"Mama says this is her favorite place in the whole house," Fin said. "Mine, too."

"I can see why." The porch faced west, toward the mountains. The wide screens and the length of the porch gave a panoramic view of open ranch land.

Maybe this is what Willem wanted, Abbie thought. Acres and acres of possibility, but farm crops rather than cattle between the zigzag of fencing. She forced her mind to shift to Rudy, uncertain how she was going to break the habit of wondering about Willem.

She opened the book, *The Wonderful Wizard of Oz*. "Where did we leave off?"

"Toto!" Fin said.

"Oh yes." Abbie found the page and handed the book to Fin. He began to read, stumbling on a few words but easily gaining momentum. In her years at an *English* school, the Amish parents sought alternative assignments if they felt an *English* book was disparate from their educational goals. She read American history and biographies but never anything as fanciful as this book that enchanted Fin Wood—and would have enchanted Levi Weaver if he ever had the chance to read it. It certainly was imaginative, but Abbie did not see how it would prepare Fin to someday run his father's ranch.

A door opened, and Louise Wood appeared with a tray. "I thought you might enjoy some refreshment."

"Thank you." Abbie took the glass of lemonade that Louise offered.

"I haven't seen your friend Willem lately," Louise said. "I hope he is not unwell."

Abbie had not seen Willem in three days, not since he dropped her at Rudy's farm on Monday afternoon.

"I pray not," Abbie said. "I don't always see him often myself."

"Oh? I rather thought you two were sweet on each other." Louise handed her son a glass and set a plate of sugar cookies in front of him.

Abbie fought the blush creeping into her cheeks. "There was a time when we considered one another in that regard."

"Have you had a falling out?"

Abbie dodged the question. "I hope to always count Willem among my friends, but I have recently accepted the proposal of another man."

Louise smiled. "Of course a young woman as lovely as you would have suitors. I hope you will be very happy with your young man."

Abbie returned the smile. "We are quite compatible."

Fin pushed the book into Abbie's lap. "It's your turn to read."

Abbie waited for the stunned expression on Mary Miller's face to fade.

"I know you weren't expecting this," Abbie said. "Neither was I. But I know it's the right thing."

Mary shrugged. "It is the way of the Amish to keep courting private. Albert and I did not even drive home from singings together in Pennsylvania because we didn't want our families to speculate."

"How did you court, then?"

"We managed to find a few minutes here and there at a picnic or an auction." Mary stood on her porch and pulled her shawl snug. "In our old district the people came together all the time. I don't understand how you and Rudy courted, though. We don't even have church out here, much less singings or auctions."

Abbie tilted her head to think. She had not even thought they were courting. "It started with his calf, I suppose. We were both afraid she wouldn't make it. I fell into the habit of looking in on her when I stopped by with bread. More and more, Rudy was in the barn when I got there."

"So this is why you did not leave with your parents."

"Not really." Abbie rolled her bottom lip in but immediately pushed it out. She did not want Mary—or anyone—to think she harbored doubt. "I stayed behind because I wanted to remain with the community. I came to be a settler, and I mean to settle."

"Even if there is no community in the end?"

"The end of what, Mary? Does God's will have a timeline?" Abbie searched her friend's eyes for what she really meant.

"Come inside," Mary said. "I'll make tea."

Abbie waved off the suggestion. "Thank you, but don't go to the trouble. I've had a long day already."

"I heard about your position on the Wood ranch."

"It's just for a few weeks," Abbie said. "But I am tired, and Rudy is bringing me some milk and cheese before supper."

Mary's smile looked forced. "Another time, then. I pray you and Rudy will be as happy as Albert and I are."

Abbie shuffled to her buggy and watched as Mary called for Little Abe and herded him into the house. Too late she realized Mary had meant to tell her something over tea, and Abbie had been too distracted to listen.

For three days Willem festered over Abbie's peculiar behavior on the day her parents departed. No matter how many times and how many ways he explained away her reticence toward him, he was not satisfied. At least once each day he marched to the barn resolved to saddle up his stallion and go make sure Abbie was all right. Every time, though, he put the tack back on the wall. She might not even be there because of her work schedule, and during the wagon ride home from the depot she had adamantly resisted offers of help ranging from subtle generalities to specific chores.

And going to the Mennonite church service—even though the Millers participated as well—had set his course away from her. At least that was her opinion, and it was pronounced enough that she would rather get her milk and eggs from Rudy Stutzman. She had managed to leave his bread that week without encountering Willem, even though he had not left the farm in three days. Willem had not expected she would treat him so cooly so quickly.

On Thursday afternoon, Willem decided to muck the stalls thoroughly, as if clearing soiled straw would also clear his mind. By the time he heard the sound of the approaching buggy, betrayed by snorting horses, Willem had worked up a sweat. He went outside to greet Moses Troyer.

"The news is good, *ya*?" Grinning, Moses jumped down from the bench.

"What news is that?" Willem used a sleeve to wipe the sweat from his forehead.

"The Weavers should have stayed a few weeks longer. It's a shame they will miss their daughter's wedding."

Willem cleared his throat, puzzled but determined to remain calm. "I had not heard the news."

"That sneaky Rudy Stutzman!" Moses wagged his head. "I just came from there. Who would have known he was courting Abigail Weaver?"

Yes, Willem thought. *Who would have known?*

"We all knew she was spunky," Moses said, "but I was shocked that Ananias would let her remain here once he decided to go."

"I guess they worked it out." Willem reached for the rake he had left leaning against the side of the barn.

"I suppose Ananias was determined to move before winter. Why else would they miss her wedding?"

Willem shrugged. Why indeed?

"I always thought it would be you," Moses said. His face sobered. "But considering how her father feels about the salvation of anyone outside the Amish church, I suppose I should not be surprised. She could hardly marry you and set the two of you against each other."

"I thought you had an open mind on that question, Moses." Willem twirled the rake between his hands.

"I do. It's Ananias who doesn't."

The knock, though not insistent, jolted Abbie out of a doze she had not meant to fall into. For a moment she listened for the footsteps of her mother or little brother on the way to answer the door. Standing up, she raised a hand to the back of her neck to rub the spot where it had gone stiff while she slept with her chin on her chest in an upright chair.

"Coming!" she called, unsure how long she had slept. It must be Rudy with the eggs and milk. She snatched her prayer *kapp* from the side table and put it on her head before she reached the door.

He stood there with downcast face and wounded pools of murky green where his eyes should have been.

"Willem."

"I wish you had been the one to tell me, Abbie."

Abbie stepped outside. "I'm sorry." Her murmured statement was more than words.

"I would have understood."

"Would you?" She challenged his gaze. "You wanted me to go to the Mennonites with you. You went even when you knew I couldn't. Wouldn't. Would never."

"Never is a long time, Abigail."

She straightened her shoulders. "Don't scold me. You have no right."

"I gave that up." Willem shifted his feet in the dirt. "I didn't realize your growing affection for Rudy."

"I did not realize it myself until recently. But I have found myself in the position of having to make several decisions I never expected to make, and I have no regrets."

Willem stepped away from her. "I know what it will mean to you to be married in the Amish church. I wish you every happiness."

"*Danki.*"

She covered her mouth with the back of her hand and she watched him stride away from her and mount his horse. The moment had come to truly find release from his hold on her heart.

CHAPTER 43

The sight of him made Abbie smile.

Rudy, not Willem. Rudy made her smile.

When she drove gently onto his land on Friday morning, he was on a ladder scrubbing the outside of the window at the front of the house. She had cleaned the inside of the glass more times than she could count in an effort to keep the dust blowing in from the plain from coating every inch of interior surface, but cleaning the outside was not part of her housekeeping duties, and Rudy had never raised a sponge. When she asked him about it once, he said he saw no gain from the chore. The wind would only blow dry soil against the panes before the day was over, and most of the hours he spent inside the house were after the sun was low enough in the sky that he had no reason to look out the windows. Yet here he was, scrubbing glass.

From the fourth rung, he dropped his sponge in the bucket at the foot of the ladder and grinned.

"Why, Rudy Stutzman, what has come over you?" Abbie let the reins go lax.

He climbed down and came to stand beside the buggy. "I won't be a bachelor much longer. Figured it was time I learn to behave like a man who cares what pleases a woman."

Sentiment filled her throat, making her words hoarse. "I would never ask you to change anything about yourself."

"You didn't. But a man can decide." He offered her a hand to help her out of the buggy.

She reached under the bench. "I found a jar of cherries *Mamm* left behind and made a pie. It's still warm."

When he took it from her, he cradled her hands along with the pie plate. The tingle that started in her fingers and flowed up her arms startled her.

"I don't think *Ordnung* forbids having pie in the middle of the morning."

How had she never noticed the twinkle in his blue eyes before? Or the depth of the dimple that would be covered with a red beard once they were married?

"With *kaffi*?" she asked.

"If you like." Rudy gestured toward the door. "Come and see what I've done inside. I will start the *kaffi*."

"You've done something inside?" Abbie felt like a curious schoolgirl and spurted ahead of Rudy.

Behind her, he chuckled. She turned her head and smiled at him over her shoulder. Only five days ago her mother had urged her to recognize blessing when it came. Now she did.

Mailing a single letter seemed like a feeble excuse to go into Limon. It was possible Willem would find something of interest in the mercantile, but less likely that he would decide to part with cash for the purchase. Determination to come up with a credible down payment for additional acres magnified his sense of stewardship. Every dollar mattered.

And so did the letter. It might be his best hope. When he left Ohio, Willem's father gave him the value of his share of the family farm. They both knew the money would go further in Colorado than Pennsylvania. Willem never asked for another penny—until now. He proposed a business arrangement—a loan, not a gift. He would even include his father on the title of the new land if that was what would satisfy either the senior Peters or the bank officer. And since he did not know when a specific need would draw him to Limon again, Willem chose to make the trip just to mail a letter.

Outside the post office, he tied his horse to a hitch and fingered the envelope. The laboriously crafted words ran through his mind.

It took him three drafts before he felt secure that he did not sound alarming or in need. The matter was one of timing and opportunity.

"Hello, Willem." Jake approached. "What brings you into town?"

Willem tapped the letter against an open palm. "A letter home."

"I'm sure your folks will be glad to hear from you."

Willem nodded and glanced at the post office.

"Something wrong, Willem?"

"Wrong? No. Why do you ask?"

"You seem distracted. Do you have regrets about attending the service last Sunday?"

"Of course not. I was grateful to be included."

"I heard about Abbie and Rudy," Jake said softly.

"I knew how she felt about your church."

"Still."

Willem scratched one ear. "I'd better mail my letter. Then I'm going to ask around about odd jobs. Maybe somebody needs help getting ready for the winter."

Jake brightened. "The Melton Wood ranch does. I just heard this morning that they lost one of their ranch hands."

Willem shook his head. "Abbie is working for them."

"I know. But you'd be out on the ranch, not in the house. It couldn't hurt to inquire."

"I can paint," Rudy said. "Fresh white walls. You would like that, wouldn't you?"

"You don't have to do that, Rudy." Abbie scraped up the last bit of pie from her plate.

"But you would like it, wouldn't you?" Rudy watched her face for the slightest light of pleasure.

She broke down and smiled. "Yes, I suppose I would."

"Then I'll do it. Next time I go into town I'll order the paint."

"You don't have to do all this, Rudy." Abbie reached across the table and took his hand. "We agreed we would get married without a lot of fuss. A simple start."

Rudy downed the last of the coffee in his cup. "And we will. I don't see how a clean coat of paint will complicate anything."

He did not tell her that he had started a list of what he wanted to do to make his house, which could barely be construed as a cabin, into a home. He would have to do something about the sagging, creaking bed, for instance, but it would be unseemly to speak of that. And she deserved to have matching shelves on the kitchen wall spacious enough to hold more than a dented stockpot and the one iron skillet he owned. The sale of a cow or two would provide some cash for immediate needs and perhaps allow him to hire someone to make drawings for expanding the cabin. He should have spoken up sooner. He should have risked telling her how he felt or asked her how matters stood between her and Willem. Now he would never know if she might have accepted him without first finding herself in the confusing circumstances of her parents' abandonment of the settlement.

But he had not. And it did not matter, because he would do his best to make sure that Abbie never found reason to regret her decision to marry him. She might not love him the same way she loved Willem—or at least had loved Willem—but the blessing of her affection in any form was more than he deserved.

He wondered what his own face would look like once a full grown beard covered it to indicate his married status. A year from now there could be a baby on the way. Rudy hoped all their children would have Abbie's gentle features.

The only thing missing was a church to raise their children in. The Chupps. Eber and Ruthanna. The Weavers. All gone from the community's midst. Willem was as good as gone to the Mennonites. Rudy and Abbie would have to lean on the Lord to see them through the years without church. Even as Rudy told himself that God was faithful and gracious in His will, he yearned to sit on a bench in a room full of men and women who shared his desire for worship.

Willem shook Melton Wood's hand on the wide porch of the Wood house. "I appreciate your seeing me so quickly."

"No point in wasting time," Melton said. "I need a hand. If you're serious about wanting the work, I'm happy to take you on.

You did a good job digging coal for us."

"How soon would you want me to start?" Willem tilted his head and scratched behind his ear.

"Let's see." Melton looked up at the overhang shading them. "This is Thursday afternoon. I think Monday will be soon enough. How is that for you?"

Willem nodded. "That would work well. I have to confess I've never worked on a ranch before."

"But you're a farmer," Melton said. "I need somebody to help me look after the fences."

"I can fix fences," Willem said.

"I have no doubt." Melton's tanned face scrunched as he narrowed his eyes. "I meant to do a lot of repairs over the summer that I never seemed to get to. Too many sick animals to tend to. Then last week a half-dozen head wandered off of my land through a break in the barbed wire, so the matter has become more urgent. It's expensive to lose cattle just when you have them fattened up for market. I was lucky to recover them."

"I'm only too happy to help with anything that needs doing."

"You haven't even asked what the job pays." Melton's mouth turned up.

Willem scratched behind his ear. "I trust you to be fair."

"Most of the hands live on the ranch as a good part of their pay, but I'm sure we can come to an agreement that is fair to everyone. You can take your meals here if you like. My foreman will pay you in cash twice a month."

"Do you mind if I ride around this afternoon and get a better idea of the layout of the ranch?"

"Not at all. It's not a large property as ranches go, but you should still be careful not to wander so far that you can't get home to look after your own animals."

Willem extended his hand again. "I won't disappoint you."

"I wouldn't take you on if I thought you might." Melton shook Willem's hand. "I'll walk you back to your horse."

As they walked down the steps and into the open yard, Willem glanced around in involuntary speculation about where Abbie spent her time when she was here.

CHAPTER 44

I'll copy the letter over so it's not so messy." Abbie smoothed the corner of the page she had crumpled while she wrote at Rudy's table on Monday morning. They had selected the minister in Ordway they thought would be most able to get away for a trip that was likely to take four days even if the minister did not stay for a visit with the Amish families. Abbie did not expect that he would, given that no one had come even to preach in such a long time.

"Why don't you read it back just to be sure we've thought of everything?" Rudy straightened his chair up against the edge of the table.

Abbie cleared her throat.

> *We greet you in the faith that binds us together.*
>
> *We are Rudy Stutzman and Abigail Weaver of the Elbert County settlement. God's will has become plain to us, and we rejoice that God leads our hearts to be wed. Our hope is to speak our vows before the end of November. We are writing to you because we could not see ourselves as truly married in the eyes of God if we could not be married in the Amish church we both love so dearly.*
>
> *Following the custom of our people, we know the harvest must be in before we turn to our celebration. As you know, the drought in our county has pressed our labors from every side. Our farms have yielded little to harvest, but we share your joy*

that Ordway's crops have been abundant. We pray God blesses your family through His gracious provision in these busy weeks.

May we ask you to pray about whether God might lead you to come to Elbert County to lead our wedding service? Being married here, among the families who share our settlement and our future congregation, is the desire of our hearts.

We implore you in the name of Christ to consider this ministry to our shared people.

Abbie looked up. "You don't think it sounds too strong?"

Rudy twisted his lips in thought. "Maybe we should offer to travel to Ordway after all."

"Are you having second thoughts?"

"Would it not be satisfying to be married in an established congregation?"

"But they would not be *our* congregation," Abbie said. "Who would want to come if they don't even know us? I don't want our families here to think we are turning our backs on them at one of the most important moments of our lives."

"Of course you are right." Rudy's volume dropped.

Abbie studied his face. "I don't want to be right, Rudy. I want us to be of one mind."

He patted her hand. "We are. We'll send the letter just as it is."

"It will only take me a few minutes to copy it fresh," she said. "We should both sign it, don't you think?"

"Yes, let's do that. I'll pour some more *kaffi*."

Abbie watched his movements as he stood, turned to the stove, and reached for the pot. They had talked about these questions several times in the week since she accepted his proposal. Why had he chosen this moment, when they were writing such an important letter, to sound uncertain?

He was in one of his funks, she decided as she copied in a firm hand the words they had chosen carefully. One of his moods. It would pass. She would have to get used to them and learn to respond with patient words—or patient silence.

When she finished writing, she handed Rudy the pen. "I think the husband's signature should come first."

He scratched his name onto the paper and returned the pen. "Do you still plan to mail the letter yourself?"

"When I go to work I'll be halfway to the post office in Limon," she said. "But if you would rather take it—"

"No. Your suggestion is sensible. You take it."

Abbie gave Fin Wood a stern look. "You heard your mother. It's time for your rest."

"All I do is rest." Fin slumped in his chair and crossed his arms. "We didn't do anything."

"We played four games of checkers, cleaned the bottom of the bird cage, and read thirty-six pages in *The Wonderful Wizard of Oz*. I'd hardly say that's nothing." Abbie wondered what Levi was finding to complain about these days. "If you don't rest in the afternoons, the doctor might send you back to bed."

"I can't make myself be tired when I'm not." Fin scowled.

"You might find you are tired if you just close your eyes for a while."

"I want to feed the new calf."

She wagged a finger at him. "You know your parents don't want you to leave the house yet."

"When?"

Abbie softened. "As soon as your parents give permission, I promise our first outing will be to the barn."

"When are you coming back?"

"Tomorrow, first thing."

"Promise?"

"Promise." Abbie stood up and gathered her things. The letter to the Ordway minister lay in the folds of her shawl. She had not been willing to leave it in the buggy out of her sight. "I'll tuck you in before I go."

Despite his protests, a few minutes later Fin dropped off, and Abbie padded out of his room. She stopped in the kitchen to let Louise know she was leaving and then went out the front door.

The stallion tied up outside the barn caused her to look twice. Yes, the ears were right, and the spot on the left flank. It was

Willem's horse. Abbie did not know what his business was on the Wood ranch, but she scanned the open area around the house and hoped to get her buggy turned around before stallion and rider were paired again. She whistled for her horse in a nearby pen—and then slammed a hand over her mouth in regret.

Abbie dashed to the mare and tried to urge it through the gate.

Too late.

Willem came around the corner of an outbuilding. "I thought I recognized that whistle."

"Hello, Willem." Abbie slowed her pace. It would seem rude to hurry now. "I'm surprised to see you here."

"I'm working for Mr. Wood today."

"I thought you finished digging his lignite long ago." Abbie patted her horse's neck to keep her hands busy.

"I did. I'm going to fix fences for a while, and then we'll see what else needs to be done."

"I see." He was after money, no doubt so he could buy the Weaver farm.

"I was hoping I would run into you," Willem said.

"Willem, I'm going to marry Rudy. There's nothing to talk about." She picked at the harness.

"Abbie, listen. I have something to tell you."

She said nothing and did not look at him.

"The Yutzys have decided to leave," he said.

Her eyes shot up at him. "What?"

"I only heard about it on Saturday. The bank is about to repossess their land. They have no hope of catching up on their loan."

Pain sliced through Abbie's middle like a blacksmith's fired chisel. Willem caught her elbow.

"I knew how you would feel," he said. "I wanted you to hear it from me before the rumors start flying."

"I suppose you're going to try to buy their farm, too." She shook off his touch. "Don't think I can't figure out why you want to work here."

His face fell.

"I'm sorry." Abbie composed herself. "That was an awful thing to say, especially after you found this position for me when I needed it. Please forgive me."

"Of course I forgive you. I'm sure the news about the Yutzys is upsetting."

"It's no excuse. Let me make amends. Do you need anything from Limon? Since I'm halfway there I'm going in to mail a letter." And then she would be up half the night baking the bread she would deliver to Willem, Rudy, and Martin Samuels on Wednesday as usual. She could not give a whole day to baking now. Two evenings would have to suffice.

"Thank you, no," Willem said. "If you're writing your parents, perhaps it is not too late to send my greetings along with yours."

"Rudy and I wrote to Ordway," she said, looking away again. "To the bishop."

While the loaves were rising and the oven warmed, Abbie spread out the quilt on the floor of the front room. Her father had not left much furniture, so she had plenty of space. With a pair of scissors in one hand and a lamp in another, Abbie crawled around the edges of the quilt to be sure the binding was securely stitched and to trim off excess threads that caught her eye. When she had been around the entire perimeter, she sat back on her heels. Considering that she had made the entire quilt without benefit of a frame, she was pleased with the result.

Other than its physical appearance, the quilt was nothing Abbie had expected it to be. It had twelve blocks because the settlement had begun with twelve households. With the imminent departure of the Yutzys, and including Willem's departure to the Mennonites, five of the twelve would be gone. Every household had contributed at least a few patches of fabric to this quilt, and as she stitched the triangles together she prayed for God's clear blessing. She had chosen a tree of life pattern because she wanted each family to blossom and grow in faith and prosperity. Instead, one by one, the families felt the weight of discouragement that reshaped their vision. Branches bent and broke.

This quilt was supposed to cover the bed she would share with Willem. Though Abbie had been forced to abandon that expectation weeks ago, she had not reoriented to the image of this quilt covering Rudy's bed. But what else did she have?

The quilt could still carry meaning. It could still represent a fresh start, a growing faith. In addition to praying for the families that left, Abbie could pray for the unknown families who would come. She could pray for a marriage she had not expected but nevertheless welcomed. She could pray for the safety and security of God's will.

Smelling the yeasty fragrance of the burgeoning bread dough, Abbie got up to put the first batch in the oven.

CHAPTER 45

The sleepless night persuaded Rudy.

Perhaps it was the bed and knowing, when he let himself reach down inside himself, that he could not ask Abbie to sleep on it. But her father had sold the family's beds, and Abbie was sleeping on a narrow cot. Between them they did not even have a decent bed.

Or perhaps it was the news that the Yutzys were giving up. Rudy had spoken to Isaiah himself, and he had not even tried to say that since his farm had failed it must be God's will for them to move somewhere else. He just said he was giving up. Too discouraged to keep trying. Another square of Abbie's quilt would wilt before it blossomed.

Or it might have been the approaching Sunday, the second Sabbath in November, and so many weeks without a worship service that Rudy had lost count. He had been right, those months ago, when he sat in the barn with all the other men and prodded the council to speak forthrightly about why the settlement still had no minister of its own. If he had been successful, instead of letting himself be silenced or influenced by Willem's unflustered demeanor, the Amish households might have found the spiritual unity that seemed beyond their grasp. Noah Chupp might have stayed. Rudy and Abbie might have taken a buggy down the road to their own minister to speak in person, rather than labor over words that might still be misunderstood. They could have heard their banns read in their own congregation. Now even if a minister came from Ordway, would the banns would be read at all? Who was there to hear them?

He lay in bed, awake, with his eyes closed and picturing the fullness of his home congregation shoulder to shoulder on the benches, the mothers with babies on their laps and small boys beaming their delight at being old enough to sit with the men. He heard the robust harmonies of the hymns, smelled the hams baking in the kitchen, watched for a glimpse out the window of the horses gathered in their own circles in the pasture with tails swishing.

Rudy missed going to church.

He did not have to open his eyes to know that dawn was no imminent promise, but he rolled over and lit the lamp. If he did not put his thoughts on paper before the morning milking, they would torment him all day.

Abbie was grateful for Saturday. Louise Wood did not expect her on Saturdays, and Abbie was certain Mary Miller would welcome a leisurely visit. While it was still warm, Abbie wrapped up a small cake she had baked as a treat for Little Abe. Louise had given her a basket of apples, and Abbie put half in a sack to take to Mary, who made the best *schnitzboi* of anyone Abbie knew. They might even work on baking together while they talked about Abbie's wedding plans. Abbie planned to cut out the pieces of her blue wedding dress that evening and begin spending her evenings stitching them together.

Abbie put the cake and apples in the buggy and slid her arms into the sleeves of a thick sweater. If it were not for the devastation the incinerating summer had wreaked on crops, the blistering days would have seemed a distant memory, a harmless turning of the seasons. She shook off the thought, determined not to let even the departure of the Yutzys dampen her wedding preparations. With her mother and Ruthanna gone, Mary was Abbie's closest friend in the settlement.

The horse established a steady trot, and Abbie's work at the reins was easy. The distance between the farms closed while she daydreamed, and Abbie nearly missed the turnoff. A last-minute tug turned the horse toward the Miller home.

Abbie tied the reins loosely over around a post and fished out the cake and apples from under the bench. She knocked on the door, listening for Mary's cheery "Come in" or Little Abe's giggle.

Instead, Mary came to the door and stood in its frame.

"Good morning." Abbie started to step up into the house, but Mary did not back away from the door in welcome.

"Hello, Abbie."

Abbie lifted the cake in one hand and the apples in the other. "A treat for Little Abe and something for your *schnitzboi*."

"You shouldn't have bothered."

Mary's voice sounded distracted.

"It's no bother," Abbie said. "Is everything all right?"

"Abraham is not feeling well," Mary said.

"Nothing serious, I hope." Still holding her gifts, Abbie tried to look past Mary into the house.

"I'm sure it is not." Mary took the food into her own arms. "You know how little children are. He is too excitable. I think he just needs a quiet day."

Abbie nodded. "I promise not to play rough with him."

"Forgive me, Abbie, but I think it is better if we don't have company today."

Abbie blinked. She had not thought of herself as company at Mary's house, but easy friends who looked forward to breaking up their own isolation. "Can I help you with anything?"

"Thank you, but no. I'm just going to keep Little Abe in and quiet today. Thank you for the food."

"Of course."

Mary closed the door.

A moment later, Abbie was back in her buggy hating the thought that she had offended Mary and did not know what she had done. There seemed to be nothing to do but go home—or to Rudy's. Surely he would be happy to see her.

Willem walked along the tracks behind the depot in Limon, wondering why he had not seen the obvious before this. Most of the people who lived within the city limits of Limon had some connection to the Union Pacific or the Rock Island Railroad. The rail companies had tracks that crossed in Limon, and freight cars and passengers cars had to be coupled and uncoupled day and night. Baggage handlers loaded and unloaded trunks and crates. Willem was as strong as any man. If he started on the Wood ranch early in the morning, he could still offer a few hours a day to one of the railroads and get home to his animals before the milk cows got desperate. He could save enough for his down payment even more quickly. It was worth an inquiry as soon as his work at the ranch settled into a routine.

He turned up the collar of his jacket. The early November Saturday harbored a threat of winter Willem had not detected before now. A graying sky, a temperature reluctant to warm appreciably since sunrise, and a wind hopping from one ridge to another across the plain carried reminders of the change in seasons. Willem did not see how winter could be more harsh than summer had been this year.

He walked the blocks toward Main Street, where he had left his wagon to be loaded with several rolls of barbed-wire fencing. He would take advantage of the opportunity to check for mail. If he could predict his mother's rhythm accurately, he was due for a letter.

The postmaster looked at him as soon as Willem entered the building. "I've got two for you this week."

"I'll be glad to have them."

The postmaster rummaged through a cubbyhole and handed the contents to Willem. "Are you still collecting mail for the Weaver farm? I have you on file as authorized, but my understanding is they've left town."

"Their daughter stayed behind."

"Ah. Then I suppose there is no harm in giving you the mail addressed to them. It's just one letter, actually, and it's addressed to the daughter."

The return address flashed through Willem's mind before he

saw it, but it was too late to withdraw his open hand.

Ordway.

Abbie would be anxious for this letter. And he was heading back to the Wood ranch where she was working with Fin today.

CHAPTER 46

Louise Wood glided into the sitting room, where Fin was teaching Abbie to play chess. Relieved to have a reason to interrupt the puzzle of the boy's explanations for how players were permitted to move the various pieces, Abbie looked up and smiled at Louise.

"Mr. Peters just came from town," Louise said. "He asked me to give you this letter."

Abbie's eyes widened when she saw the return address in block letters. "The bishop!"

"The bishop can only move on the diagonal," Fin said.

"I don't think that's the bishop Abbie means." Louise's eyes sparkled when she turned up the corners of her mouth.

Abbie turned the envelope at a right angle and back again. "Thank you. I'll just put it with my bag." She stood up.

"Fin," Louise said, "why don't you come in the kitchen and help me fix some tea?" She winked at Abbie as she reached to take Fin's hand.

"But it's almost lunchtime," Fin said.

"Then we'll see what we can find for lunch."

"When can I eat with the ranch hands again?"

"Not yet."

Louise and Fin turned the corner into the hall. Abbie immediately slid a fingernail under the flap to break the seal. If the news were bad, she might regret opening the letter while she was supposed to be working. But she hoped the news was good, and she did not want to waste a minute wondering about it and not knowing.

Abbie unfolded the plain white paper and held it along the sides. Scanning just the first few lines allowed her to let out her breath. He was willing to marry them.

She started again and read more carefully. He was happy to consecrate their marriage, but he preferred a date in the middle of December rather than the end of November because of previous commitments. He was mindful of the added risk of inclement weather that might impede his travel, but he was confident God's will would of course be plain in the events that transpired. The wedding of Abigail Weaver and Rudy Stutzman would take place as quickly as possible.

He said yes.

The bishop was coming.

With Fin leading the way with a bowl between his hands, Louise carried in a tray of cheese, ham, and bread. As she set it down on the table beside the chess set, she raised an eyebrow.

Abbie grinned.

"Let's eat lunch, Fin," Louise said. "Then I believe Abbie has a matter she needs to take care of this afternoon."

Abbie's buggy clattered into Rudy's barnyard. She did not wait for a full stop before leaping down in two steps and leaving the reins lax. Chickens in the pen pecked at the ground outside the coop just as they always did, some of them clacking at the disturbance Abbie's arrival brought. Eight cows—no, nine, counting the calf—grazed in the pasture as they always did. The new calf, fully weaned, was with the others. The horses—all but one—meandered on the other side of the field. The trough outside the barn was full of water.

"Rudy!" Abbie clutched the bishop's letter and spun in a circle looking for some indication of Rudy's whereabouts. "Rudy!"

She looked first in the barn, where it was obvious Rudy had mucked and laid down clean straw. With no animals in the barn, he had even left the door open. Fresh air gusted in behind Abbie as she looked in every stall.

Next she let herself into the chicken pen to make sure he was not cleaning there. The day's eggs had been removed, but Rudy left no other sign of recent presence.

She ducked a head into an outbuilding where he kept a plow and a few other large farm tools, but it was dark and dusty.

"Rudy!" She called louder this time. "The letter came!"

She strode to the house, knocked sharply, and entered. Rudy had cleaned up since Saturday. Their visit had been brief. Rudy claimed a headache, making Abbie wonder if Little Abe and Rudy shared an illness and giving her hope that Mary Miller had not been avoiding her after all.

The kitchen wall had been scrubbed down since then, and the scrap bucket emptied—probably what the chickens were pecking at. The bed was tidied, and both chairs were tucked under the table at precise angles. The floor had been swept so recently that it bore not even a faint layer of dust. Abbie smiled. She appreciated the effort he was making, but she would make sure he understood that she did not mind doing the housework. After all, she had been keeping house for him for a long time already. Nevertheless, it was nice to know he would not start their marriage taking her for granted.

Abbie lit the stove and pulled the coffee canister off the shelf. She might as well have a cup while she waited for Rudy. If he was out in one of the fields, he would not be long, since he had no harvest. When the coffee was ready, she filled a mug, chose the chair facing the front door, and sipped at regular intervals.

The afternoon descended into early darkness. Every time Abbie thought she might as well go home and save the joyous news for tomorrow, she believed surely he would step through the door at any moment. The cows would need milking, for one thing. A man dedicated to building a dairy business would not put his cows at risk.

She lit a lamp and foraged in his food bins. When he came through the door, she would greet him with a meal. Before long she had a potpie of green beans and potatoes in the oven.

The darkness deepened, and the howl of a coyote pierced her solitude. Rudy would never leave the calf in the pasture exposed to the coyotes. Abbie pulled the lantern with the sturdy handle off a shelf and transferred flame. She had to get the cows in.

And milked.

She knew how to milk a cow, of course. And she was fairly certain she knew Rudy's system for caring for the milk until he could distribute it in the morning or churn it into butter or cheese. The truth was, though, that her family had never had more than two cows, and her brothers had taken on the milking as soon as they were old enough. Even Levi had milking duties. While she assumed she would learn to help Rudy with the milk after they married, she never had before this.

Where was Rudy?

For the first time in this interminable afternoon, Abbie was frightened. She tightened her sweater around her midsection and carried the lantern out to the pasture. Wherever he had gone, Rudy had taken one horse, but riding without a wagon he would have nowhere to hang a light when he came home in the dark.

By the time Abbie finished the milking—which she was sure took her far longer than it would have any of her brothers, including Levi—and got all the animals settled in safety for the night, Abbie's nascent fear had multiplied into terror for Rudy's well-being. The meal in the oven dried out beyond consumption, and Abbie made another pot of coffee to drink while she sat upright at the table the entire night. She regretted now that she had let the daylight seep away while she sat cheerfully expecting Rudy to walk through the door when she could have been out riding through his fields as the first step in making sure he had not fallen ill or into harm.

She had milked the cows later than they were used to, and now she would rush the next interval by disturbing them before dawn. As soon as daylight broke, she intended to be looking for Rudy. She tended to all the animals and left them in the coop and the barn when she struck out on her search. Before the sun had transformed from pink threads to bright orange, Abbie was certain Rudy was not on the farm.

Her heart thudded against her chest wall as Abbie admitted she would have to seek help. She rode to the Millers' and interrupted their breakfast.

"Have you seen Rudy?" she asked a surprised Albert at the door.

"Today?" he asked.

"Or yesterday." Abbie's brain muttered a scrambled prayer. *Please, God, let Rudy be all right.*

"What's wrong, Abbie?"

"I'm not certain anything is wrong." Yes, she was. "When did you see him last?"

Albert shrugged. "Last week."

The weight in Abbie's stomach threatened to explode. "If he drops by today, will you let him know I was looking for him?"

"Of course. But I don't expect him."

Abbie got back in her buggy and gauged the sky. It was still very early. She had several hours before Fin Wood would be watching out the window for her arrival. *God, show me what to do.*

She was going to have to ask Willem. It only made sense. Other than the Millers, Willem's farm was the nearest. She took a deep breath, steeled herself, and drove the buggy back out to the main road.

The fluster of activity in his coop told her he was collecting eggs. Even Levi could do a more deft job of getting the eggs without upsetting the hens. Abbie pulled up beside the coop.

Willem had never seen Abbie so pale. Urgency coursed through him. "What's wrong?"

"Have you seen Rudy?"

"I'm. . .keeping my distance," Willem said. "I don't want to complicate matters."

"It's not that." Abbie twisted the reins around her hand. "I can't find him. I waited for him all day and all night at his farm, and he never came home."

"But the animals—"

"I did what I could. The animals are fine for now." Abbie's voice cracked. "I've been all over his farm, and over to the Millers'."

"What about his deliveries?"

"I can't think about that. Besides, I don't know who all his customers are."

"I meant, maybe he mentioned something to someone."

"I wouldn't know where to start, Willem. But something is very wrong."

Willem set the bowl of eggs he was holding on the ground and brushed his hands against his trousers. "What about the *English* authorities?"

Her eyes clouded. "So you agree something is wrong."

He wanted to reach up to the bench where she sat to stroke her cheek and reassure her. Instead, he slipped his fingers in the horse's bridle. "You're not a hysterical woman, Abbie. If you feel something is wrong, then something is wrong."

"What can the *English* authorities do?"

"Make inquiries. Try to determine what he has been doing the last couple of days. If you could find Rudy's account books, they could start with his dairy customers."

He saw the tremble in her nod.

"I think I know where to look," she said.

"Come inside and wash your face," he said. "Pin up your hair. We'll find it and then go into Limon together."

CHAPTER 47

Abbie wanted to know the minute Rudy returned. He *would* return. She would not allow herself to consider another answer to his disappearance.

The police officer in Limon, Mr. Shelton, was too calm. He took down the information Abbie provided, including the list of Rudy's dairy customers, and promised he would let her know when he had some information.

How long would it take? she wanted to know. What did he plan to do? Who was he going to talk to? How soon would he start? She explained where she lived, where Rudy lived, where she worked. Would he promise to send a man out to find her as soon as they knew anything at all? The most the officer did was arch an eyebrow and write a few more words on his form.

Willem had to take her by the elbow and guide her out of the police station before she heard any satisfying answers. Somehow she managed her hours with Fin, though he expressed exasperation at her lack of progress in understanding the rules of chess. Because she had ridden in with Willem that morning, she had to wait for him to return from the far reaches of the ranch. She said good-bye to Fin when it was time for his afternoon rest, telling herself she would go outside and walk off her nervous energy. In the end, she stayed near the house. If she roamed the ranch, how would an *English* officer know where to find her?

Willem drove her home, though the buggy was hers.

"I want to wait at Rudy's," she said when Willem started to

turn onto the Weaver land. "If. . .*when* he comes home, that's where he will come."

Willem redirected the horse. "I'll do the milking."

"I can manage."

"But you don't have to."

While Abbie worked alongside Willem, he was three times as fast at every task.

"In the morning," he said as they finished the last cow, "we'll have to find some use for some of the excess milk or pour it out."

"Seems a shame to waste it," she said.

"We both have jobs," he reminded her. "Neither of us has time to try to find Rudy's customers or churn butter. We should focus on keeping the cows producing."

"You're right." Whatever had happened to Rudy, he deserved to come home to healthy animals.

"I'll be back in the morning."

"You don't have to do that. I'll manage." Abbie rinsed her hands in the trough outside the barn and turned to his expectant face.

He met her gaze and moistened his lips. "The turn in your relationship with Rudy surprised me. I'll admit that. But it doesn't mean I don't care about him. Or you."

She swallowed without speaking.

"I'll ride one of Rudy's horses home for the night and be back in the morning in time to milk."

"Let's play chess again." Fin made a face at Abbie the next morning. "You don't seem to be learning the rules very well."

She forced a smile. How could she explain to a housebound eight-year-old that two sleepless nights and a missing fiancé meant she had no mental energy for absorbing the rules of chess?

"We should read today," she said. "Your mother is particularly concerned that you not fall behind in school." Fin's reading had improved enough that he might not notice she was not listening carefully.

"I don't want to do math," he said.

"We won't today." The last thing Abbie's brain wanted to do

were the multiplication tables. "Your mother suggested that we read *Around the World in Eighty Days*. It might be an interesting way to learn some geography."

Fin turned around in a dramatic fashion. "I know where the book is."

They read for most of the morning in the library. When Abbie felt the boy's efforts lagging, she took the book from him and tried to inject some enthusiasm into the task. She had never read the book before, either. It was far too fanciful for an Amish education.

It was almost lunchtime when Louise interrupted them. Abbie put a finger under the line she had been reading and looked up.

"We have a visitor," Louise said. "He said he is here for you."

Rudy! Abbie snapped the book closed and stood up.

"I've put him in the sitting room so you can have some privacy." Louise gestured and Abbie paced across the hall.

"Mr. Shelton," she said when she saw the officer who had taken her report about Rudy's disappearance.

He stood in a casual stance with his hat in one hand, resting on his leg. "We have some information."

Abbie trembled. "Have you found Rudy? Is he all right?"

"As far as we know he is quite well."

She exhaled relief.

"Apparently he decided to take a trip."

"A trip?"

"It was quite a simple matter, actually," Mr. Shelton said. "This is a railroad town, after all. People come and go all the time."

"Rudy hasn't left the area since he arrived four years ago. He hasn't even been to Colorado Springs or Denver."

"The railroads keep records, you know, and the ticket masters have developed excellent memories. Since there are so few Amish men around here, it wasn't a difficult inquiry."

"What are you saying, Mr. Shelton?" Abbie crossed and uncrossed her arms.

"We traced him to a Union Pacific passenger train that left on Tuesday morning. Apparently he had a voucher from some time ago and decided to cash it in for a ticket."

"But his farm! He would never go off without making sure his animals were cared for."

"Have they been cared for?"

"Well, yes. Mr. Peters and I have been looking after them."

"Then it seems Mr. Stutzman knew what he was doing." Mr. Shelton reached for a slip of paper. "And it seems he sold the horse he rode into town to a railroad employee, tying up loose ends."

Abbie closed her eyes to calm her breath. "We are engaged to be married. Something must have precipitated his sudden departure."

"I cannot speak to that, Miss Weaver. That is between the two of you. We consider this a closed matter because there seems to be no indication of foul play."

"But where did he go? Can you at least tell me that?"

"It was an easterly train. His ticket would take him as far as western Missouri, but of course he could have gotten off anywhere."

"Can't you find out?"

"It's not a police matter, Miss Weaver."

The mare resisted Abbie's urge for speed, but she pestered the animal until it responded to commands with sufficient conviction.

Gone.

Rudy was gone. Abbie had refused to believe the officer's conclusion for two distracted hours until she could extricate herself from Fin's attention and barrel toward Rudy's farm. If he was really gone, he could have no objection to her looking through every stack of papers, every shabby drawer, every drooping shelf for the truth. She remembered now seeing the crimped corner of the voucher one day while she was cleaning. That was months ago, and in all this time Rudy had never again spoken of leaving. Now she was supposed to believe that he had after all.

Leaving the horse in the yard, Abbie stomped past the chickens and yanked open the door. With hands on her hips, she narrowed her eyes and looked around for the clue she had missed. Rudy had left the place tidy, but Abbie had been camped out there for two days and left evidence of her presence. She began by gathering the odds and ends of her belongings into a compact pile and stacking them on one chair next to the front door. A shawl, a soiled apron, the schedule she had scratched out for taking care of the farm chores. Then she moved the coffeepot from the table to the back of the stove and shifted the pots and dishes she had left drying beside the sink to the shelves above it. A tattered quilt went back to the foot of Rudy's bed.

Now the cabin was as he had left it.

And Abbie realized what was wrong. The pile of papers Rudy always left on the table, on the end that doubled as his desk, was gone. The notes about milk production, the quantity of seed he hoped to plant in the spring, the record of how he had weaned the calf. Abbie had supposed Rudy cleaned up to please her. Now she realized he cleaned up to say good-bye.

She hunted for the stack. If he truly was abandoning the farm, he would have no reason to take it, but the papers might give some clue of his intent. Abbie stood and stared at the three narrow drawers that housed Rudy's meager wardrobe. As soon as she tugged on the bottom drawer, she knew it gave easily because it was empty. The middle one was as well.

The top drawer yielded the papers, with a letter tied closed in twine laid on top of them. Shaking, she pulled the twine away and unfolded the letter.

Dearest Abbie,

First, I want you to know that my affection for you is more profound than I imagined possible. The greatest joy of my life is the moment you agreed to wed.

Second, I want you to know the depth of my admiration for your commitment to the success of the Elbert County settlement. You could have taken the easy road and gone east with your family, but your determination is relentless.

And now for two truths. I was utterly surprised when you accepted my proposal. For so long I thought it was the only thing that could tie me to this land. I have given my farm the best effort I could, and quite possibly, given time, I would have succeeded.

But I am not your Willem. Success would not be enough. I need the church as much as you do, and I am afraid I don't have your patience or optimism. So I have used my train ticket after all. I could not bear to ask you to come with me. I was too afraid you would say no and I would have to face the truth that your acceptance of my proposal was not based on mutual affection after all. I could not bear to know that for certain.

I ask you not to look for me. I am not sure where I will go, but I know there will be a robust Amish congregation wherever I end up. On a separate page, I am leaving instructions about the animals.

Fondly,
Rudy Stutzman

The knock on the door startled her, and for a flash she wanted it to be Rudy.

But of course he would not knock on his own door.

Willem stepped into the cabin. "Mrs. Wood said you didn't look well when you left today."

Abbie handed him the papers and stumbled to a chair. Willem scanned the letter before sliding it under the document below.

"He's left you the livestock," Willem said.

Abbie exhaled and spoke hoarsely. "What do I want with dairy cows when I have been abandoned by two men?"

"I'm here," he said quietly.

"I always thought you and Rudy were different as night and day." She stared out the front window. "Now I see I was wrong. Neither one of you could choose the life that included me."

CHAPTER 48

Willem twisted the barbed wire in place and snipped the excess off one end. Johnny, the ranch hand Melton Wood had sent out to help him was a young man, probably not any older than Reuben Weaver. But if he had grown up nearby, he might know the answer to Willem's question.

"If I wanted to sell a half-dozen milk cows around here, who do you suppose might be interested in them?"

Johnny straightened his thick gloves and prepared to handle the roll of wire. "Not too many folks. Milk cows are not the same as cattle raised for beef. The feed's not the same."

"Can you think of anyone?"

"Maxwells, maybe."

"Maxwells?" Willem raised his eyebrows.

"Brothers. Jason and Raymond. They'll buy most any kind of livestock and then try to turn a profit."

"So they'll take horses, too?"

"As long as they aren't ready to be horse meat."

Rudy's horses were healthy, and one was still young as far as horses went. Most of the cows had ample calving years ahead of them.

"How do I find these Maxwell brothers?"

"On a ranch a few miles northeast of here. Other side of Limon."

Northeast was the wrong direction for going home, but he would have to do it. Rudy's intentions were clear, and Abbie needed prodding to take action. She would run herself ragged trying to take care of all those animals by herself, and for no purpose. Rudy was not coming back.

Willem braced to lift the roll of wire. "Come on. We need to finish our quota early today."

The Maxwell ranch was farther out of Limon than what Willem would have called a few miles, but by the time he realized Johnny's estimate had fallen short, Willem had invested too much time to turn back. His stomach grumbled for a late supper by the time he found the ranch and sorted out which building to approach.

"I hear you might be interested in some dairy cows," he said to Jason Maxwell.

"Maybe. How many?"

"Eight. And a calf."

"The only one of your people who has that many dairy cows is Rudy Stutzman, and you're not him."

Willem resisted the urge to point out that Jason Maxwell might not know as much about the Amish as he thought he did—except he was right on this point.

"Those are the cows I'm talking about. I am inquiring on behalf of Mr. Stutzman."

"We don't pay agent fees."

"I'm not asking for anything. Mr. Stutzman is a friend."

"We looked at his cows once." Jason narrowed his gaze. "He turned us down."

"Circumstances have changed."

Jason's eyes perked up. Willem held his tongue. He would say nothing that might compromise the value of Rudy's livestock.

"I'll tell you what," Jason said. "We'll come and have a look. Tomorrow before supper."

Willem nodded. "We'll be ready."

"You'd better not be wasting our time."

Abbie sighed and turned away when she saw Willem's stallion through the open barn door on Rudy's farm the next afternoon. She sat on a three-legged stool with her skirt arranged for clear access to the cow's udder and leaned her head into the animal's side. Only two minutes into the milking, and still not as fast as her brothers, she calculated she could keep her head down and her eyes averted for twenty minutes. If Willem had not left by then, she would move on to the next cow.

"Abbie," he said.

She did not answer.

"You can ignore me if you want to, but it won't change what is about to happen."

Abbie bit her lip in determination not to speak.

Willem picked up an empty bucket in one hand and a stool in the other. Abbie glanced out of the side of her eye and saw him inspecting the cows to determine which ones still needed to be milked.

"I made some inquiries." Willem situated himself beside a cow. "Jason Maxwell and his brother are coming in a few minutes to look at Rudy's livestock."

Abbie flared. "It's none of your business."

"Rudy wants you to sell. I am going to make sure you get the best value."

"I didn't ask you to find a buyer. Neither did Rudy." She listened to the rapid rhythmic squirts of Willem's efforts against the metal bucket.

Willem named a number. "If they offer you at least that much just for the cows, I think you should take it. Don't let them try to get you to throw in the horses."

"You're not listening, Willem. It's none of your business."

Squirt. Squirt. Squirt.

"When I heard you were going to marry Rudy," Willem said, "I thought I could accept that you were none of my business. But that has changed, hasn't it?"

"I'm not giving up on Rudy."

"Abigail."

Squirt. Squirt. Squirt. She was nearly keeping pace with him now.

"I just need time to find him. Eventually he'll go home to his parents. To his home district."

"He asked you not to look for him."

"I should never have let you read that letter."

"But you did. We can't undo what's done. Rudy is gone."

Abbie leaned her head harder into the cow's side, though her hands slowed. Underneath the rhythm of Willem's steady milking, she heard the hoofbeats. Two horses.

"They're here," Willem said softly. "I'll bring them in. We'll start with the cows and then see about the horses."

Willem had been surprisingly accurate in the number the Maxwell brothers would eventually offer for the cows, including the calf. Abbie met the gazes of the Maxwells with an unflinching lack of expression.

"We are mighty curious about why we are not dealing with Mr. Stutzman." Jason picked at his teeth with one finger.

"The reason does not matter," Willem said. "Miss Weaver is a legal agent for the sale."

"Maybe so," Jason said. "But if you want our full price offer, we'll need some proof of that."

Abbie looked at Willem and took a deep breath before she relented and got up to retrieve Rudy's document from the house, leaving the three men leaning over the fence watching the horses in the pasture. When she went back outside, she took a lantern with her and dutifully held it above the paper while Jason perused the details in Rudy's handwriting.

"Are you sure the livestock are not securing any debt?" Jason asked.

Abbie had no idea. She turned her face toward Willem.

"He bought them free and clear," Willem said. "One at a time when he had the cash."

"He is a good businessman." Jason handed the papers back to Abbie. "It's getting too dark to inspect the horses tonight. We'll come back tomorrow. My offer on the cows is good until then."

Abbie waited until they rode away before she spoke. "I haven't decided to sell. You can't force me."